the kid table

the kid table

andrea seigel

BLOOMSBURY

NEW YORK BERLIN LONDON

First published in the United States of America in September 2010
by Bloomsbury Books for Young Readers
www.bloomsburyteens.com

For information about permission to reproduce selections from this book, write to
Permissions, Bloomsbury BFYR, 175 Fifth Avenue, New York, New York 10010

Library of Congress Cataloging-in-Publication Data
Seigel, Andrea.
The kid table / Andrea Seigel.—1st U.S. ed.
        p.   cm.
Summary: Explores the quirky dynamics in an extended family
full of close-knit cousins who both help and hinder each other as they
celebrate holidays and momentous occasions together.
ISBN 978-1-59990-480-1
[1. Families—Fiction.   2. Cousins—Fiction.   3. Interpersonal relations—Fiction.]   I. Title.
PZ7.S4562Ki 2010   [Fic—dc22]   2010004540

Book design by Nicole Gastonguay
Typeset by Westchester Book Composition
Printed in the U.S.A. by Worldcolor Fairfield, Pennsylvania
2 4 6 8 10 9 7 5 3 1

All papers used by Bloomsbury Publishing, Inc., are natural, recyclable products
made from wood grown in well-managed forests. The manufacturing processes
conform to the environmental regulations of the country of origin.

For my dad, Larry
1948–2009

THE
FAMILY TREE

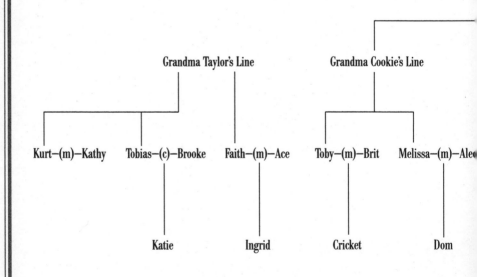

Grandma Taylor's Line   Grandma Cookie's Line

Kurt—(m)—Kathy Tobias—(c)—Brooke   Faith—(m)—Ace   Toby—(m)—Brit   Melissa—(m)—Ale

Katie   Ingrid   Cricket   Dom

KEY

(m) married
(rm) remarried
(c) complicated

Great-Grandma Cecily's Line

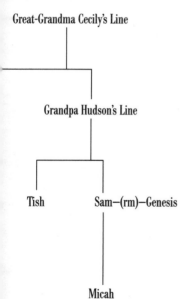

Grandpa Hudson's Line

Tish   Sam—(rm)—Genesis

Micah

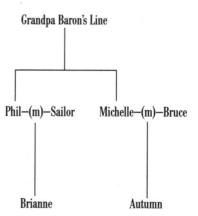

Grandpa Baron's Line

Phil—(m)—Sailor   Michelle—(m)—Bruce

Brianne   Autumn

the kid table

PART I

THE BAR MITZVAH

CHAPTER 1

My earliest memory is fuzzy, not because of time, but because I'm looking out of a full-body jumper. It's sea foam green. My mom has cinched the hood so tight that my vision is a fleecy porthole.

I am at a collapsible poker table with the other babies—my cousins Cricket, Dom, Micah, and Autumn. And then there's also my cousin Brianne, who's two years older and capable of cutting her own food, and she has suddenly burst out, whining, "Why do I have to be at the Baby Table?"

The grown-ups, sitting along the longest, biggest hunk of wood (in my mind, it's like they chopped down a five-hundred-year-old pine for their Christmas table), stop their discussions and look toward us small ones in exile. Concern is all over their faces. Years later I'll learn this is the meal over which Autumn's parents have announced they're going to divorce.

My hands and my mouth are two of the few parts not restrained by imitation wool. I bring my fingers to my lips and start blowing kisses at the faraway adults like crazy.

They laugh. They squeal, "Cute, cute girl!" They clap like *they're* the ones who should be at the Baby Table.

I learn that it can be so easy to make people feel happy.

Hands down, I was considered the most charming of the younger set until a month ago at the Labor Day barbecue, when Brianne managed to convince my extended family that I might be a psychopath.

During the Frisbee toss, I accidentally hit a robin in the head midflight. What are the odds? The bird dropped to the grass and my cousins and aunts and uncles and half uncles (and girlfriend of the half uncle) and great-aunts and lone living grandma and parents closed their circle in upon it.

A moment of silence, then—

"Has anyone noticed that a lot of animals die around Ingrid?" asked Brianne.

"A hamster here or there," I said. "Both accidental."

When I was ten my Siberian hamster, the nastiest little asshole you'd ever meet, choked on the piece it bit off my finger. I still have a dent in my left pinkie. My dad replaced Jaws with a Syrian hamster, and Sweetie was a licker, not a biter, so it's tragic that she came along right as I was entering my body-glitter phase. The vet took one look at the shimmering foam on her lips and pronounced my lotion the probable cause of death.

A few dead goldfish—but come on, goldfish are notoriously death-prone. Our family dog, Long John, died last year while I was the only one in the house. But that was old age. He just happened to be napping in my bed with me when he left this world.

"I have," said my aunt Kathy (related by marriage to my mom's half brother Kurt). "I've noticed that."

Brianne was just about to start her sophomore year at Pepperdine, where she was an undeclared psychology major. She was the second most charming of the younger set. I knew this was her jockeying for pole position.

My dad was standing next to me, and I reached into his pocket and took a penny from the change that was always jangling there. Placing it over the robin's upward eye, I said, "If I hit that bird on purpose, then someone get me to the Olympic Frisbee team. Fast."

"There's an Olympic Frisbee team?" asked my cousin Dom, one year younger than me. "How *gay*." Dom was constantly saying that things were gay to try to force a confrontation about his sexuality, but probably the majority of the family already assumed.

Over lunch, Brianne continued her efforts at amateur diagnosis.

Holding a BBQ chicken wing and staring at it thoughtfully as if it had come from the robin, she asked, "Has anyone noticed that Ingrid doesn't seem to feel guilt or remorse when she kills animals?"

"That's not true," my mom said, probably less in my

defense than in belated prevention of negative vibes. Lately she couldn't stand hearing anything downbeat. "She cried when Long John—"

Stopped, thought.

"No, that was me."

"If you love something, you set it free," I said.

The attack continued throughout the meal.

Over watermelon: "Have any of us ever seen her truly upset? Isn't it weird how even-keeled she's been over the course of her life?"

Seventeen years is not a life, I thought. I had plenty of time to crumble, just not a good enough reason yet.

"I'm getting bored with this," I said to Brianne, who was sitting directly across from me at the Kid Table. Still the collapsible poker contraption, it traveled everywhere, and where it couldn't travel, it was re-created in spirit.

Over the years the Baby Table had evolved into the Kid Table, even though it now had a baby again: my four-year-old cousin (barely), Katie, illegitimate child of my half uncle Tobias and his on-again, off-again girlfriend, Brooke. For some reason, my extended family stopped having kids after my gang, all only children. Either we were enough for them, or we hadn't been enough to encourage more.

Excited, Brianne held a finger in the air. "Proneness to boredom! Need for constant stimulation!"

The adults, sitting at their never-ending plastic picnic table, leaned forward, taking her more and more seriously.

∞

Over sweet potato fries: "And the promiscuousness . . . ," she pressed on.

My dad, pretending not to hear this one, squeezed ketchup onto his paper plate long after it had completely covered his fries.

Cricket finally looked up from her food, which had been preoccupying her. No, torturing her. Every time she put a fry in her mouth, she looked as if she were inwardly screaming, "Why would you do something so stupid?" I wanted to defend her, but what can you do to a pile of fries? It wasn't like the time a tank of a girl bullied Cricket when our parents left us in day care together during a Club Med vacation, and I knew how to help then. I told the tank I'd overheard her family saying that they didn't love her, and that made her depressed and scared enough to stop making Cricket depressed and scared. I don't know how I knew it would work like that for the tank, but it did.

Of all my cousins, Cricket was the closest to me, both at the Kid Table and in my heart.

"You're slutty too," she lobbed at Brianne.

"See? Thank you, Cricket," I said.

After this, Brianne seemed to drop the subject, maybe because her sluttiness was far more committed than mine. I had a tame habit of dry humping with whoever might be around and recently showered, but Brianne was a cut above. I'll give her that edge. At her high school graduation party she got with three of the waiters supplied by the catering company.

Conversation returned to normal, normal being talking trash about the family members who hadn't decided to show.

That day the topic was my second cousin, Tish. "Still steaming about that chain e-mail," said Aunt Kathy, rolling her eyes.

But Brianne wasn't finished. She'd only been waiting for Aunt Kathy's brownies, everyone's favorite, to bring it all home.

"What's really interesting is that psychopaths," she said, crumbling a chunk of brownie between her fingers, "are cold inside, but you'd never know it unless you're trained to recognize this type of disorder, because outwardly they're very, very charming."

My relatives looked from Brianne to me, the connections locking in their eyes, her bullet points adding up to something in their minds, just like triple cherries on a row of slots.

Well, she had me there.

In October my uncle Kurt had his bar mitzvah. Uncle Kurt was forty-six. He decided to bar mitzvah himself after spending the past year cheating on my aunt Kathy. Having gotten so caught up in his mistress that he forgot he already had another life, suddenly he wanted to start over. He'd told my mom it was time to become a real man.

But then he got so busy with making things up to Aunt Kathy and running his Blimpie's franchise that he had to forego the actual bar mitzvah ceremony because he never got around to learning his routine (or converting to Judaism). So he was just skipping to the party part.

At eight we arrived at the Hilton in Costa Mesa in formal wear. It was cocktail and hors d'oeuvres hour, and the ballroom doors were still shut. Mom went over to congratulate Uncle Kurt for unknown achievements. Unable to resist, Dad turned back around to go look at a red Lamborghini that had pulled into the valet driveway right as we were coming into the hotel.

From every direction my relatives were staring at me. Or it was more like they were trying to stare through and into me, struggling to figure out if I would bring future shame to the family (well, more shame—we already had some question-able members) or injure their pets when their turn came to host Thanksgiving. I knew I had to do something to get them back on my side, but there were just so many of them. I was trying to come up with a way to restore the most affection in the least amount of time. I thought about giving the ladies cheek kisses and whispering, "You look like you're still losing weight." And then for the guys I could do the fake-jabbing thing I sometimes pulled out because they all seemed to love it and didn't care if it got repeated straight down the line.

But my relatives were really eyeing me, and I was worried they'd question my intentions. It felt like if they looked long enough, they'd finally look right through me. Back in sopho-more science I learned that theoretically, if you keep your hand on a wall for eternity, eventually your hand will pop out the other side. That's how I felt about their eyes and my personal-ity. So I just gave them all a big smile at one time. I swept that smile across the crowd of them like a searchlight.

I would have to win them back later.

Or maybe, I considered, there was something to letting

them think the worst of me. For sure I was having to do a lot less whispering and a lot less jabbing.

I walked to the seating assignment table to pick up my place card, even though I knew exactly where I'd been put. The cards were topped with artificial glistening snow—Uncle Kurt loves to ski. In fact, he met his mistress on a lift in Vail. I scanned the row of *B*s: Ace Bell (Dad), Faith Bell (Mom), Ingrid Bell, me.

A chin nestled my shoulder. I tipped my cheek against Cricket's.

"Where are we?" she asked.

I picked up my card and opened it. "The Bunny Slope."

"Oh no they didn't," she said, voice rising.

I found the card of little Katie. I tipped it to look inside. The Bunny Slope.

"Forever young," I sang.

Turning around, I saw that Cricket had dropped maybe twenty pounds since I last saw her at the barbecue. That was barely over a month ago, and that was too much lost weight for that amount of time. Her cheekbones looked like tomahawks. She swam in her stretchy black tube dress; even the Lycra couldn't keep up with her compression.

"Cricket—"

I wasn't about to whisper in her ear that she looked like she was still losing weight. I was about to pull her under the place card table and not let her crawl back out until I knew what was going on with her inside.

"Do they not see we have *chests*?!" she yelled before I could start in on her, and she's not usually a yeller. She's more the type to drop just the right sentence in just the right place at just the right time, keeping her volume mellow. I couldn't remember an instance of her just losing it without warning—not even when the tank undid Cricket's best lanyard at Club Med— and I was taken aback by the sudden change in her personality. Part of the reason we'd always been close was because we both had trouble understanding why people did so much yelling.

I hardly recognized her. But I also wondered if she'd ever felt that same thing about me.

"Speaking of chests, where did yours go?" I asked, pressing both hands to her disappeared boobs.

"Where is he?"

"Who?"

"Cousin Kurt." My uncle, her cousin. Her mom is my mom's aunt's daughter. Not important. Important: where'd the boobs go and why?

"Cricket," I repeated, but just then a waiter approached us with a tray of four-cheese quesadillas. Traditional Jewish fare, I'm sure. Dipping the tray right under Cricket's chin, he, a full-on white guy, asked, "Ladies—*quién desea una quesadilla?*"

Cricket was already cranky and angry, as people end up being when they're subsisting on breath mints, and the waiter's offer tipped her into a full-blown rage.

"We've grown up! We've changed! They can't just put us aside forever!" Her face, more taut the more upset she became, was fully unrecognizable. If she'd been making that face walking down the street, I think I might have passed her. The waiter instinctively pulled the tray back in front of him and kind of used it as a shield. He backed away with the quesadillas.

"It's just a seating arrangement," I said, shrugging. "And they're just our relatives."

"It's a fucking insult!" she—well, she yelped. Like a puppy. I'd heard her cussing in a lazy way before, but never out of real emotion. She looked at me cagily, both of us knowing something was very wrong. And then she stormed off, elbowing the waiter on the way, presumably to chew out Uncle/Cousin Kurt.

After the yelp, whoever wasn't already looking was looking now.

A hand clamped down on my shoulder. My cousins are a sneaky bunch, always approaching from behind.

"What's her problem?" asked Micah.

"I don't know," I said, watching Cricket's shoulder blades go. But when I turned I saw that I had yet another cousin in a visibly declining state. Micah was wearing a suit jacket without anything underneath, and I was staring into his shaved chest. In short, he was topless. Anything to keep up the illusion that he was the family's loose cannon and our rebel with a cause—that cause being, being the family rebel.

I poked him in the space between his nipples. "*You* have a problem."

"The others here yet?"

Searching the growing crowd, I put back on a vacant,

even-keeled grin, maybe just to freak them all out. I was in my new party dress and my hair was slicked back with my dad's gel. More and more it was seeming like a fun idea to be dangerous for the night. After all, if I'd learned anything from the commercial for Britney Spears's perfume, it was that hotels are hotbeds of mystery and intrigue.

Scattered in the midst of my family were adults I vaguely or didn't recognize. Probably a few Blimpie's higher-ups, ski partners, old college buddies. From the looks of them, maybe some former mistresses. At the barbecue, Brianne had also warned everyone that psychopaths have an inflated sense of self, but I thought that even the people who hadn't been there appeared to be eyeing me cautiously. My relatives talk.

I continued to scan the partygoers. Concerned face, concerned face, concerned face, concerned face, concerned face, concerned face. Grin.

Tucked among all the concern, there was someone giving me back my exact same expression. My grin was fake and his grin was fake, but together they weren't, because together they said, "Hey! Your grin is fake!"

He looked about twenty. In my family, that's Bunny Slope territory, and we rarely had visitors to the Kid Table. Was he an especially beloved Blimpie's employee? One of the unknown's sons?

Behind him, Autumn and Dom were at the bar, bartender passing them Shirley Temples.

"They're over there, getting their drink on," I told Micah as a waitress approached with individual nacho plates. She lifted and presented me one without me so much as glancing toward the tray.

"For you," she said. "From the young man with the—" Suddenly her composure quit and she dropped into an almost conspiratorial whisper. "Listen, these are his words, and usually I wouldn't use this sort of language in front of a guest, but you're young and cool, right?"

"Right," I said.

Back in her professional voice, she said, "From the young man with the shit-eating grin."

I looked across the room, where he was watching, straight-faced.

"Aren't these free?" I asked.

"Well, yes."

"Classy," I said, took the plate, and bit into a chip, staring back at him. Then I don't even really know why I felt compelled to do this, but I returned my gaze to the waitress and said, "You have an amazing figure."

Blushing, she told me when the minichurros came out of the kitchen, she'd return to serve me first.

CHAPTER 2

"Fantastic bar mitzvah. Do you happen to know where Cricket went?" I asked Uncle Kurt.

Last I'd seen of her she'd been yelling at him, "You expect me to celebrate your becoming a man when you can't even recognize I've become a woman?!"

I guess this outburst seemed far more scandalous than it actually was to the attendees who weren't related to us—I heard an unfamiliar guy muttering to another that she must be the mistress. Then I lost sight of her in the mob and lost sight of the grinner too. By nine the area was so crowded that it was as if our family had joined up with the reunions of five more.

About Cricket, Uncle Kurt shook his head no while grabbing the arm of a woman trying to squeeze through a wall of bodies near us, forging a path with her giant clipboard. He was sweating badly, and I wondered if this was how he looked when he told Aunt Kathy what he'd really been doing all the times he said he was volunteering at the big-cat rescue.

"How much longer?" he shouted to the woman. She was sweaty too. "My bar mitzvah should have started already!"

"They're just stringing the last of the lights!" she promised.

In addition to all the waiters and waitresses circulating with the *bocados*, the entertainers had showed up and were also working the room. I hadn't come across all of them yet (it had taken me twenty minutes to inch toward Uncle Kurt, only ten feet away), but to my left a mime was twisting animal balloons.

Stuck behind the giant clipboard, I turned toward him and smiled.

"Hi there," I said.

I thought that under the pancake foundation, he looked like he might not be half-bad. Maybe he could go into a bathroom and get washed up. (I don't believe in God, but I do believe that cleanliness is next to whatever makes the world go round.)

He didn't say anything since his profession doesn't allow it. He just blew into a long, peach balloon and shook it around in front of my face, raising his painted eyebrows.

"You want me to tell you what to make me?" I guessed.

The mime nodded enthusiastically.

"What we're doing here, it's making me feel like I'm Timmy and you're Lassie."

He pantomimed panting.

"Okay, why don't you make me a Lassie, then?"

As the mime began to twist the balloon, I smiled at him and said, "Good boy. Good boy." He was extremely deft with his hands, and in under a minute he'd created something resembling a dog.

When he held out the balloon, I detected a certain sparkle in his eyes, a more interesting message coming from underneath the makeup.

"She wanted a collie," said the grinner, stepping next to me. "That's more of a poodle." He stood so close that his shoulder was touching mine, but he looked at the mime and not me.

The sparkle in the mime's eyes quickly became a spark. It glowed, "You dick."

Turning toward the grinner, I was just about pressed flat against him because of limited space.

"Who are you?" I asked.

His hair looked as if it had gone three too many days without shampoo, and a greasy, wayward piece of bang had fallen in the path of his left eye. Underneath his unbuttoned sport jacket, he was wearing an old white undershirt that wasn't going to be white soon if he didn't invest in some bleach. It was like he'd purposely gotten dirty for the party the way that most people purposely do themselves up. I began to wonder who he was trying to piss off. The one part of himself he couldn't dress down was that he had beautiful, flawless skin, and standing that close I discovered he smelled pretty great, like a combination of Nilla Wafers and leather.

Looking at me, he tucked the wayward bang behind his ear. He had kind eyes. A mean mouth.

"Trevor."

"Nice to meet you." I held out my hand, but he didn't see it—we were *that* near—so I found his hand, grasped it, and shook it for him. "Ingrid. How do you know Uncle Kurt?"

"Friend of the family," he said.

"My family?"

Another long balloon, this one green, was suddenly waving in the gap between our noses. We looked to the mime, who was impatient for the next request.

Trevor turned toward him. "Chesapeake Bay retriever," he said.

The mime's painted black lips parted to reveal some impressively straight, white teeth. I'm guessing braces as a kid and then he got into bleaching as an adult. "We were in the middle of something," the mime snapped.

"Yeah, I know. You'll have to finish being creepy later," said Trevor.

Like I said, hotels are hotbeds of mystery and intrigue, so I went with Trevor as he pulled me through the crowd toward the lady who was drawing caricatures. I just knew right away that we had something bigger in common than what you should usually share with someone who feels good to you. Going off my friends at school, that's usually a favorite band or a teacher you both hate. When I looked at the mime, I just thought about getting him a washcloth for that greasepaint, but when I looked at Trevor, whose hair and shirt should have made my head spin with Pantene and Clorox, I could only think about how he'd grinned at me and why he'd done that. The mime was taking everything too seriously.

On the trip to the caricature lady I whipped by my mom, who was tucking one of the hotel's embossed napkins into her clutch. A few months before, she'd started getting into scrap-booking and had begun taking whatever from wherever we went so she could preserve it later. I squeezed her arm as I passed.

"Hey, Mom!"

Looking up, surprised, she said, "Hi, honey. Having fun?"

Trevor had already wedged himself between Autumn's parents, now fourteen years divorced but newly dating each other, and all I could see of him was his hand in mine. I was still moving with him.

"Starting to!" I called back. From behind I could hear my mom asking, "So you're not bored? Good! Or is that just because the party is constantly stimulating?"

The lady was drawing my cousin Tish as a sexy nun. Cartoon-Tish's habit had a slit going almost all the way up to her cartoon-vagina, and I knew Tish wasn't going to be happy when she saw the likeness because she's pretty much a prude. That chain e-mail leading to her boycott of the Labor Day barbecue, originally sent from Half Uncle Tobias, contained a list of all the different things you can call a vagina. (Aunt Kathy was scandalized by it too.)

"Looks good, Tish," I said from behind the easel.

"But does it look like me?"

"I think she captured your eyes. This is Trevor."

He raised his eyebrows in a "Hi."

The lady signed the drawing by Cartoon-Tish's bare foot, then pulled it from the clip and handed it over. Tish took one look at herself, dropped the paper like it was a printout of Half Uncle Tobias's e-mail, and walked away.

"Who's next?"

I put my hand near the bottom of Trevor's back to let him know he could go first, but he took it up in his again and pulled me toward the chair.

"Do you have another chair?" I asked the caricaturist.

Trevor told her, "We'll share."

I took half and he took the other half, and we looked at each other and grinned that we fit.

"So what do you want to be?" asked the lady.

I suggested to Trevor, "Why don't we do either cop and robber, or cowboy and Indian?"

Looking to the caricaturist, he said, "She's going to be throwing a Frisbee, and I'm going to be a robin flying by."

I stared at Trevor's profile, and I felt half of a smile creeping up on me. He already knew more about me than I knew about him. And I felt like the best way to catch up to him was to let him be the one to react first, so I could quickly learn something else.

He still didn't look at me but raised his eyebrow and sang, "Psy-cho kill-ah."

I heard the lady start drawing, her marker squeaking on the paper.

He started singing the next part of the song with all the fa's.

He liked the same band as my dad; that's one thing I learned. "You've been talking to my family," I said.

"I told you, I'm a friend."

"Well, you can't think I'm a psychopath or you wouldn't want to be sharing a chair with me."

"All I know is that I had to meet the person in the room most likely to hurt me if I got too close." Hurt him how, I wondered.

"Sweetheart?" asked the caricaturist.

"Yes?" Trevor and I both answered.

"The sweetheart in the dress," she clarified. "Do you want to be wearing something specific while you're throwing the Frisbee?"

"What I have on right now is fine."

"Never done one like this before," the lady said, reaching for the red marker on the table next to her.

"I like your dress," Trevor said.

"Thank you. And you have great skin," I said.

"Thank you."

"We should have asked her to draw me as a shampoo girl and you as the client at my sink."

I saw his grin out of the corner of my eye, and it didn't feel fake from where I was sitting.

"Ingrid!" Again, a cousin was coming from behind. I turned and saw Autumn, who was waving her arms at me like we were on opposite sides of a stadium, even though she was only blocked by Brianne's grandma. The caricaturist said, "Sweetheart, I need you to look forward. I'm not done with you."

"One second, please," I told her.

Ducking down so she could come kneel by the chair, Autumn said, "Micah said you were looking for Cricket. I just came from the bathroom and I saw her shoes in the stall next to mine, but she wouldn't say anything and she wouldn't come out."

I got up from the chair. To the lady I said, "Sorry. I know you're going to do a great job without me." To Trevor I said, "Come find me later."

The women's restroom smelled overwhelmingly of baby powder. My aunt Kathy was at the diaper station, organizing her purse (such a gross choice of counter space). I gave her a pat on the back as I passed and went right for the stalls. When I crouched down, I found Cricket's crystal sandals in the farthest one at the end.

I got onto my hands and knees and crawled under the door.

Cricket had made herself a tarp over the toilet with about fifty of the waxy sanitary covers. I grabbed my own collection from the dispenser and made myself a pad on the floor.

"What's going on?" I asked.

She sighed, her eyes going a little bit watery. "I can't go back out there."

"Because you yelled at the bar mitzvah boy?"

"Because of the churros." The same tortured look came over her again, the one I'd first seen in the presence of the sweet potato fries. It hit me that she was becoming scared of food like I was scared of making my way in a world where everybody could see right through me. We stared at each other. "They just kept coming by and by and by, and they smell so . . ."

"You don't have to worry anymore," I said. "They're long gone."

Her whole face brightened. "Really?"

"They ran out of churros twenty minutes ago. I have a contact on the waitstaff and she personally delivered the news." This was actually the truth. I was glad to be able to tell it to her.

Then Cricket's face clouded again. "But are the waiters circling with something else now?"

"No." I shook my head. "They're done serving the hors d'oeuvres. Come back out with me."

Her waxy covers crinkled as she shifted around, trying to come to a decision.

"Okay," she finally said, and I was relieved I didn't have to give her a talk like my parents used to give me when I was convinced there was a portal from hell in my bedroom closet.

Aunt Kathy was applying a flattering nude lipstick in her compact mirror when we walked out of the stall, and she did a double take at the two of us.

"I didn't see you come in, Cricket," she said. "You look—"

"That lipstick color is fantastic on you," I told Aunt Kathy before she could finish.

"What a charming thing to say," she mused, as if trying to solve a math problem in her head, wanting to believe me, except for those warning signs Brianne had chirped in her ear. I pulled Cricket out of there before Aunt Kathy could spend any longer considering what I was up to.

When we returned to the cocktail party, there was no more food in sight, which was making some of the guests mad, but Cricket was able to take a deep breath. Seeing the crowd with refreshed eyes, I realized just how drunk everyone was. My dad was still talking about the Lamborghini to Half Uncle Tobias as if it were a girl.

"I'd take her out late at night when there was no one else around," he was saying. "Hi, hon. Cricket."

We stayed and hung out with them, mostly because tunneling farther in would have taken more energy than Cricket seemed to have. I kept one eye on her and the other on a magician working the edge of the room. He tried to appear out of nowhere, but I'd seen him hiding behind a column a second before.

"Good evening, ladies! Do you happen to have a dollar?" He tipped his hat. "I'll turn it into a hundred for you in less than a blink."

I reached into my dad's change pocket. "I'm sorry, the best I can do is a quarter. Can you turn that into a dollar?"

Squinting, the magician said, "Ummm."

From behind, there was a stroke down my hair. "Ingrid! Cricket!"

We turned around to say hi to Brianne. She was wearing a long, white silk dress—it was bridal. I thought it was a little heavy-handed, like the good cowboy wearing the white hat in a movie.

"Like a virgin," Cricket said.

Brianne ignored her because she never knew what to say back when Cricket took aim. "I want you to meet my boyfriend. He goes to Pepperdine with me." Then she tugged on a hand and Trevor emerged from a cluster of mistress types. He didn't look surprised or guilty or ashamed to see me, but completely at ease. In his right hand was a rolled-up piece of paper that was probably the drawing of us.

"It's nice to meet you," he said.

I broke into my most electric smile. There was nothing better to do. "It's nice to meet you too," I said.

Just as my own smile was about to fail me for the first time since I could remember—and my mind was swimming, so I couldn't even really remember when that specific occasion was—the eight doors to the ballroom flew open to reveal thousands of twinkling white lights. The band inside erupted into a spirited rendition of "Celebration" (come on!).

"Everybody in!" yelled Uncle Kurt over the music. "L'Chayim! Did I say that right?"

CHAPTER 3

The thousands of small white lights didn't only twinkle across the ballroom's surfaces, they hung suspended in the air. I couldn't make out a single wire. It was just dazzling snowflakes frozen in time. The guests rushed by me because I had frozen too, and the rustling of their dresses and suits sounded kind of like winter blowing through. Maybe I even forgot where I was for a second.

"This is so beautiful," I said to no one, but the party planner must have been nearby because she heard.

"God, *thank you.*"

I hadn't meant to start working on her. But once she was there next to me, I realized how much I wanted one of the centerpieces to take home and stare into while falling asleep. I couldn't help but gently work on her then. They were large snow globes, the size of regulation basketballs at least, and inside were tiny, glowing ski lodges. The light coming from them was phosphorescent to the point of almost being green. They were the kind of sight that made me want to believe in things, like how I used to believe in Santa Claus for a minute. I have no memories of that minute, but my parents say it exists, unless I was pretending then too. But I wanted to believe—just in anything. Just in believing, I think.

"I can't take my eyes off the centerpieces," I told her. "They're like what churches are supposed to be, if you know what I mean."

We stared into the twinkling lights for a minute until the party planner's assistant came to get her, panicking because there was a problem with something called the challah. "It looks like it's *French* braided," she said, and together they ran off to the kitchen. I was thinking of moving on too, but then the band shifted from "Celebration" to "Silver Bells," and I became rooted even deeper to my spot at the top of the room. That had always been my favorite holiday song because, well, we're the Bells (Brianne had pointed this out as more proof of my narcissistic tendencies, but she also said that no one's even sure if there's a real distinction between true narcissists and psychopaths anymore, anyway).

I was growing more and more perplexed by the second. Something was nagging at me, but it still could have been anything, because when I searched my mind for the problem, it went blank. I was perplexed by what it was that I was believing in so strongly even as I felt myself doing it. My chest was swelling, but for what? Cricket's sudden fear of appetizers? Was it wonderment at the song choice, which had me nearly hypnotized with anticipation for the line about Christmas time.

The band was playing the music of the first verse, their lead singer, an incredibly short woman with tall-woman hair, improvising over it.

"What is that I hear?" she half sang, half talked into the microphone in a sultry voice. "Something ringing?" She bent forward and her hair shut like a curtain around her nose. "Getting clo-ser?" From having watched reruns of *Def Poetry Jam* on HBO, I recognized that she was veering in the realm of spoken word from the stress on the second syllable. "Could those be dinner bells?" On cue, waiters, both male and female, emerged from the far wall holding platters of dinner salads.

I was perplexed by Brianne's new boyfriend.

"Silver bells!" belted the lead singer.

I really was.

Then, with more emotion, "Silver bellllllllllllls!"

I was trying to sort through how strangely Trevor had acted toward me, as I stared into a room that looked like the combination of a blizzard and a galaxy.

Transfixed, I cocked my head and waited for what was to come.

"It's bar mitzvah time . . . in the ballroom!"

And there I had the line I'd been waiting for.

Then I felt someone I believed to be him touch my shoulder, but I didn't look back. I didn't twist around.

Instead I decided to move on again. I veered to the left, and there was the Kid Table.

∞

It wasn't the actual Kid Table that still got dragged from event to event, the round, white plastic table with teeth marks around its edge because all us kids had gone through a stage of liking to chew on it. Even my dog, Long John, had gnawed on the table when he was a puppy and I'd sneak him into my lap to feed him. Uncle Kurt scolded me once for feeding Long John a king-size Hershey's bar, but I was too young to know about dogs and chocolate and was definitely not trying to kill him.

The table was still a Kid Table, nonetheless, smaller than anything else in the ballroom. The other circular tables sat twelve, but only seven chairs had been squeezed around ours. You could tell it was meant for six, max. They'd put the table in the farthest corner from the open bar, nearly pressed up against the eastern wall and backed into an artificial pine tree sprayed with a fat layer of faux snow.

The singer of the band scatted, "Take your seats, do-do-do. Every-bod-y take your seats be-cause the sal-ad's here" over a drum effect that sounded like branches swishing across the roof of a car.

The only one *sitting* at "The Bunny Slope" was little Katie. Her head barely reached the table and she seemed bewildered by the bar mitzvah. You could merely see the top parts of her eyes over the tabletop, but they gave off enough alarm you could figure out what was going on with the rest of her.

Cricket, Dom, Micah, and Autumn stood behind their chairs as if they were protesting the table. Cricket grasped on to the back of hers, looking weak. I stepped behind one of the two remaining seats.

"You look weird," said Micah, one of his nipples peeking out from his suit jacket like a third eye joining in the observation.

"And you're dressed unseasonably," I pointed out.

Autumn was studying Katie from across the table. "Katie looks weird," she said in a low voice for us. Then in a higher, sweeter voice, she asked, "Katie, honey? Are you feeling all right?"

Being four, Katie could talk—and fluently—but she stayed silent, her eyes scrambling as they fought not to slip below the tablecloth's horizon.

"Maybe she needs a booster seat," Autumn considered.

"Yeah, that's exactly why she looks like the party's kicking off with a child sacrifice and she's ours," Dom said, watching Katie like she was the best movie he'd seen in a while.

"I mean, this whole thing *is* really weird. So why shouldn't she be so freaked out?" asked Micah. "You, on the other hand—"

At first he looked over at Cricket, and it seemed like he was going to bring up how weird it was to see her looking like the love child of a ghost and a skeleton. But she was looking over her shoulder, watching one of the waiters lower a salad plate at a big table. We all watched her, worried, but she didn't notice the table had gone quiet. And then maybe because Cricket looked weird in a way that was real, Micah refocused on me.

"You're freaking me out for some reason. I've never seen your face do that."

"Do what?"

"Dom, tell her what her face is doing."

Dom shifted his attention from Katie to Micah, and he got this weird look on *his* face like he suddenly was remembering something he'd meant to say earlier but never got the chance. "Hey, you look *really gay,*" he told Micah.

"Why are you starting with the gay stuff? There's no one at the table to hear you who doesn't already know."

Dom had come out to the Kid Table originals when he was eleven, confessing he'd been having reoccurring dreams of Leonardo DiCaprio holding him tight on the prow of a ship. Ever since we were around thirteen he'd been calling out a wide spectrum of things as "gay!" around the adults, his list including cargo pants, laser eye surgery, laminate countertops, and Splenda. He refused to just come out and tell them. He said that would be anticlimactic after having worked so hard to accept himself.

I think what he was hoping for was one of our relatives snapping and getting the whole production going. The fear was that if he came out himself, the adults would fake smile and pretend to be supportive but never look at him the same way again. He said he needed a parent, an aunt, an uncle, his grandma . . . *someone* to melt down uncontrollably so that everyone could have an authentic catharsis.

Micah said, "Katie doesn't know what being gay means, and even *she* knows you're gay. Right, Katie?"

No answer from Katie.

"I should really sit next to her," Autumn said, and went over to the chair to her right. Ever since Katie had come along, Autumn spent so much time mothering her that sometimes the rest of us forgot she wasn't forty. When around her, I had the impulse to say things like yes, school was great, and yes, I was looking forward to graduating, and definitely, it had been unseasonably hot out lately.

"Let's all sit," Cricket said with a sigh, turning back toward us. "Let's all sit at the Midget Slope."

We did and when we were all in our chairs, one still remained empty.

"Where's Brianne?" asked Dom.

It was only then that I realized Trevor was going to show up at our table and sit right across from me. He was going to eat there, drink there, and exist there. We were going to spend the night facing each other. I hadn't put it together yet.

Except that couldn't be the case, I realized, because there was only one seat left and it was Brianne's. But then where was Trevor being sent off to? I didn't think my relatives were big enough prudes, aside from Tish, that they'd separate Brianne from a guy she was most likely sleeping with. If they were that uptight about her honor, they wouldn't have let her get within spitting distance of the buffet line staff at her graduation party.

And then my usual grasp on logic must have escaped me for a minute because I had the thought that they were so cool about Brianne's love life that Uncle Kurt or Aunt Kathy or whoever did the table layout had given her and Trevor a single chair to share. They'd said to themselves, "Ehhh, if we put eight chairs around the table, we have to go up a size and spend another couple of bucks. They're already doing it, so she can just sit in his lap."

"B-ann's over there," said Katie, finally snapping out of her waking coma.

"Welcome back, kid," said Dom.

I looked over my shoulder, and it wasn't hard to zero in on the bridal dress in the room, even amid all the snow. The planner had done an amazing job of creating depth through texture and lighting. The whites of the surface decorations had either a slight blue or green tint to them, and the dangling lights put out a trace of old-school incandescent yellow. Nothing was truly, fully white, except for Brianne.

Trevor was next to her. They sat at a table for twelve.

They'd been put with Katie's parents and a number of couples I didn't recognize, probably Blimpie's people. Brianne was leaning in close to the woman next to her and their temples were practically touching. They seemed to be having a serious conversation about the napkins, or at least that's where their eyes and fingers went. Trevor had his arm around the back of Brianne's chair. He was staring in wonder at the glowing centerpiece, or at least that's where his eyes had gone.

Sometimes you can be looking at something and not really see it, so that's why it took me longer than it really should have to understand that Brianne had been excused from the Kid Table.

"She's not sitting here?" Micah asked, and in that question all the normal swagger had gone out of him. This was no time for bullshitting. I shared in his mystification.

"Well, that's good for her," Autumn said, but I thought with some uncertainty.

It's not that I'd assumed that I'd be sitting at the Kid Table until it couldn't follow me into the convalescent home. I hadn't given the endgame that much thought, but I guess I just assumed one day, when we all looked no younger and no less burdened than the adults around us, one of our parents would fold up the table and put it in any one of our garages. It was just where you sat until you finally looked at your parents, your aunts, your uncles, and suddenly you had the same problems as them.

I tried to rack my brain, thinking what could have been the big sign that said to Uncle Kurt or Aunt Kathy or whatever mastermind had done the seating arrangements that Brianne was now one of them.

"Is it because she brought a boyfriend?" asked Dom.

"She's done that before," I said. We'd just made room for him . . . and him, and him, and him. I thought about age, about the arbitrary yet cemented landmarks that dot the road to thirty, after which, from what I can tell, either everything becomes a wash or you just try to make it seem that way. She had already been eighteen at the last few Kid Tables. She wasn't yet twenty-one. What's nineteen?

It's nothing.

"What'd she do that's so great?" wondered Micah.

Brianne had already been to college for a year now, so it wasn't higher education. This wasn't her special occasion, so her seat at a normal-sized table wasn't a "queen for the night" throne. I'd only spoken to her for a second outside in the cocktail area, but she didn't seem any wiser or any more mature to me.

Cricket was more of a laser than a person as her eyes burned a line across the room to Brianne, a line I could practically see quivering in the air. "What's her table called?"

None of us could answer.

Then, in an almost plaintive voice, she asked again, "What the hell could the name of it possibly be?"

"Just like that, huh?" Autumn wondered as I asked myself, what is it that could have warranted Brianne's and Trevor's places among couples who were ostensibly sharing lives, even mixing their gene pools? Was she pregnant? Maybe that was it, that you had to be carrying a kid to leave the Kid Table.

But as I watched a waiter pour Brianne a glass of champagne and then as she drank it—evidently, another perk of an adult table being that you didn't get carded, along with the extra leg and arm room—I knew she wasn't that stupid or that selfish, no matter how many times I'd tried to cast her in both those lights.

She raised her champagne glass to Trevor's and they clinked them. For whatever reason, I badly wanted to hear that resulting sound, but it got buried under all the voices and the band's dinnertime smooth jazz.

The woman next to Brianne made an "awwwww" face, meaning "awwwww" at Brianne and Trevor, and Brianne looked at Trevor like I've never seen her look at anyone before. Like she wasn't worth it. Like she was the grateful one.

Then I knew. Being in love was what got you ejected from the Kid Table.

"Oh my God, my dad just kissed my mom on the lips,"

Autumn said, not in the "ewwwww" way you'd expect of the daughter they'd made together, but with wonder and hope, pure and simple. "It was short, but he did."

I shifted my attention over to their table. I'd prefer watching even parents like Bruce and Michelle make out over certain other couples.

∞

The waiters brought salads to the Kid Table last; by then some of the adult tables were already being cleared of their plates and forks. This whole time Cricket had been craning her neck, and when our waiter lowered her salad in front of her, she gasped in horror.

The other cousins were busy arguing over dinner rolls because the basket came with only two of each kind (wheat, sourdough, Hawaiian, olive), and obviously everybody wanted sourdough. That misguided basket selection had my aunt Kathy all over it.

"Oh! This has dressing!" Cricket pulled back in her chair as if an alien had popped out the belly of her salad plate.

"Yes, miss," said the waiter. "It's a very light balsamic. It's very subtle, very good."

She begged, "Please take it back and ask them to make me one plain."

The waiter lifted his shoulders and did the string-pulling-at-bottom-lip move with his mouth to convey his lack of influence in the kitchen. "The salad was pretossed this afternoon, so they can't really do that. It's all mixed together already."

Part of me knew that I should stay focused on Cricket. Another, louder part was distracted by the twinge I was still experiencing from when Trevor said it was nice to meet me. I have no short- or long-term memory for pain, none, which is a good part of the reason why I'd rarely made any of those signs of unhappiness my relatives apparently wanted more of. If it ever occurred to me to cry over something or someone, by the time enough moisture collected, I was already past the point of tears. So then I'd just blink, making my eyes shine. Brianne had pointed out this frequent glint in my eye as part of the psychopath's surface charm. But I was still feeling that twinge, and this was new.

I couldn't help but look over my shoulder for him. He was in the middle of taking off his jacket, but he froze. His eyes jumped from somewhere off in space to me, like I'd dialed him up. Brianne's seat was empty.

He mouthed, "Hi." It didn't have any jokes in it. He said hi to me like we'd known each other twenty years and this was just another night out for us, stuck on opposite sides of the room.

I stared at him until I had to blink.

"What's the main course?" Cricket was asking. Slowly, I put my head back on straight.

The waiter brightened. "You guys," he said, meaning the denizens of the Kid Table, "get a special dinner that the bar mitzvah boy—" He stopped. "—man? The bar mitzvah man ordered just for you: *quatre-fromage* macaroni!"

Cricket and I both knew a little French from the summer our families took a joint vacation to Disneyland Paris, and at the name of this dish, the wildness left her face and she looked at the waiter as if *he* were the one who'd come unhinged. "You're putting four. *Four* cheeses on the macaroni."

"I know—it's so, so good."

Cricket said quietly to herself, with what sounded like revelation, "Then I can't eat." It was disconcerting to me, like hearing from a member of a cult who believed the government was using pasta to track brain waves. She was being nothing like herself. This was unfair, I realized, but I wanted to believe that I mostly understood who that was.

Right then a woman I'd never seen before approached our table with a toddler sleeping in her arms. "Hi, guys!" she said. "I'm Nancy, one of your uncle's oldest and best college friends, and this here's Alexander." She sort of tipped him toward us, making him give an unconscious greeting. "As you can see, this party's a bit much for him, but we're from Toronto, and I didn't want to leave him with a strange sitter in a strange hotel in a strange country, you know?"

She dropped the kid in the remaining chair, where he slumped down like a professional drunk. His tiny suit was one of the more depressing things I've ever seen in my life. Katie eyeballed him with suspicion.

"Don't have too much fun!" warned Nancy as she left.

I took Cricket's napkin, still folded on the table, and laid it out across her lap. "There's a restaurant off the lobby. I'll get you a dry salad."

∞

But before I could head for the restaurant, there was someone I needed to talk to. Her chair was still empty and now Trevor's was too. Scanning the ballroom, I immediately spotted her at the open bar, which had been covered with glittered batting to look like a naturally occurring mound of snow, but she was even whiter than it was.

"Brianne," I said, and she glanced back at me.

"Thank you," she told the bartender as he passed her a blue cocktail. Then facing me, "Guess I don't need to be carded."

Cricket was the one who could have come up with the perfect response there, something about the bartender recognizing Brianne's inner hag. I was more the type to go for the obvious. "I'm sure he was too busy thinking about the party favors you promised him later."

"Ha, ha," she nonlaughed. "You saw my boyfriend. No one but him gets anything from me."

What I liked best about the contest between Brianne and myself was that at the very root of it, we were competing over the love of people who already had to love us anyway, so what we were really striving for was true excellence in the field. It was art. But when you're in the midst of a struggle to survive—a basic one, I mean—and you only have the energy to focus on essentials like getting food, or getting food for your cousin who's no longer eating anything that contains oil, fat, or toppings, you no longer have time for art.

"Brianne," I started over.

"Yeah?" she asked, resetting.

"In your psychology classes, they teach you how to deal

with specific problems, right? Like what you should do so you don't make a mistake and make the person worse?"

She took a sip. "Kind of. I'm in low-level ones, so it's been mostly a lot of memorization of signs and disorders."

I nodded to indicate that would have to be good enough. "What's the best way to approach someone who you think might, judging by the looks of them, be having a problem with—"

"Cricket," she said.

"Right," I said.

"What's happening with her?"

"She's suddenly scared of what food will do to her, and I don't know why. She'll agree to a salad without dressing, though, so I'm about to go grab her one, but I was wondering if that's enabling."

"Well," Brianne said, all signs of bitch having dropped from her face, "I think you're supposed to encourage her to eat, just eat. That's what's important. And I'm pretty confident you make sure you're empathetic about how hard food is for her, but you don't pretend that you don't notice."

"I'll get the salad, then."

"Yeah, I think you should."

We were nodding together in unison, convincing ourselves of the soundness of the plan.

"Okay, I'll see you later," I said and borrowed her drink for a second to take a sip before handing it back to her.

On my way out of the ballroom I passed Dom's mom, Melissa, who was just hanging out near one of the closed double doors, leaned against the wall, her arms folded across her massive breasts, simply taking it all in.

I stopped before pushing on the nearest door. "Hi, Melissa."

"Oh, hi, Ingrid. This is really something, isn't it?" she marveled.

"It is," I said. "It's really such a gay event."

Melissa looked at me out the corner of her eye, squinting. "You kids use that word a lot. I didn't know it had come back into fashion—I mean, in that way."

I tipped my head from side to side to convey that that was a distinct possibility. "I guess so," I said, walk-ing out of a winter won-der-land.

CHAPTER 4

I know it sounds odd to say I learned how to handle relationships with people from my dog, but I did. Before him, I didn't spend all that much time thinking about how I was—as a person, I mean—but then my parents got me Long John after I swore to them I wouldn't get sick of him in a week. I quickly learned they had nothing to worry about, because how could I? He was a different dog every day. Every part of the day.

Like he'd bring in a dead bird from the yard (he killed birds deliberately, and no one in the family thought he had psychological issues) and wipe its guts all over my bedroom carpet. I always liked a clean room. So in the moment he'd do this, I would feel that I hated him from the very bottom of my soul. I'd yell at him and take away his bird-prize, and I could see he hated me back. For a second, maybe I wanted him to roll over and die. And for a second, I'm sure he wanted a gigantic dog to come along and treat me like a bird.

Then in the afternoon, I would get tired of being angry, and I'd lie down on the carpet—after my mom had helped me clean it—because I liked to keep my bed just for nights. Long John, who would have been sitting on the window seat, staring out at our block, would turn his head toward me.

"Come here, boy," I'd say, lazily tossing up my arm in invitation.

He'd be lazy too, and he'd jump down, one set of paws at a time. After trotting over, he'd buckle to the floor and put his head on my stomach. I'd pet him until I fell asleep. The thought I'd have before I fell asleep was that relationships shift. They do.

And then as I grew up, I became a person who knew this. If my mom was pissed at me for lying to her about where I'd been, I just looked into the future, when she'd be over it. As she yelled at me about how she wouldn't be able to trust me for a really long time, I'd think back to how I'd felt with Long John sleeping on my stomach. By that point of the day, I loved him more than ever, and I couldn't remember what it even felt like to be angry.

Then I'd think ahead to that time my mom was talking about, knowing it was coming sooner than she thought. Patience became this thing I lived by that was real and productive.

What I learned from Long John was that we're all simply caught up in our own shit, and from then on, I didn't take things personally anymore. Long John never really hated me. He hated that he didn't have his bird. I didn't really hate him. I hated a dirty carpet. It's that way with people times a million. If I was ever about to flip out at something someone said or a guy who'd chosen another girl over me or a fight I'd just been in or a table I'd been placed at, I'd remember how little that second of hatred for my dog had meant to me and how quickly it had passed.

Anyway, that's why I didn't really have a history of crying. That's also why I was planning on ordering Cricket additional food along with her plain salad, even though I knew she might leave the party hating me because she thought I was working against whatever it was she was trying to achieve. Should I have been upset knowing that?

Regardless, I wasn't.

When I saw the hotel restaurant was a California bistro, I said, "Oh good," because no one fetishizes the salad like us Californians; my options had just expanded way beyond the Caesar. I planned to throw in as many low-calorie ingredients as possible, reasoning that enough slices of cucumber had to add up to *something* in terms of nutrition.

The bistro was set in an atrium with palm trees all around, and walking in, it was as if I'd lost half of a year of my life, skipping right to summer. The hostess (in a sundress) stood at her podium in front of the bar.

"Can I place an order for take-out?" I asked.

Pulling out a menu from a secret cubby in the back of her podium, she handed it over. "Sure. Do you need a second?"

"No." I ran my finger over the list of salads, mentally collecting ingredients. "But it's going to be custom. Is that all right?"

She did an endearing shrug that let me know she was indifferent to the integrity of the menu. "Probably."

"Great. I'll take a—"

She began to write.

"Mixed Green Caprese, minus everything but the mixed greens and the cherry tomatoes—"

"No dressing?"

"Definitely no dressing." I continued, "Plus the seared ahi tuna from the ahi tuna salad, no wasabi mayonnaise. Plus the green beans. Plus the cucumbers from the farmer's market salad, plus the shredded carrots, and also the—" Looking up, I asked, "Radishes are basically air, caloriewise, aren't they?"

The hostess nodded. "Basically. Once I went on an all-radish-and-pickle diet. It worked great."

"Forget the radishes," I said. "Plus the cabbage and oranges from the Chinese chicken salad." I read through the crab salad, but the healthiest thing in it was avocado, which I knew might push Cricket over the edge, and then she wouldn't eat the rest. "Okay, that's it for the salad."

"Anything else?"

"Can you see if the chef wouldn't mind broiling a piece of chicken and steaming a piece of white fish? Any kind he likes. His choice."

The hostess flipped her wrist. Dom performed that move a

lot with his gay pronouncements, exaggerating it to the point of making himself look like he was throwing a softball. "Yeah, we do that kind of thing all the time for kids when they come in here because they won't eat flavors."

"That's it, then," I said. "Thank you."

She ripped the paper from her pad. "I'll go put this in. You want to wait here? It won't be long."

"I'll wait."

It was only when she stepped away from the podium to go punch in the order that I saw that Trevor was sitting at the end of the bar. He was eating a hamburger with one eye on me. I happened to know it was Kobe beef from having spotted it on the menu.

"Come sit with me," he said—or he mouthed. I don't know. I think I heard a sentence.

I went over and sat on the bar chair next to him.

"Why are you eating here?" I asked.

"They're serving lamb kebabs."

"Not at my table."

"I'd rather be there with you, then."

His suit jacket hanging over the back of his chair, he was down to his undershirt, which I could now confirm as a Hanes because the cotton was so thin I could read the tag straight through it.

I said, "I don't know why you've been flirting with me when you're with my cousin."

He did some more shit-eating grinning and said, "I don't know why you're sitting here if you don't want more flirting because you're concerned about Brianne."

I put my elbow on the bar and rested my chin on my fist. "I didn't come sit over here to flirt. I came over here because, I'm going to admit it, I'm perplexed about what happened over cocktail hour . . . s."

That moment was exactly when I knew we were becoming real trouble because we weren't being cute. Neither of us was arching an eyebrow stupidly. Neither of us was saying anything clever or playful. We were just talking like we shouldn't.

"I saw you," he said, shaking his head.

I thought there was going to be more to that, but he stopped and took a bite of his hamburger. It didn't matter that the rest didn't come, because I pretty much knew what he was saying without it. This was what I was talking about when I said we had things in common. Things like the channel our brains were tuned to.

"Yeah, I saw you too, but I'm not playing at being a couple with someone you grew up with and shared every major life milestone with, you know?"

He held up a finger, indicating that he needed me to give him a second to swallow. Then he said, "I'm not playing at being a couple."

"No?"

"Brianne and I are a couple. What kind of person would I be if I came to a party with your cousin only to decouple from her because I had this need to flirt with you?"

"Arguably," I said, "a better one."

Here he paused to drink his clear something. His bending forward sent a couple pieces of hair, heavy from shampooing neglect, tumbling over his forehead. He took his hand and swept them back. That small move had something totally individual in it. I wanted to watch it again. "I knew about you already, before I saw you. Brianne wants to use you as the case study for her final paper."

We circulate a family-wide newsletter at Christmastime, with every subfamily contributing a few paragraphs about what they've been up to over the course of the year (which is a redundant exercise, since we all already know what each other has been up to), and it wasn't unlikely that an excerpt from this study might show up under Brianne's section.

"When you two get back to your dorm or wherever you're going later, you let her know that I loved my dog," I said.

"I heard you killed him."

"No. I loved my dog."

Trevor went on to repeat back almost the exact same diagnosis Brianne had delivered about me at the barbecue, but he rambled through it, like none of it was important. Like he didn't see the problem in me that the rest of them were starting to. He stopped in the middle of the part about my promiscuousness to take another bite of his burger.

After swallowing once again (his neck was so long and thin that his Adam's apple looked painful when he did, reminding me of girls who put gargantuan breast implants under not enough skin) and wiping his mouth with a napkin, he said, "Then Brianne pointed you out to me when we got here. I don't know what else to tell you, there was something in putting the face to the name."

"You sent over nachos."

"Do you like nachos?"

"What did you want?"

"To meet you, obviously."

With his fork, spoon, and knife, which had been sitting unused next to his plate, I performed an artless demonstration. I tipped the fork—him—into the spoon—Brianne—and said, "All you had to do was ask Brianne to make the introduction." Bundling their two utensils, I swung them over to the knife, me. "But you waited for her to do it later, and then you pretended not to know me." I pushed the fork and knife up a little. "You wanted the two of us to have a secret."

"It doesn't matter what I want." He sighed, tapping his finger near our two utensil stand-ins. I'd rested my chin back on my knuckles, my right elbow propped on the counter, and he ducked his head to look up from under me. "Do you want to hear that my connection to you was so instantaneous that it rendered whatever I have with Brianne meaningless?" He let the question hang there for a second, like he wanted me to say yes and that would actually be a relief. But then he quickly added, "How psychopathic of you."

His hair had fallen forward again. The pieces hung over his eyes. They pointed down to the mean shape of his mouth, which I found particularly tremendous.

"No," I said.

"Do you want to hear that I'm going to break up with Brianne and come pick you up from high school every day instead?"

The mention of high school took me aback. It hadn't even occurred to me before then that maybe the reason he'd decided his flirting and his lying was compatible with his relationship with Brianne was that I was too young to make it real.

I pulled my hand out from under my mouth and, bothered by the hair hanging in his eyes, pushed it back from his forehead with spread fingers. Not gently, exactly. I was trying out his move. I kept my hand there, pinning his bangs against the top of his head. His eyes widened for a second. I felt that he had such a wrong picture of me that I immediately had to fix it. I said, "In an alternate world, where you weren't with my cousin, you would already be making out with me in one of the elevators or hallways. Don't kid yourself."

When I heard myself say the word "kid," which hadn't been on purpose, it seemed to hang in the air. I'd never thought before about how kidding yourself was just assuming everything would turn out all right if you just kept on how you'd been doing. That was being a kid.

"You're naive," he said, but I thought it was in a wistful way, like that's actually what he wanted in a girl. Or maybe that was just me being narcissistic again.

From behind us the hostess called, "Excuse me? Your food is ready." I let go of Trevor and got out of the chair without looking at him another second.

When I came up to the podium she passed me a white plastic bag, knotted at the top. "How did you want to pay for this?"

My mom had told me that Uncle Kurt and Aunt Kathy

were staying overnight in a luxury suite to make their night really special, so I had the hostess charge Cricket's food to their room. I don't know what family's good for, if not for essentials like that.

CHAPTER 5

As I was reapproaching the ballroom, I saw my mom plowing mounds of snow from the place card table into her evening bag. In the illustrated fairy-tale books I'd had as a kid, the kings would do the same thing with their piles and piles of coins, sweeping them into the folds of their robes. But this was fake snow, and my mom was hoarding it like it was going to take care of her and my dad and me forever.

"Hi, Mom," I said, joining her. From inside the party, the band was doing "It's Raining Men," except, according to the singer, it was snowing them instead.

She glanced over. "Hi, honey. This stuff feels pretty realistic except for not being cold."

I took some into my hand and sprinkled it in the air. "Very soft. What are you going to use it for?"

Pausing her sweep, she framed out a scrapbook page on

the table so I could picture it. "First, I'm going to glue gun a layer around the edges of the invitation, so the card looks like it's just lying in the snow, just happened to be discovered like that." She started collecting again. "Then I think I'll put some in sandwich baggies and secure them to a page with staples, but I'll cover the staples with ribbon—don't worry."

"Why would I worry?" I asked. I'd heard from a lot of people that I was the one they'd want to be around in an emergency because I wouldn't lose my calm and I'd get everyone safely out of the car, the door, the building, ten seconds from earthquaked collapse. But saying this to my mom, I wondered if I'd just stand there, telling everyone not to worry, figuring whatever would come to pass, would, and we'd sort ourselves out then. If we weren't dead.

"You're naive," echoed from the back of my mind.

Maybe it was time to start worrying about my mom, who had begun to spend more time at the past year's occasions collecting stuff to remember them by than just creating automatic memories by accident. By, you know, just hanging out at her table.

"Are you doing okay?" I asked, but I knew that wasn't right. That wasn't what I should have asked.

My mom packed the snow down in her bag so she could fit in some more. "Of course." She looked at me with the quickness of a bird. "Are *you* doing okay?"

"Of course I am."

"Great party," she said.

I repeated the same back to her, and it was like we were clinking an empty toast, using that phrase.

When I opened the door to the ballroom, the volume of the band was nearly deafening.

Inside, my dad was in the center of the dance floor, making the face he makes when he's preparing to backflip; he looks like there's a thought he can't grab hold of. I hadn't seen him actually leave the ground since a family-wide trip to the beach when I still put my life in the care of Floaties.

I looked to the Kid Table, and Cricket was sitting there with her eyes shut. She was basically alone because the only other holdout was Alexander, and not only was I pretty sure he didn't have his words yet, but he was also still unconscious.

"Hi," I yelled over the band, placing the three stacked Styrofoam containers down in front of her.

Her eyes flickered open. "What's all this?"

"Your greens and lean protein," I said.

She opened the lid of the top container so nervously it was like she thought a severed head was inside. The flickering candles at the table added to the feeling of horror she'd successfully created around a halibut filet. "Did butter touch this?"

I took the rest of the containers and flipped open the lids, the Styrofoam creaking loud enough to go over the chorus. "I'm going to give you a choice—do you want to talk about your problem or do you want to eat?"

Her expression contracted into the one that people make

when they're about to lie by making *you* seem troubled. "I don't know what problem you're talking about. And I don't know when you became my mother."

I was about to counter that I was nothing like her mother, Brit, who has such a hatred of confrontation that when she walked in on me and Cricket, both eight, studying her and Toby's copy of *The Joy of Sex* they used to keep under their four-poster bed (after that day, it disappeared), she simply said, "Good, you girls are practicing your reading."

From what I could guess, Brit was letting her daughter waste away without saying anything, but I reasoned that nothing could come of pointing out our many differences besides another thing to fight about.

"Well, I don't know who you think you're kidding, but no, there isn't butter," I said. "Just steam. Just air and water."

Still, Cricket put aside the chicken and the fish and pulled the salad closer to her, and it kind of broke my heart to think that she didn't trust me. Until I reminded myself that this wasn't about me, that it was more realistically just mistrust of food altogether.

Poking around in the salad I'd Frankensteined together, she gently removed the strips of seared tuna and then happily speared a green bean on her fork. "Crunchy. I can't believe you located fresh vegetables in the midst of this raging squall."

I told her, "I have to take care of my people."

The room burst into wild applause and whistles, and I looked over to see my dad hopping backward, finding his balance after landing his flip. When he was steady, he threw his arms all the way up into the air and turned himself around in a circle.

He was shouting, "Did you see that, just like how I used to?"

The drummer took this opportunity to launch into a solo. "Can we get that man a prize?" asked the lead singer, almost stepping on her hair as she bent over to get nearer to the crowd.

I thought it was a rhetorical question, but then two guys and two girls in sequined tuxedo jackets and shorts combos came dancing out from the four corners of the room, one appearing from behind the fake pine nearest the Kid Table (he had better skills than the magician; I'd had no clue he was there). When a dancer reached my dad, she presented a glowing medallion from her glowing fanny pack and hung it around his neck.

He seemed proud of it, seemed not too old for it. Uncle Kurt started another round of applause, and I joined in the clapping.

Without missing a beat, the singer went straight into a disco arrangement of "Let's Hear It for the Boy," and the hired dancers began weaving through all my relatives and all the strangers, passing out glow sticks to the guys and glowing jewelry to the girls.

"Come on, let's go dance," Cricket said.

I looked back over at her. "Now?"

"No, at the wild after-mitzvah. I hear Uncle Kurt's throwing a kegger up in his suite."

"You took two bites."

"That's two bites more than I was going to eat before you

went and got me the salad," she said, and what was especially messed up was that I understood this was her way of thanking me for what I'd done.

"I need to pee. You go ahead, I'll be out there in a minute," I told her.

"We're okay?" she asked.

"Of course."

She nodded and walked toward the dance floor, undoubtedly just to burn off more calories.

I made like I was going in the direction of the doors until Cricket was occupied with a dancer sliding the glowing bangles onto her minuscule wrist, and then I slipped along the back wall, behind the trees, and snuck over to the table where Cricket's parents sat.

They were looking at something together on Toby's Black-Berry, and I took the empty seat next to Brit.

I made my face blank so they wouldn't read any concern in it. "What's up, you two?"

"Ingrid," said Brit, planting a hand on the top of my head and smoothing my hair for a moment, even though it couldn't have gotten any smoother if she'd borrowed an iron from housekeeping. "You look beautiful tonight."

"You look stunning," I said, fingering the beaded strap of her cocktail dress in appreciation.

Toby turned the BlackBerry screen toward me. "What do you think of this?" On screen was an infinity pool, the sun appearing to melt into it. "You think you and Cricket would like to float around in that next summer?"

Brit raised her eyebrows, also wanting my vote.

I whistled at the photo and shook my head at the beauty. "Well," I said, "I think Cricket has obviously developed an eating disorder."

Both Brit's and Toby's smiles faded in unison, and although this confirmed they were as reluctant to address Cricket's problem as I'd suspected, it still was kind of a touching display of how seriously they were bonded together. "Ingrid, that's a terrible thing to say," said Brit before Toby could. "Terrible."

"Look at her," I said.

Neither did.

"She just decided to get on a health kick," Toby corrected. "To better herself."

Brit shakily took a sip of her wine, and in that motion, I knew I'd successfully hit a nerve. "Why would you come over to us and want to stir up trouble for her? When she considers you like a sister? You're taking something very innocent, very positive, and manipulating—" She stopped. Her gaze flickered from one of my eyes to the other, evaluating.

"Cricket's fine," said Toby. "What motive could you possibly have by starting a rumor—" Then he stopped too.

I put my elbow on the table and pressed my left fingertips against my cheek. I hated that I'd had to come to Cricket's parents, that I was like Lassie—yes, Lassie, again—who saw the danger and who could yap her head off about it, but who didn't have the means to actually do anything. They lived with her. They made the pancakes on Sunday mornings. They had legal power over her for another year.

"Cricket has an eating disorder and you need to get her help," I said. "You know you do, or you're going to hate yourselves later."

I got up from their table and shimmied onto the dance floor, where, as soon as Cricket saw me, she held out her arms and jokingly beckoned me to her. We clasped hands and danced like that, laughing and twirling each other as we'd done for years and years, ever since we were old enough to stand upright. From the side I caught sight of her parents watching us. They stood very still, their shoulders touching. When we locked eyes, neither smiled. Ironically, the song being run through the singer's party filter was James Taylor's "Your Smiling Face." Cricket pulled me in toward her, wearing a smile that wanted me to meet her in the absurdity of everything around us. I smiled along as if I hadn't just gone behind her back. It wasn't hard.

A few more songs into the set and Micah was onstage with the band, straddling the empty mic stand like, as Cricket put it, "a girl with major daddy issues." He now had a collection of glow necklaces illuminating his bare chest, and when Dom came over to us, jaw slack and palms upturned, I told him, "You don't even have to say it."

"But . . . right?!" he demanded. He started to dance with us, but his heart wasn't in it.

"Yeah," Cricket said.

Next to the singer's bottommost curls, Micah got down on his knees and did a backbend.

Dom borrowed Cricket's laser-beam stare from before and

sent it straight at Micah's throat because his head was missing, hanging somewhere behind him like a Pez dispenser with a faulty spring. "All that's left is for one of the professional dancers to come and limbo over his nose."

I shrugged. He wasn't completely wrong.

"If he's going to act *that* gay," Dom snarled, "then how are they supposed to recognize that I'm the one they're supposed to out?" Being the only two boys at the table, Micah and Dom had come up with a code of honor for themselves back in third grade when they decided girls were gross. Even though Dom stayed with that decision while Micah was only tired of the ones at his school trying to kiss him so much, the code was that they'd always stick together against the world.

Cricket, her stamina failing, put an arm around Dom's shoulder and they swayed together. "He needs to cool it—you have dibs on causing the shitstorm in the family this year." She pointed at me. "That goes for you too, Ingrid. You also need to convince them you're mentally squared away."

Dom and I traded a quick look that I took to mean we could say the same for Cricket but weren't going to.

"No problem. Worst comes to worst," I said, doing a fancy little step, "we'll put some contact solution in my eyes, and I'll fake cry at Thanksgiving."

∞

As the party winded toward its demise, I was feeling about ninety years old, so the logical thing to do was to go and sit with my grandma Taylor at the Life Alert Table. In many ways, it was the sister table of the Kid Table, the other side of our forsaken coin; you got there by being old enough to have need for a button to push in your shower in case of emergency.

Technically, she was my stepgrandma Taylor, my mom's dad's second wife (and Uncle Kurt's mom), but she'd been sending me a five-hundred-dollar check every birthday since my parents opened my childhood Wells Fargo savings account, and that erased the distinction as far as I was concerned.

"It's the time of the night the hair comes down," she said, unclipping the pin holding her updo. Her hair, stiffened by age, didn't come down as much as tip over.

I tried shaking out my slicked pompadour. "I'd love to join you, but I'm gelled within an inch of my life." I pulled two of the empty chairs over to us with my leg, those places having been abandoned by a great-uncle visiting from Maine and his in-home aid. We kicked off our heels and put our feet up on the seats.

We watched the dancing, everyone looking like better versions of themselves. Their cheeks were flushed and their eyes were shining as if they'd been out in a real winter.

"You're young," Grandma Taylor said out of the blue.

"Youngish," I conceded.

"This should be a dramatic night for you. When I was your age, there was no night spent in a dress and set to music that didn't bring either tears or almost unbearable elation." She clasped her hands to her heart and dipped back the chair a little.

"It's not my night," I said, meaning that this was Uncle Kurt's occasion for emotion.

"Then something *did* happen?" she asked, misunderstanding.

What could I say?

Say, "Oh, Grandma Taylor, you see something sad's been building up in me tonight. Here's as far as I've gotten with it: I really feel like I want to believe in believing. Do you get it?"

"No, nothing," I said, bringing her chair, now rocking, forward again with a concealed push from my hand. "I've had a nice time tonight."

Grandma Taylor cringed, sighing. "People your age shouldn't have nice times . . ." and didn't seem to be finished, but then her gaze went past mine.

I turned my head to follow it, figuring that Uncle Kurt was topping off his party with a real showstopper. On the way over to the hotel, my dad had told me that it was Jewish tradition for the bar mitzvah guy to go up above the partygoers' heads in a bouncing chair; my dad thought he might be called upon to hold a leg because he'd been working out a lot. I wouldn't have been surprised to see Uncle Kurt being lifted into the room in a metal chair from a disassembled ski lift.

Except who my grandma was looking at was Trevor. He was pulling up an abandoned chair.

"Hello, there," Grandma Taylor said, extending her hand.

He shot the briefest glance at me, then took her hand and held it between the two of his. He had to reach across me to perform this gesture, and his left arm felt wrapped around my waist. I had an impulse to clasp on to his forearm. I killed it.

"I'm Trevor," he said. "Brianne's boyfriend."

"She's a good girl. I'm Taylor, Brianne's . . . it gets compli-cated. Just call me Taylor."

"It's nice to meet you."

She raised an arched eyebrow at me, bemused. "Nice." When it became clear that no more introductions were com-ing, she asked, "Do you two already know—?"

"We do," Trevor said.

I returned to watching the slow dancers. "Well."

He leaned toward me. "Do you want to?"

"Want to what?"

"Dance."

Lowering my voice and bringing my lips as close to his ear as I could without touching it, I said, "You have some nerve continuing this in front of my grandma."

Turning his face to do the same into my ear, he just nearly missed kissing me, but I looked forward in time. "Let's reset."

"You say that—" Now I was speaking through an almost closed mouth, like the actress who plays Serena on *Gossip Girl*, so my grandma wouldn't think she was being left out of a con-versation. "But you're still acting exactly the same."

He stood and stepped in front of me. He had Grandma Taylor's attention now. "Please dance with me."

"You should," Grandma Taylor chimed in. "You're young—you should be dancing."

I scanned the ballroom to find out where Brianne was and located her white dress over near the bar. Along with the white-striped shirt right next to it. She was talking to the mime, actually talking, which I didn't think he was allowed to do, but rules always break down at the end of a night. Their conversation looked more intense than one you could have on the subject of twisting balloons, and I guessed she was psychoanalyzing him. "You chose a career that doesn't allow you to have a voice because your father . . ." The greasepaint on his face shone nearly as bright as she did.

"What do I care?" I said to Trevor and stood up.

As Trevor was already leading me toward the floor, Grandma Taylor said, "Too bad he's taken, but maybe you'll get a good dance out of him at least."

We took a spot next to Autumn's parents. They were dancing like high schoolers: her arms were hung around his neck, her face resting in the crook of his neck. His hands were interlocked, resting on the curve of her . . . I want to say "ass," but I can't because it was Autumn's mom. I checked once more and Brianne was still talking to the mime.

I slipped my hand into Trevor's and we held hands a little differently than we'd done approximately four hours ago. I folded mine into the space between his thumb and forefinger; he closed his as much as he could. That took care of one arm.

The other I placed gently in the middle of his back, expecting that he'd press his against the small of my own. But instead he lay his palm firmly in the space between my shoulder blades, so I couldn't bend away from him at all.

Once we were like that, he began to tell me, "When I was little, I had a huge crush on my older brother's girlfriend." I tried to pull back slightly to make eye contact, but his hand kept me to him. "There are a lot of years between me and my brother. I was probably ten. In that case, he must have been twenty-one. Her too. He brought her to a family wedding, and she had on this short black dress, but that wasn't it—it was that it was low. Very low. No other women there had on anything like it."

Because he wouldn't let me pull back, I turned my head toward his, but his eye was so close to mine that it was a dark blur I couldn't make any sense of.

"I asked her to dance," he said, "and she humored me. So we did, and I held her in the correct way, and I made her laugh, and she told me, 'If you were only two years older.'" He paused. "I didn't understand that was her making a joke until much later."

I slipped my right hand out of his and took my left one from his back, so he was the only one still holding on. "Why are you telling me this? Why couldn't we just have danced?"

The singer belted out a final "ooh-ooh-ooh." The song was over.

There was a moment's lull that made it possible for me to step away from Trevor before Uncle Kurt jumped onto the stage. He took the microphone right out of the singer's hand.

"To your seats, please. To your seats!" he commanded while motioning with his free arm for the party planner to raise the lights. She brought them up halfway and suddenly everyone was a bit more sweaty and a bit less glowy than they'd appeared the second before.

I walked toward my chair at the Kid Table without looking back.

Everyone was already there (pretty sure Alexander had never left), and Katie was on Autumn's lap. We exchanged looks around the circle like links completing a ring.

"Quiet, please. I'm going to need absolute quiet." Uncle Kurt stood there and waited for his silence until it kind of came. There was still rustling taffeta and forks scraping the icing dregs from eaten pieces of cake, but we all shut up, probably more from being tired than anything else.

He took a deep breath. "I'd like to thank all of you for coming here to celebrate my bar mitzvah tonight. For coming to celebrate what you probably thought was my manhood—"

Cricket nudged me with her foot under the table.

"Or even just my forty-sixth birthday. Or maybe you're just here for the free dinner." Big laughs from the Blimpie's associates and from no one under forty. Micah pretended to go to sleep. "But the reason that I'm here is to celebrate my wife." No more laughing; everyone knew what they'd been through.

Uncle Kurt slid the microphone back onto its stand, shaking his head. Loudly, he said, "I don't want to do it on this. It makes it sound like a comedy routine."

When he started again, everyone had to lean forward to hear him.

"It's hard for me to believe I didn't lose you, Kathy," he continued without the speaker system. "I made myself sit down yesterday and think about how close I came. How had I lost my mind like that? I'd become a man who'd forgotten what it was like. To see you coming toward me down the aisle, the snow falling behind you in the windows." I hadn't known they'd gotten married in the snow.

"Just yesterday, when you went to get your nails done, I simply let myself feel you gone. Then when I heard the garage go back up—" He stopped himself. A few seconds later he didn't complete the thought but instead fought to speak through a voice choked with emotion:

"Kathy!"

He seemed to be searching for more words, his mouth opening helplessly, nothing coming out until once again, this one like a prayer sent across the ballroom to her:

"Kathy!"

I understood why so many people at the tables around us were tearing up, hearing him say her name. It was a heart-breaking act. Believe me, I know it was. Even Cricket's eyes gleamed. Micah lifted his head. Autumn nodded encouragingly. Dom looked less moved, but he respectfully bit the insides of his cheeks.

Uncle Kurt's sadness and his desperation were very clear to me. In some part of my brain, I could even feel them vividly. But another part was laughing.

Out loud.

It wasn't that I thought Uncle Kurt's speech had been all that funny. In fact, I didn't know what it was that was making me laugh so hard and so uncontrollably—authentically, from the gut—as I was doing it and as my relatives were gaping at me in horror. (Just like that, I was under renewed suspicion.) It was only later during the car drive home that I started to put things together. It was after Trevor and Brianne, standing at valet parking waiting for Trevor's car, watched me climb into the back seat of my parents' coupe.

I had been laughing because Long John had flashed through my mind again. An imaginary scene had popped into my head: me going to Aunt Kathy the day she found out about Uncle Kurt's infidelity, the day she must have been out of her mind with hurt, and me sitting her down to comfort her with the lesson of *me and my dog*. All of a sudden I knew it wouldn't translate if I tried to share the thinking that worked for me. I got this glimpse of myself from the outside. I saw myself failing to help her understand why I believed so much that you could dissolve any feeling, whether stirred up by your husband or your pet. Same either way. That's the thing it turned out I believed in. And then it all seemed absurd and naive, so I'd laughed.

I leaned back in the rear of my parents' car, the luminescent snow globe resting on my lap. (The party planner had guarded it for me like a mama tiger as the guests began to leave and take whatever they thought they could get away with.) My dad and mom didn't talk. The radio was off, but the freeway hummed. For the first time in forever I thought I could cry, but by then it would have been a waste.

PART II

THANKSGIVING

CHAPTER 6

We were very late leaving for Thanksgiving because my mom wanted to get down memories that didn't exist yet. She was calligraphing the names of all the relatives in attendance into her scrapbook, and although her list would prove to be wrong, this activity was partially what was stalling us from finding out someone was missing.

Another factor in the holdup was that my mom got busy photographing the four dozen Austrian Chocolate Balls she'd made for dessert before they went to the real table.

"Do me a favor and pretend you're taking one," she said when I came into the living room, eating a container of Easy Mac because I couldn't wait for dinner anymore.

Humoring her, I dipped my hand into the crystal bowl. She took some close-ups.

"Is my hand convincing you it wants this cookie?" I asked. "Maybe I should tense the knuckles."

"No, don't lift a finger," she deadpanned. "I'm sold."

While waiting for her to get her shot, I considered how many little details could change between her prediction and the near future. The bowl could break as she was carrying it to the car. I could lose my modeling hand in a kitchen accident right before dessert. Not even the whole hand, just a finger. Not even the whole finger, just a tip. Or the telling detail could even be one of a million things far less dramatic, like the way the cracks in the icing were going to deepen over the next few hours.

Regardless, the two remaining Bells were in no particular hurry to get to dinner either. Right around the time we should have been leaving, my dad decided to go swim laps in our pool. I knew he was serious about these laps because he'd put on his goggles and the swim trunks with the green racing stripes down the sides.

As for me, it wasn't like I was really looking forward to schmoozing my adult relatives, assembled for the first time since Uncle Kurt's bar mitzvah the previous month. I'd be right back to where I was as I walked into the hotel after the diagnostic barbecue, under careful watch and feeling some kind of oppressive but vague pressure to act normal (meaning not how I'd normally act). From looks I'd received after cracking up at Uncle Kurt's speech, I had an idea that even my older male relatives, who had been less alarmed by my light approach to life before, now thought I was dangerously insensitive. I also had an idea that when men find you insensitive, that probably required a mind-blowing amount of damage control.

Plus there was the fact of seeing Trevor, who had called once only to say, "Never mind." After he hung up, I'd stared at the phone for a minute, trying to will it to give me something more.

I'd tooled around the house all day, in no rush to get dressed or comb my hair or pay any attention to the time, which had slipped out from under us like it was still summer. I even dozed off for a few hours on the window seat in my bedroom, the sun beaming right into my face.

The best tactic seemed to be to never glance toward a clock when my parents were in the room and to make no mention of where we were supposed to be. I used to pull the same con when I was little and wanted to stay up past my bedtime. As eight p.m. crept nearer, I'd relax all my limbs, sending out the unconscious impression that everything was totally cool. I wouldn't check to see if I'd made it past the hour; other people can sense the tiniest signs of agitation. No asking to stay up later or bargaining or begging or throwing tantrums or doing so much as quietly vibrating with excitement. Instead I just behaved as if it were the most natural thing in the world I was still awake for the doink-doink of *Law & Order.* At that sound in particular, my mom would realize how late it had gotten and exclaim, "It's ten! Why didn't you say something?"

I would say, "It's ten? Wow, really?"

Relationships and bedtimes shift.

On Thanksgiving, it was also a sound that reminded my mom time had slipped her by: the phone. Aunt Kathy was calling, wondering when we were going to grace everyone with our presence.

"Ace!" my mom called out through the open sliding door. "We're super late!"

My dad pulled himself out of the pool (doing some quick push-ups on the edge) and called back, "Then I'll skip the shower!"

As he walked into the house, my mom lifted her camera and began taking pictures of him, not posing or doing anything ridiculous, just moving through the room.

"For the scrapbook page?" I asked after he'd gone.

"Family album," she said, looking at me with puzzlement for not understanding her system.

It was Brianne's family's turn for Thanksgiving, and they lived almost an hour north in Manhattan Beach. For whatever reason, my extended family had made like an army conquering Southern California, so no one had put their home base in the same city. Not that most of our cities were all that identifiably different, but I think it seemed important to our parents' identities for them to find a place and pretend to make it their own. All of us Kid Table members went to different schools and had totally separate lives the majority of the year, but we called each other at least once a week to hear the rundown, to talk about who we didn't like among our school friends, because we safely could. As long as you didn't talk about family gossip, then talking to a cousin was like talking to a priest.

Before the bar mitzvah, we'd all been following the stories about a girl that Cricket hated, Yael, because Yael hid behind the tennis clubhouse when everyone was doing laps, then joined in on the last one to make it look like she'd been in first place all along. The coach stayed on the court, and so all he saw was Yael sprinting in victoriously through the gate. Cricket wasn't a tattletale, but she was thinking she might have to hit Yael with a wayward ball. Each of us cousins had received e-mails from Cricket since the party saying that she was stressed out and busy, but no one had had an actual conversation with her. We had no idea if she'd gotten her revenge.

By the time my dad hit Ocean Drive, the sun was just a bar of neon separating sky from water. Down near the shore I could make out the silhouettes of a family, and I guessed they were probably from out of town because one of the outsider's California dreams is that the water stays warm all year.

We pulled up to the Stillmans' three-story contemporary on the waterfront, a house that Cricket believes they picked because Phil and Sailor (no kidding) misunderstood the concept of choosing a home that "reflects yourself." She was convinced they'd taken the approach literally and bought the most reflective property on the block—where the house wasn't concrete, it was made up of mirrored panels that gave it the feel of an elevator turned inside out.

Being beachside, the parking on the block was so scarce that Phil and Sailor had hired a valet just to park our relatives' cars. The guy couldn't have been much older than me, and even though he didn't need sunglasses, what with the sun being so low, he was wearing Ray-Bans that made him look as if he were doing this just for the cute factor of matching the house.

As my dad handed over the keys, he told the valet, "If you happened to total the car, I wouldn't be all that angry. I've been thinking about a Lamborghini."

When my dad started up the driveway, the valet popped up his sunglasses to make eye contact with me. "Is he kidding?"

"Only halfway." I looked him up and down, smiling as if I liked what I saw, even though I saw nothing beyond a nice-enough-looking guy somewhere around my age.

"I'll be here all night," he told me.

"You're a comedian?"

"What?"

"Never mind," I said. "You shouldn't be alone on a holiday. Later I'll bring you out some breasts and legs."

I'm not sure that one connected either.

Whenever there was a holiday involving the preparation of food, all the women crowded in the kitchen, even the ones who had no clue how to warm Pop-Tarts, which made me feel a little crazy. It was like we were participating in a tradition that had never come from us—I mean both the girls *and* the guys—and it had robbed us of making new ones that had something to do with who we really were.

The men would gather in the TV room to watch football,

even though I knew half of them didn't follow sports. Dom, who would have rather been watching the *Twilight Zone* marathon, would be resigned to pointing out how gay the stretch pants, tackles, and touchdown dances were—which, yes, is valid commentary. But if he could have just gotten that agenda out of the way, then he could have talked about all the things going on in his life, all his secret interests like lasers and Guinness beer that contradicted the flaming message he was trying to send.

Micah, not athletically inclined either, also sat with the guys on the couches, when I happened to know that he'd prefer to be in the kitchen, piercing his nose with a fork or making a shirt from Saran Wrap.

The truth was that most of us probably didn't want to be in either the kitchen or the TV room but had weird, intuitive preferences for off-limits rooms or even nooks throughout the house. If we'd let ourselves go, we might have discovered there was something to who was a home office and who was a master bathroom and who felt most themselves hanging out in the dead space just off the front entryway, my favorite.

That's where Micah and Dom met me when I came in. They were happy for a reason to leave the game. Back when they were little, their dads tried to stick them on a peewee football league together, but Micah was only interested in what he could do with greasepaint and Dom would just stare up into the sky, looking for something better out there. If aliens landed right then, he thought he'd be embarrassed for them to find him in the middle of an activity he couldn't defend. I still hadn't decided what game face I was going to put on to say my hellos to the adults.

"Lag much?" asked Dom.

We took a seat on the metal sculpture that looked a lot like it had dents specifically meant for asses, except every time we'd ever gotten caught on it, we were told this wasn't the case. The sculpture was uplit by halogens recessed in the concrete floor, and since the entryway was pretty dark otherwise, the light made the three of us look just a tiny bit evil.

"I'm the last one?"

"No Cricket or Brianne yet," Micah said, tugging at his pants. When he'd sat, they rode so low on his hips that I had to diligently interpret the shadow above the zipper as a trick of the halogens and not his happy trail.

"Brianne's in traffic," Dom explained. "No idea where Cricket is. Autumn's in the kitchen. I'm in pants with a normal rise."

Simultaneously, there was an "Ohhhhh!" from the men in the TV room and an "Ahhhhhh!" from the women in the kitchen, both suggesting that there had been mild slip-ups in their respective activities. Maybe a dropped ball; maybe a dropped turkey.

"Is Brianne bringing her boyfriend?" I asked with no interest in my voice.

Dom shrugged. "I assume she is. I saw you dancing with him at the bar mitzvah. Is he an okay guy?"

"Yeah, he's okay," I said.

"That's it? What's his story?"

I had never kept anything like this from my cousins before—in fact, they could probably tally the guys I'd ever been interested in more quickly than I could, and I could do the same for them. During our regular conference calls, when we were finished talking about who we didn't like that week, we'd move on to who we thought was decent. But I couldn't talk about Trevor. Why? Well, there was the simple fact that he was Brianne's boyfriend, but more importantly, I thought he was the only one I might have ever been authentically interested in.

"I wouldn't know," I said. "You should ask Brianne."

It was as if saying her name produced her because in the next second the front door opened and she blew in, exhaling dramatically like she'd walked down from Malibu.

"Speak of the devil," Micah said.

"Her ears must have been ringing." I punned, "A Bell talking about her."

"I'm here," Brianne told us, unbuttoning a cream trench coat, "so let's not talk about me like I'm not."

I stared at the door, waiting for Trevor to come through behind her. Maybe he was a smoker. Mostly he'd smelled of Nilla Wafers and leather, but he seemed like he could be a smoker. I could live with it. Maybe he was outside, having a cigarette before he came in with a hard and fast smile for everyone, except he'd slide me the one again that said, "I know you know." The men in the TV room would claim him. Even though I didn't have any information to back this up, I was positive he didn't give a shit about football.

"I can't believe how many people are still on the road at this hour." Brianne sat down on what, as kids, we'd decided was the head of the sculpture when we'd decided it was an elephant, although Brianne's mom had quashed that theory since. ("Absolutely not." She'd laughed in horror. "Why would I have put an *elephant* in my house?")

Brianne knew her mom would kill her for doing that. She wasn't so bad sometimes.

Dom squinted out the window behind us into what was now officially night. "Cricket must be stuck too. They're never the last to arrive. They'd think it looked bad."

"Have any of you talked to her the past couple of weeks?" I asked.

Brianne shook her head. "She didn't return my call, but she had all those tennis tournaments, didn't she?"

Regardless of tennis tournaments, the time she lost her voice to strep throat, and even the month her parents took away her phone privileges for calling this guy she'd met on our cofamily trip to Paris, Cricket always returned my calls. This time she hadn't.

I'd chalked this up to the tension between us at the bar mitzvah, which we'd pretended had gone while we were dancing, but which returned just as we were hugging good-bye. I could feel every bone in her back. She'd stiffened as if she could feel me feeling them. Then we weren't squared away. We didn't say anything and there were no smiles, but we did slide each other looks that said I knew and she knew, and there was no getting around it.

When she didn't call me back, my first thought was that I'd let our relationship settle back into place over a month, two months, however long, and we'd be fine. That's the belief that occurred to me naturally. But then I began to feel guilty for believing, no matter what, that things would be okay, because I considered that this faith might have only been the doing of the terrible grin that had long been plastered across my brain. It smoothed over the bad. It was always convincing me to relax, that everything in the world was only temporary.

Micah remembered. "Hey, I just texted her yesterday when I couldn't sleep because I thought she'd be up."

"Did she text you back?"

Appearing to realize this in the moment, he shook his head. "No."

"She hasn't returned any of my texts for a while," Dom realized too. "Shit, what do you think is going on with her? The weight loss, and she was so hyperemotional about everything at the bar mitzvah. Now she doesn't want to talk to us?" He pointed a finger at an imaginary her. "She's not allowed to do that."

"Let's call her, see where she is," Brianne said, pulling her phone out from one of her trench pockets. She started to dial but then stopped. Looked up at me with her own realization. It was already a night of group epiphany, and we hadn't even gotten to the table, where those usually occurred.

"You call from your phone, Ingrid." She dropped her phone back into her pocket. "If she's going to pick up for any of us, it'll be you."

I looked ahead, toward the glow of the rooms that were approved for use. "I don't think that's the case."

There was the swishing of wool on metal as she turned toward me.

"What is wrong with you?"

"Wrong?"

"Care, Ingrid. It's Cricket, and you're supposed to be thick as thieves. So care and get out your phone."

I turned my head sideways, and Micah and Dom were also watching me then, Micah with expectation, Dom with puzzlement. I was hoping Trevor would walk in at that second so everyone would look elsewhere.

"Oh, those puppy-dog eyes, Micah," I told him and reached down for my bag; I was wearing a minidress with no pockets. "I'll call."

We were all quiet as I hit Cricket's name and my phone dialed hers. I pressed speaker, so they could hear it ring. Except that didn't happen because there was a pause, a click, and then her voice mail message came on, saying, "This is Cricket. If you don't leave a message, you're no friend of mine," followed by the beep.

I pressed the end button.

"Her phone's off," Micah said. "That's on the weird side of things, right? It's not like she's sitting in a movie theater— this is Thanksgiving, if you know what I mean. You put a feather in your hair, and you do it."

We all glanced over at him. I hadn't noticed before because the hallway was dark and the recessed halogens washed us out, but now that I really looked carefully, I saw Micah had attached some light pigeon feathers to the bottom of his already shaggy hair.

"I think it is strange," Brianne started, but before we could get into a discussion of Cricket's normal cell phone practices, a shadow appeared in the hallway leading from the kitchen. It had a confident buzz cut and an hourglass figure.

"Kids! Get off the sculpture!" yelled Sailor, her heels clicking as she ran to save its patina from our ass friction. "Brianne, I could kill you! You know better!"

"I do, and I don't." Brianne laughed, jogging in her own heels to meet her mom in a hug. "But Happy Thanksgiving!"

As they were rocking in an embrace, Sailor lifted an arm from Brianne to motion to the rest of us. "Butts up."

"Seven up," Micah sang, getting up while hiking up the waist of his pants with one hand. As he did, I noticed that the upper portion of his butt really had been touching Sailor's work of art. Oh well, I thought. She had a professional maid service.

Now with just an arm slung around her daughter's shoulders, Sailor commanded, "Everyone back to the party. Ingrid, come join us in the kitchen—I've got something to keep you busy."

"But, Mom," Brianne said and laughed more, "isn't the turkey already dead?"

My job was placing minimarshmallows in an even, decorative layer over the yams.

However, as much patience as I had for emotional discomfort, I had zero for these kinds of details. When Sailor went to check on the dinner rolls in the warmer, I turned the bag of marshmallows upside down and dumped them over the casserole dish. I had one ear on the kitchen conversation, one listening for Trevor's entrance into the other room. He was really taking his sweet time. Autumn, in what looked suspiciously like an Easter dress, was tossing the string beans with sliced almonds, and she gave me a tenderly scolding glance.

"Come on. You've got to smooth them out with your hand. They're all over on one side."

"Have you talked to Cricket lately?" I asked, figuring that if Cricket had only been able to deal with the least judgmental and most nurturing of our bunch, it would have been her.

"No, not lately." Her eyes widened with concern. "The day after the bar mitzvah I called her to tell her I was there for her if she needed anything, and I don't think she liked that."

"So how's Trevor?" I heard Sailor asking Brianne.

The guys in the TV room erupted into cheers. I heard my dad's voice rise above the rest with a sharply pronounced, "Booyah!"

"Don't feel bad about it, none of us have heard from her," I told Autumn as Brianne told Sailor, "He's great. I don't have a bad thing to say about him." She took a bite of the carrot stick that she was holding between her fingers like a cigarette. "Besides that I hate he has to be up in San Francisco."

So he wasn't outside smoking? In the instant I found out he wasn't coming, disappointment sped through me. The bulk of it wasn't disappointment that he wasn't coming to our Thanksgiving. It was disappointment that I didn't feel relief at hearing this news. I was hoping I would have. I touched the bone in the middle of my boobs.

"I'll take care of it," Autumn said, gently arranging the marshmallows into a converging spiral.

Sailor said, "Well, he has a family too. He didn't just drop out of nowhere."

It felt like he did, though. Like he was his very own thing without any ties.

"True," Brianne said with a nod, chewing still, "and you never want a guy who isn't on good terms with his family. That's always a danger sign."

"Hello!" called a voice from the entryway. "We're finally here!"

"Oh, yay," said Sailor, wiping her hands on a dishcloth in preparation for another hug. "Now we can start dinner."

Brit came into the kitchen, removing the silk scarf from around her neck, and both Autumn and I craned our necks for Cricket, who should have been behind her. Toby would have already made a right at the hallway fork.

"Hi, hi, hi," Brit sang, moving through the room and doling out kisses on cheeks.

"Where is she?" asked Autumn.

"I don't know," I said.

We waited, watching the doorway.

CHAPTER 7

I rose from my seat at the kitchen table and headed directly for Brit, who was leaning against the island and touching the ringleted ponytail of Katie, buried and shy in Brooke's arms. I placed my hands on Brit's shoulders and turned her toward me. "Brit, you made it." I smiled. "Happy Thanksgiving!"

I saw the flash of wariness in her eyes. Then she caved into me for a hug.

"Happy Thanksgiving, Ingrid." Needing saving, she averted her glance from me to my mom, who was peeling husks from a stack of corn in a bowl. A minute ago, I'd seen her folding one of these husks and placing it in the pocket of her skinny jeans.

"Faith," Brit said, her shoulders turning. "Happy—" She attempted to move on to where my mom was, on the other side of the island, but I kept her in place with my hands.

"You too," my mom returned, blowing a kiss and then getting up from her stool to carry the corn out to the dining table.

Brit's wariness sharpened into unease. Wherever Cricket was, I knew Brit was also nervous I was about to acknowledge the last conversation we'd had, and not the part about the infinity pool.

"Where's Cricket?" I asked, tilting my head.

She blinked too much. "She's on a trip."

"A trip? How nice. But a trip over Thanksgiving?" I smiled again, infusing it with a little bit of confusion. "What kind of trip happens over Thanksgiving that doesn't involve your family?"

"Would you like some wine, Brit?" asked Sailor, offering her a glass.

"I would," Brit said. I released my grip on her shoulders so she could accept it with both hands. Then she looked about to try to wander off, so I placed a hand on her forearm.

"You were saying about the trip—"

"Tennis," Brit said, taking a sip, her eyes darting to the left. She was holding the glass in her right hand, and although I'd never paid attention to which one she wrote with, I thought that was probably a good indication of hand dominance. An episode of *CSI: NY* had taught me that when a right-handed person's eyes go to the left or the upper left, odds are decent the person's constructing a made-up idea. In other words: totally lying. "A tennis trip to a camp back East."

"They're going to play tennis in the snow over Thanksgiving, *really?*" I asked as if I were fascinated and not a bullshit detector.

"It toughens them up."

"We should at least call her from the table as a group, so she knows we're thinking about her."

"The camp doesn't allow phones."

"That *is* a tough camp."

"Grandma Cecily!" she called to my great-great-aunt, who was wobbling out to the dining room with a huge salad bowl sometimes in her upturned palms and sometimes in the air because her wobbliness had it hopping like a Mexican jumping bean. "Let me help you!"

"I've got it," her grandma said, removing one of her palms to wave Brit away.

Eyes darting back to me for the shortest instant, Brit then rushed to get her hands on the bowl and a reason to leave the kitchen.

I turned to survey the women in the room, evaluating who was most likely to have the inside track on Brit's secret. Dom's mom used to be close with her, but they drifted apart when she confronted Brit about her growing feeling that Brit didn't like her husband. Rather than have that conversation, Brit found a new shopping partner . . . in Autumn's mom, but she had lips that sank ships, and Brit wouldn't have trusted her with her original hair color.

My great-aunt Cookie *had* to know the true whereabouts of her granddaughter, but she was deaf. My sign language was so bad that even if I could draw the information out of her with my limited vocabulary, I seriously doubted I could interpret what she'd revealed.

So who did Brit talk to? (Besides Toby. Going into the TV room to grill him would put him just as on edge as if I'd followed him into a public urinal.) My gaze hopped from woman to woman, my brain checking them off with no's, until it happened to cross my mom. She and Brit talked frequently because Cricket and I did, or used to; what they had in common was us.

Remembering my mom working on her scrapbook earlier that day, I couldn't believe she would have been so crafty as to write down Cricket's name when she knew Cricket wouldn't show. That seemed out of character, that level of maneuvering.

Still, I figured it couldn't hurt to ask and watch the direction her eyes went in when she answered.

"Mom?"

She walked over and kissed the top of my head. "Yeah, honey?"

"Why isn't Cricket here?"

Taking a visual sweep of the kitchen (eyes going in every direction), she asked, "She isn't?"

"No," I said, shaking my head. "Brit says she's at a tennis camp in the snow."

"A tennis camp in the snow?" My mom cringed. Then she looked me straight in the eye, blinking at a natural rate. "As if organized sports weren't already bad enough."

I shrugged. "That's what Brit says." My voice trailed off as my gaze now landed on my cousin Tish.

Tish.

Her bond with Brit had become tighter over the past couple of years because of their shared social conservatism. I don't mean political social conservatism, like they were both into prayer in school, not into gay marriages, and gigantic fans of Arnold Schwarzenegger. I'm talking about "social" in terms of parties and family gatherings, and "conservatism" in terms of being easily mortified. I think they started looking at each other differently when they realized that they both had a problem with embarrassment. Tish gets embarrassed because she hates sex talk or anything "inappropriate," and Brit, while she has no problem with sex jokes, gets embarrassed whenever she feels exposed, and so that's the magic that brings them together. I knew that recently they'd had a spa day.

Tish wasn't exactly the easiest egg to crack, though. I wouldn't be surprised if she associated loose lips with being loose elsewhere. But thankfully there was a memory nagging at the corner of my brain, a story I'd heard the previous Christmas about how Tish used to really, really, really like her cocktails back in college. So much so that with a few in her, she supposedly became a different person.

I slipped from the kitchen into the dining room, where, as expected, the collapsible poker table had been unfolded. There it stood, the original Kid Table. Per tradition, a bowlful of nonalcoholic punch shimmered in the middle, the ladle with the glass turkey for a handle resting against its lip. Picking up a tumbler from my spot, which had been designated with a leaf place card, I filled the glass halfway with punch. Then I took the glass over to the minibar assembled by the Adult

Table and splashed (or maybe the verb I should use here is "dowsed") it with vodka. And then I couldn't have timed things more perfectly because just as I'd stepped away from the bar, Tish walked into the dining room with a pitcher of water.

"Tish," I said, sipping on the punch and making a face of deep thought. The mix of juices was so strong that the alcohol hid well beneath them. "Something about this tastes funny to me this year—maybe a new ingredient? Here." I extended the glass to her. "Does it taste funny to you?"

She put down the pitcher and accepted the tumbler. After taking a sip, she pursed her lips and mirrored my deep-thought face. "I don't usually have the kids' Thanksgiving punch, so I can't say if it's different." She took another sip. "It's strong, that's for sure." Another sip. "But it's not bad." Another sip. "Not bad at all."

Dinner had been delayed well past the latest possible time anyone expected it, per usual, and all the ice in the water pitcher had melted away. My family always underestimated the time it took to thoroughly and safely cook a turkey. As a result, we always ended up readying the table with warm dinner rolls and crisp salad and cold drinks way too early, and then we mourned these things as they cooled, wilted, and approached room temperature.

Lightweight Tish, having finished off the punch, had definitely become a different person, a chattier one, except she wasn't spilling about what I needed to know. Every time I tried to drop in Cricket's name or bring up the strangeness of a tennis camp in winter, she would spin off on tangents, revealing moments of her life that I'd never heard about before. Which were interesting, but unhelpful.

Like when we'd taken a seat on the concrete steps leading down from the dining room into what Sailor called "the entertaining area," and I said, "I really wish Cricket were here," Tish told me, "Back in school I was listening to Pink Floyd's 'Wish You Were Here,' and I was so wasted, I thought they were talking to me—to *me*, Ingrid. So I took my roommate's MasterCard from her wallet and charged myself a plane ticket to England—"

"*Cricket* has always wanted to live in London," I said emphatically. "If Cricket were to go to England, she might end up leaving the *tennis* behind and getting into *cricket*."

For a few seconds Tish laughed hysterically, which made me optimistic. So maybe she was a little bit too amused, but she still appeared to be clear enough for a two-way conversation.

Then suddenly, she stopped laughing and refocused, turning her shoulders toward me as if about to take me into her confidence.

I turned inward too, sending a message that I was creating a safe space for her delicate information.

We looked each other carefully in the eye.

Tish's voice lowered and, serious, she said, "You'd think that once I got on the plane to go to London, I'd stop being wasted . . . but they had lots of little drinks on the plane, Ingrid. *Lots.*"

I sighed and reclined against the step. She wasn't finished. "*Lots* of itty-bitty bottles."

"Uh-huh," I said, removing the empty tumbler from her hand. "Let me refill this for you."

"That would be remarkable of you," Tish slurred. "I know this family says some things about you, and I know some people in this family think maybe the way you are is some shifty, shifty act, but—" Before she could dole out the back-handed compliment, it was as if her mind were a View-Master and someone had clicked her back to the previous slide. "So I get off the plane in London, and Pink Floyd is still singing to me, and so I decide I've got to somehow get to David Gilmour's house—"

I cut her off. "I'll be right back, okay?"

She lifted both hands and twirled her hair into a bun, knotting it in on itself. I'd never seen her throw her hair up like that, and instantly I could picture how she must have looked a decade earlier, rolling out of bed and dragging herself to a nine a.m. class. "Okay," she agreed. "See you soon— wait, they say 'alligator' for 'see you later,' so why isn't there an animal for 'soon'? Why? See you soon . . . *baboon*. That's good."

Passing through the kitchen, I loaded the tumbler in the dishwasher. To my mom, I said, "Tish wants some coffee. Regular."

"Now?" She crinkled her nose. "Before dinner?"

"She's really tired today, pretty out of it. In fact, she might not even remember asking for coffee. But she should definitely have a cup or two."

"All right. I'll brew a pot."

As my mom went to the pantry to get the coffee, Sailor called out, "One minute to turkey, everyone!" Clock ticking, I went from the kitchen, down the hallway leading past the TV room, and into the guest room that Sailor used for visitors' coats and bags. Tish had been a bust, and I didn't have time to start in on someone else, and that was even if I knew who else to start in on. I shut the door behind me.

When Brit arrived she had been wearing a scarf, making wearing a coat entirely ridiculous in seventy-degree weather, so I didn't bother trying to personality-match her with any of the women's outerwear pieces piled on the bed. She hadn't been carrying a purse, however, which meant she'd dropped it off first.

I'd never paid all that much attention to what kind of bags Brit liked, so I couldn't immediately spot which was hers. Still, I had a strong inclination she went designer. Nothing flashy, though: no logos, no bright colors, no crazy hardware. She'd had on navy slacks, so I started with the navy leather Coach hobo, and imagine my surprise when I opened the wallet contained within that hobo and saw Brit's face smiling back at me from her driver's license photo. First try.

As I was digging around in her purse, looking for any interesting slips of papers or notes to self, I spotted her cell phone. I was thinking that maybe her call log could be the key to finding out about Cricket, when the door unexpectedly flung open.

"There you are!" exclaimed Brianne. Sailor and Brit were in the doorway with her. "We've been calling you to come to the ta—"

"She's going through my bag!" exclaimed Brit, turning just about as white as Cricket had been the last time I saw her.

Unfortunately, when the trio found me, I was holding Brit's hobo up in plain sight and my right hand was plunged into it, so I couldn't exactly say that I'd just been shifting bags around, searching for my own. Not to mention that my purse was still out in the entryway, not actually lying on the bed.

"Oh," I said, pretending languidly to take a closer look at the bag's material. "This isn't my mom's? I thought it was. She has one just like it."

"No, that's mine!" Brit insisted, and I shrugged and laid it down.

Eyes narrowing, Brianne asked, "Why would you be looking through your mom's bag anyway?"

"I wanted a piece of gum," I said.

"Gum," Brianne repeated, her expression turning into the one she makes when she's switching into academic mode. The best way I can describe that expression is that she looks like she's suddenly put on a pair of glasses, except she hasn't.

"Yes. To chew."

"You know," she continued, and reading her tone, I knew exactly what was about to come. "A common characteristic of psychopaths is that they have no problem with stealing.

Sometimes they even steal just to take things from others, even though the things they're taking don't have any value to them."

"Fascinating," I said, matching her tone and walking toward her and the exit. "Let's eat."

CHAPTER 8

As Sailor, Brit, and Brianne trailed me into the dining room, where the rest of the family stood around the two tables, talking loudly (we had a long-standing rule that no one sat until everyone was ready), Brianne was *still* going from behind my left ear.

"Even if you weren't intending to take something—which it kind of looks like you were, Ingrid—then we should examine the way that you thought nothing of just going through someone else's stuff. That indicates a lack of boundaries, and a common characteristic of—"

I clapped my hands over the end of her sentence and announced, "Everyone's here! Take your seats." Brianne, giving me a once-over that said we'd finish her talk later, walked over to an empty place at the Adult Table. As everyone started to pull back their chairs, I put two fingers to my chin and said, "Oh! Wait."

My relatives froze where they were. "Wait, what?" asked Uncle Kurt, midsquat.

"This just occurred to me," I mulled, keeping my fingers tapping on my chin for effect. "If Cricket can't be here with us tonight, which is really kind of depressing, except I'm sure she's having a fantastic time volleying in the hail—" Here I tipped my head to her parents, who were gawking at me as if I were about to reveal the details of what happened on their wedding night.

"—then we have an empty place at the Kid Table tonight, don't we?" I looked to Brianne. "And I know, Brianne, that you gave up your seat at Uncle Kurt's bar mitzvah, and maybe you're a little bit too old for it now, but I think I also speak for Dom and Autumn and Micah when I say that if only for this Thanksgiving, we'd really love you back."

Micah was on board. He'd been pinching out the flames on our table's gourd candles but quickly refocused and piped in. "Oh, yeah. We'd sure love you back, darling."

Dom, nodding along: "Yeah. Yeah, Ingrid, you speak for me too."

Autumn helped out, motioning for Brianne to come on back over, but I think she was being earnest.

Little Katie, bless her clueless heart, got in on the act with her adorable, plaintive, "B-ann."

Brianne had a hand on the fork at her place setting, as if holding on to it could anchor her there. "What does it matter if I'm over here, over there?"

"It doesn't," I said. "Not really. A table's a table. But for the sake of tradition."

Our family, who has no heavy religious leanings (as evidenced by the ease of Uncle Kurt's switcheroo) and no clear sense of history (we know you can trace us back to Scandinavia, but no one has bothered to do much more research than that), has always passionately responded to any suggestion of tradition.

If one year a leg of the turkey burned, which did happen one year because the ankle stub was accidentally touching the wall of the oven, then it was decided that that was a tradition. It didn't matter that no one bothered to burn a turkey leg the following year, that the tradition had died out the moment we noted it. We always thought that we were going to make something of those kinds of things. I mean, we definitely meant to carry through, even if it never happened.

The Kid Table, however, was a tradition that had carried on without effort. The actual table went up where it could. It was copied at the places where we couldn't bring it. I was sure that by reminding the adults of the one constant we'd managed to uphold, they'd send Brianne right back over like we were playing Red Rover.

I was surprised, however, that Sailor was the one to give the push. Laying her hand on Brianne's back, she said, "You should, Bee. Your boyfriend's not here. Go be with your cousins."

Then after Brianne had made her transfer back to the Kid Table, we all took our seats and began passing the dinner roll baskets.

Brianne, sitting in between Autumn and Micah, appeared more dazed than pissed. You start with one picture of how the night's going to go in your head, and when it alters, it can take you a while to adjust. Some pictures take longer to adjust than others. I know. In my case, I was busy adjusting to Trevor's and Cricket's absences, both affecting me differently but each in a big way. For Brianne, I think what she wanted was the opposite of tradition, and her move back to the Kid Table was like a waking version of that dream where you find out that you're back in a grade you thought you passed, and you can't figure out why.

Her gaze finally floating over to me, she asked, "Because I walked in on you with the purse?"

Biting into the roll Dom handed to me, I chewed and swallowed. Then answered, "It was more the dead turkey comment."

So maybe we did have one bona fide Thanksgiving tradition beyond the grade-school division of the sexes before the meal. Micah's dad, whom I called Uncle Sam even though he wasn't my uncle but really just another cousin, liked to go around the table and make everyone say what they were most thankful for that year.

You weren't allowed to say "I'm thankful for everything," and you weren't allowed to say "I don't know." You also couldn't say you were thankful for your family because that was supposed to be a given.

He started with himself, saying, "Aside from my family, which is a given, I'm most thankful the moles I had removed from my back turned out to be nothing." Dom grimaced, I guess picturing them.

Next up was my dad, thankful that "forty is the new thirty," which was similar to a joke he made once on *Love Connection*, which is where he met my mom. On their episode he told the host, Chuck, "Moccasins are the new loafers" when Chuck commented on his shoes. The show has been cancelled for a long time, but the premise was that you went out on three dates, then compared your favorite against the person the audience liked best.

My mom got 67 percent of the vote, clearly beating out Aimie and Tanya, the audience quickly picking up on the fact that Aimie had no personality, and Tanya, no matter how great hers was, could never overcome that laugh. My mom looked like a hologram next to those two. Like something unreal.

Luckily, she was as into my dad as my dad and the audience were into her. But when Chuck, bouncing his eyebrows and smiling creepily, asked, "So, Faith, do you want to tell us what happened after dinner?" my mom gave an answer that would forever cement her in my dad's family's eyes as an opportunistic tramp.

Pulling her blond hair over one shoulder, she poker-faced, "We tested out the defogger on Ace's car."

First my dad's parents, watching at home, decided she was just a tramp. Then they decided she was opportunistic because of how naturally she'd delivered that quip. Their thinking went like this: she must be leeching on to my dad's lone television appearance because she wanted to be an actress. In their minds, his getting on *Love Connection* as a contestant meant that he had star power, but my mom's role on the show meant that she was using my dad just to get famous.

Even after he brought her home to Ohio for a Christmas dinner and she told them that she wanted to be behind the camera, not in front of it (and a still-image camera at that), still a tramp. It's not that they thought she was actually running around with other guys, especially after she had me. What I took away from overheard calls and eavesdropping on fights between my parents before flights to Columbus was that my dad's family just decided a long time ago that my mom didn't have "class."

Whatever class was supposed to be. In my eyes, she was nothing but.

Anyway, that's why we spent all our holidays and big occasions with my mom's side. One time we attempted Thanksgiving with my dad's, and I saw my mom crying in a spare bedroom. I don't know why, except that it was about them.

At the Adult Table she was saying, "I'm most thankful for the new Martha Stewart craft line at Michaels. The products are great, especially the glue."

And Uncle Sam was saying, "No, come on, Faith, come on. No jokes."

"Who's joking?" she asked. "It's good glue."

For a second, Uncle Sam seemed like he was going to try to get more out of her, but then he moved on to Tish. When she told the room she was most thankful for Pink Floyd, a number of my family members exchanged baffled looks. I gestured to my mom, sitting next to her, to refill Tish's cup of coffee with the pot parked next to her mug. My mom, not making a big deal out of it, did. Like I said, class.

After that side of the Adult Table had finished with their thanks, the game jumped over to the Kid Table. Katie was supposed to be the first up, and it's not like she didn't understand the concept—I think they'd been doing Pilgrim and Indian shit with her all week at preschool—but she cracked under the pressure and went to hide under the table.

Micah was next. Uncle Sam asked him, "Mike, what are you most thankful for this year?" sounding genuinely curious.

"I don't want to do this, Dad," Micah said. "Now's not a good time." That would have probably sounded bratty coming out of anyone else, but he gave off a vibe like you were *Rolling Stone* and he was a rock star, and he was reluctantly granting you an interview after eighteen months on tour.

"Yes. You do," said Uncle Sam. "You are going to be thankful."

"Micahhhhhhh," warned his stepmom.

"Look, Katie didn't do it."

"You're acting like you're four."

Micah relit the gourd candle in front of him with a lighter taken from his pocket. "If that's what it takes." With his free hand, he pet the left side of his hair lying on his shoulder like the tail of a stole. "I put feathers in my hair. That's my gesture."

Cookie, looking agitated, signed (I'm pretty sure from the pantomiming of a lighter and cigarette) something along the lines of, "Why does he have a lighter? Sam, is he smoking now?"

I don't think this was official sign language, but Uncle Sam gave Cookie a shrugging gesture generally recognized as "Who knows?" Then he ordered Micah, "One thing."

A few of the other adults echoed how easy this was to come up with.

Micah said, "I just don't know."

"How could you not know what's good in your life?" asked Aunt Kathy.

Micah propped a knee up against the Kid Table. It wobbled dangerously, and Autumn stilled it with both hands. "I told you, I just don't know about anything important like you want to hear. A roof over my head, okay? There you go. A roof."

Uncle Kurt suggested, "He should come work at Blimpie's. He has it so easy, he doesn't know what he has."

Grandma Taylor said, "You're young. That you can navel-gaze like that and nobody at this table will fault you—*yet*—you can be thankful for that. That patience goes away."

"Who's navel-gazing?" Micah asked, lifting up his already thin and holey T-shirt to show his belly button, which sat a good four inches from the waistband of his jeans. "Except you guys."

"Shirt. Down," commanded Uncle Sam.

"Touch the ground," Micah singsonged. He was referencing the movie that our parents used to throw us in front of after the Thanksgiving meal until we were ten, *Winnie the Pooh and the Honey Tree*, which they did so they could hang out and seriously drink. Micah seemed a little melancholy to be remembering it. He'd also been like that, his face the same, when he'd seen that Brianne wasn't coming to the Bunny Slope at Uncle Kurt's. The rest of us, besides Katie, had been insulted. He'd been something else. Sad, maybe. I'd thought I detected an air of nostalgia hanging over him, but it wasn't the pleasant, heart-warming kind.

"It puts me in the mood," Dom continued the lyrics.

"For food," I finished. I had never been a big fan of Winnie the Pooh, who I thought was a big lump, especially because of a famous quote of his that had always sat wrong with me. As a kid I had an embroidered pillow in my bedroom with Pooh's head saying, "If you live to be 100, I hope I live to be 100 minus 1 day, so I never have to live without you."

When I was old enough to really think about it, I thought I'd never heard a more self-centered thing in my life. It revealed a deep, intense narcissism on the part of Pooh, a characteristic you might check off on the Hare Psychopathy Checklist as "callousness and a lack of empathy."

Missing the reference, Uncle Sam said, "Hold up, there, we'll eat, Ingrid, but not until we've heard from everyone. Your turn."

"I'm thankful that everything's basically okay in my life," I said.

I was staring into a horseshoe of suspicious minds. "Are you just saying that because of what Micah said?" asked Brianne from over to the left. "Because you're so good at giving everyone what they want to hear?"

Winnie the Psycho and Micah the Angsty were fine. I was the deviant.

Standing up from the Kid Table, I answered, "No, I said that because it was fast to say. I need to step outside and get some air. I'm not feeling so great."

As I moved down the length of the Adult Table, inching along the concrete wall, everybody was talking at me. I'd pulled a first. No one had ever gotten up before the turkey, ever.

"What's wrong, honey?" my mom asked from the other side of her table, which I heard over a lot of the same kinds of questions.

"I just need to get some air for a minute. Maybe the Easy Mac I ate earlier was bad."

As I passed by Bruce and Michelle, I saw they were holding hands secretly between their chairs. I wanted to somehow signal Autumn that she should get up and look, but I didn't know how to do that without making a scene for them; I'd just have to tell her later. Besides, once they realized I saw, they separated and pretended to mess with the napkins on their laps.

"You want me to come with you?" asked my dad.

"No, no. Just need to step outside, really." Now at the door, I called back over my shoulder, "Start without me!"

I got a whole bunch of "But we can't"s.

"Please, eat. The turkey might get cold."

When I slipped out the door, my family was still talking confusedly, but it was getting late, and I knew that if I lingered more than ten minutes, they'd have to start carving. I shut the door behind me as quietly as possible because the valet was down at the end of the driveway, listening to a glowing iPod, and I wasn't out there to get his attention.

Maybe I was the one who clung the hardest to tradition because I couldn't sit at that table without Cricket. It was like she was standing up somewhere. That was the rule—you didn't start until everyone was in her place.

I retrieved her mom's cell phone from where I'd lodged it underneath the front closure of my bra.

When she'd caught me with my hand in her bag, the phone was small enough that I could palm it while appearing to withdraw a straightened hand. I'd learned that trick from a magic book I read over and over and over again in fifth grade, thinking it would come in useful someday. I was right.

Then I'd pretended to adjust my boobs as I walked out of the guest room, and while doing this, slid the cell under my bra, keeping it tightly secured by walking with my back arched and my chest out.

The night chill had set in; it was amazing how quickly and how much the temperature dropped in the dark. I was jacketless. I could hear the ocean. Not waves or anything—it was pretty dead—but I just could hear the mass of it, the way you can hear a blanket when it's pulled over your head. The valet sang a line of a song I didn't know. That's it, though, only a line.

My hands were shaking from the chill as I opened the phone and began to scroll through the calls. Relative, relative, relative, relative, husband, a couple names of Brit's friends that I'd heard Cricket talk about before. She hated her mom's friends.

Underneath an outgoing call to Heidi, who was the mom of Cricket's best friend, Ivy, from her school, there was a number without a name. It had an area code I was unfamiliar with. Brit had called it just that morning and had stayed on the phone for thirty-six minutes.

I hit send and the number dialed.

After four rings, a bored-sounding woman answered, "Hummingbird House."

"Are you a bird sanctuary?" I asked.

"Are you trying to prank me?"

"Are you a person's home, like you're telling me this is the Hummingbird residence?"

"Are you for real?" asked the woman.

"Yes."

"No," she said, sighing, "this is not my personal residence. This is a home for girls with eating disorders."

CHAPTER 9

They had checked her in.

"Can I please talk to Cricket Dillinger?" I asked the Hummingbird House woman.

I wasn't prepared for the horror with which she responded. It was as if I'd asked if I could have the username and password she used to shop online. "No, you certainly *cannot*."

"Why's that?"

"It's after hours! Everyone's asleep."

"You're not," I said just because her tone was so aghast at my question, like being up at that hour was humanly impossible.

I could practically hear her shaking her head. "That's because I'm on overnight."

I pulled the phone away from my ear to check the time, but it wouldn't display while on a call. Last I'd glimpsed a clock, it had been approaching eight o'clock.

"You must be on the East Coast, then," I said, "unless Cricket's bedtime has reverted twelve years."

"Yes, we're in Connecticut." So Brit had been truthful about that aspect. "You can leave her a message if you like, and she'll get it in the morning."

"I'd really like to talk to her. Wake her up. She won't be mad."

"I can't *wake* her up"—"wake" being the newest cuss word. "There are rules."

In the back of my mind, I could dimly hear Brianne at the Labor Day barbecue, saying, "Another thing about psychopaths is that they just don't get rules. They find them inconvenient and often unreasonable." To be fair, in this instance, I did. It was Thanksgiving. Play a little fast and loose, Hummingbird woman—wake Cricket up.

I didn't know why I hadn't worked faster to repair my relationship with the Hummingbird woman as soon as I understood where I was calling, but I guess that's how much Cricket not being around had thrown me off. After our first couple of exchanges, I became fully aware I wasn't going to get anywhere with Hummingbird unless I came at her from the right angle. I knew that I should be flattering her, telling her how much I admired how difficult her job must be and that she must be pretty special to be able to do it. Or I should be empathizing with her, getting her into a conversation about how much it sucks to work a bad shift. Or I should have very delicately been probing what it would take to get that phone over to Cricket. I had my own checking account. Maybe Hummingbird wanted a new pair of shoes.

Still, despite this knowledge, I couldn't get myself back on track. Thus, what resulted was me yelling at Hummingbird, "She's my cousin and my best friend and I really, really miss her! Would you please put her on the fucking phone?"

At this outburst, the valet turned around to look up the driveway, pulling out an earbud, and when he saw me, he waved happily. Immediately I recognized he was one of those people who have little to no awareness of circumstances—you could be at a loved one's funeral, crying your eyes out—and so they never understand when it's not a good time.

I jerked my head at him, like, "What's up, man?"

Following a cold silence, the Hummingbird said, "I think we're just about done here, young lady." Then she hung up the phone.

I thought about dialing again and asking her to take down that note, but that wouldn't help anything. Cricket would wake up to a sheet from a WHILE YOU WERE OUT memo pad in a stranger's handwriting that read, "Hi, it's Ingrid. Happy Thanksgiving. Hope you're eating something? Talk soon," with an X in the box for "Please return call."

The valet was motioning to me from beside the reflective mailbox. I felt like I couldn't go back in and sit down at the table, at least not yet, and there were hedges to the right of me and a decorative steel wall to the left. So I walked down to him in the only remaining direction. Plus, I was still shaking, and he was wearing a jacket I thought he'd give me.

"Hey," he called when I was almost to him.

"Hey."

"What's your name?"

"Nadia." I was gearing up to possibly kiss him, just for distraction, and I liked the idea of taking on a character while making out, especially a Russian one.

"Ingrid," a male voice said from within a black car that had been idling at the curb by the opposite side of the driveway. "Ingrid."

"I'm Nick."

I turned to look. The passenger window was rolled down, but I couldn't see who was behind the wheel. I bent and put my hands on my knees so I could get a better view in.

Nick asked, "So, uh, what do you like to do for fun?"

"Who is that?" I wondered.

"Ingrid. It's me." Sometimes "it's me" can be one of the more frustrating ways an unfamiliar person can announce himself to you because it usually begs another question. This time, though, I knew exactly who was in that car.

"Who does that dude want?" Now Nick had awakened to the context around him and jerked his thumb at Trevor's car like he wanted me to get a load of that crazy guy. "There's no one out here but us."

"Excuse me," I said.

It took a second for Nick to realize I was walking away toward the car, but when he did, he was concerned. "Do you know him? Is that safe?" he called after me. "Or does he need me to park him?"

I held up a hand to signify everything was okay.

When I came up to the passenger door, Trevor reached

over and opened it for me from the inside. As I ducked into his car, the heat from the vent instantly stopped my shakes. I shut the door and the overhead light went out. I turned to look at him and saw he was wearing a white Hanes undershirt like the last time I saw him. I thought it could be the same one. He was that kind of guy, the kind who wears a shirt until it falls apart. He still needed to wash his hair by most people's standards, but I couldn't figure out why it looked so good anyway.

"What are you doing here?" I asked.

He ignored my question and leaned toward me, his face earnest. "How have you been?"

"What are you doing here?" I repeated.

"How have you been?" he repeated even more earnestly.

"No. What are you doing here?"

He smiled at how difficult we were each being. "No, really, how have you been?"

"Oh, screw you," I said, tipping my head back and staring out through the moonroof. "I'm doing fine."

"Honestly?"

Now I leaned toward him. We'd have been close enough to kiss if only one of us had closed the distance. I wasn't going to kiss him. "Why would you doubt that? Do you want to hear that I've been a little sadder than usual since we last saw each other and that it's all because of you?"

"Do you think I'm sitting out here in the car because I was hoping there'd be a chance that I'd get a look at you?"

"Actually, I do," I said.

He just stared at me until I glanced over at the house, the

front of which was reflecting the car back to us. "You should pull forward," I told him. "It's like a police mirror. I'm guessing you weren't sitting out here because you were just about to come in and join us."

Trevor considered me for a second longer, then rolled the car up past the wall of flat-topped hedges to the neighbor's walkway lantern. It was also modern, a barely glowing column of off-white, and it illuminated us just about as much as a nightlight. He left the car running, so we'd have the heat.

Once more, I asked him, "What are you doing here?"

He acted like this was the first time he'd heard the question. "That's very caring of you to wonder. I was thinking about surprising Brianne. Or I was thinking about seeing you again. Take your pick. Then I pulled up to the house, and neither seemed like such a smart idea anymore. Then I saw you."

"Don't start with the 'I saw you' again," I said.

He messed with the radio, going through stations. "I saw you bullshitting that car parker. I saw how you were tilting your head."

"You made the effort of flying back from San Francisco to come to my family's Thanksgiving, and now that you're here, never mind?"

He settled on a talk station. I don't know this for sure, but in that moment I felt like he'd picked it because if there was a conversation going on beneath ours, it was like we weren't out there alone together in his car. It was one of those call-in shows, and the woman on the phone was asking the psychologist host how she could better deal with the stress of the holidays. In previous years, she'd driven herself to a nervous breakdown.

"No, I never went to San Francisco," Trevor said. "I didn't have plans to. My family and I don't get along so swimmingly anymore."

"Why?"

"There wasn't one huge incident that would be fun to tell people about." When he looked sideways at me, there was mischievousness in his eyes that didn't make it down to his mouth. "Rough patch."

"I'm sure lying to Brianne is really going to protect your bond there too," I said.

"For someone so interested in psychology, Brianne really has no idea about all the different ways people can be fucked-up in relationship to one another." Even as Trevor was saying this about Brianne, which was arguably insulting to her, he wore an expression I could only describe as fondness. I wished I hadn't seen it. "She walks into your uncle's party, and your whole family's happy to see her. She's happy to see everyone. It's strange to stand beside that."

I looked at him. "You don't seem to have a problem being around me, and I'm just as charming."

"I said happy, not charming."

"Brianne and I are very similar."

"I know that's how you think," Trevor said, lowering the radio some because the caller was getting so loud and upset (the host had just told her to let it all out, just leeeeeet it all out), "but that's not who Brianne is. You think you two have got a competition going. You think she's as wily as you. Maybe you think even more than you."

"Wily?" I repeated. I couldn't remember if I'd ever heard that word used apart from the coyote.

"I'll let you in on a secret," he went on. "Brianne doesn't understand you. She has no idea that this game of who can be the most charming is going on. All she knows is that she can tell she doesn't know you, and she feels like she should. That's the only reason she latched on to the psychopath thing. She's excited about what she's been learning. She thinks she's onto finding the key to someone who's confused her for a long time."

It was hard to believe I could have misread all the times I saw those signs of bitch take over her face, or that I'd felt as if she and I were on opposite sides but at least in the same war, except for her reaction to her Kid Table homecoming. She'd seemed more confused than mad. I'd noticed that. And when she could have told me off for getting her put back in a folding chair, she instead had asked me why.

"What, are you studying psychology too?" I asked.

He gave me what might barely qualify as a grin but only to the people who used to refuse to smile in their old-timey photographs. "I'm a creative writing major." Then, just diving right back into it, "You enter a room, and maybe you're happy to see everyone, or maybe you're not. It doesn't matter either way. The difference is that you'll let them think you are because it's easier to deal with them like that. You think about cause and effect. Brianne doesn't."

He made Brianne sound like a saint, which was an altogether

new light in which to view her. He made me sound like, well, not a devil. Mostly, like myself. "If you're not studying psychology, why do you think you know so much about the way my head works?"

"Have you ever had a dream where you're best friends with someone you barely know? It's like you know everything about her in it. You wake up, and you still have that feeling. You see her in real life, and you still think you're best friends. Your consciousness knows better. But you don't."

"I've had that one," I said.

"I've never had a dream about you," he said. "But you're like that for me." My chest tightened. I understood what he was talking about, but I refused to say so out loud. He looked me up and down. "I like your dress." He laughed.

"Yeah, you told me the same thing when we were sharing that chair." I glanced in the sideview mirror to see if anyone had come out of the house yet to ask Nick where I went. But he was still by himself, back to listening to his iPod and admiring the moon, the stars, or a passing plane from LAX. Something bright up there.

"I remember," Trevor said.

"If you're just going to keep going back over the same lines with me, that's going to be really fun."

"It's all I'm allowing myself to do with you."

When Trevor made this kind of comment, a comment that could open the door to certain admissions or discussions that Brianne wouldn't want to hear, I knew I had to treat it like something worthless. If I decided to hold on to things that

Trevor said, things like, "It's all I'm allowing myself to do with you" or "You're like that for me," my head would be as big a mess as my mom's scrapbooking closet, where she'd started keeping every object she could *maybe* see turning into something someday, even the Styrofoam blocks the couch cleaner guys put under the legs.

I'd stare into my mom's closet and wish I could clear it out, clean the shelves with a Swiffer cloth, and then only put back the supplies she was realistically going to use. And as soon as Trevor said something to me that I couldn't make any headway with, I knew I had to treat it the same.

Also, I don't want to be so mental as to say that I was so connected to my family that I had the strongest feeling one of them was about to walk down the driveway any minute, but I did know their patience levels. Someone would be out to check on me soon. I couldn't risk it being Brianne.

"Are you sure you don't want to come in?" I asked. "I got our cousin Tish drunk by accident, and she's newly funny."

His gaze flickered up to the rearview mirror then settled back on the windshield. "No, I'm going to have dinner alone." The radio show was going to a commercial break, a classical Christmas song playing it out as the station wished its listeners "Happy holidays, whichever denomination you may be, even if you have no denomination."

"Okay. I'd better return to the table."

"You didn't get her drunk by accident."

He was completely right about me, and I let myself wonder what it would be like to be with someone who knew what I did and why I did it. Even just for a second, that idea was terrifying and thrilling. Then I noticed a fingerprint on his passenger window and rubbed it out with my elbow. "I was aiming for tipsy. The extent of her drunkenness was an accident."

Before I could open the door, Trevor reached out toward my face and it seemed like he was going to brush a piece of hair out of my eyes, but then he paused and tugged gently on it instead. My dad and uncles used to do that when I was little, when I was in low pigtails. It was a ridiculous move for him to pull. I could feel the intent behind it. So ridiculous that it might have broken my heart a tiny, tiny bit.

"Stop trying to convince yourself I'm too young for you," I said. "I think it's plenty enough that you're with Brianne."

He let go of my hair, leaned back in his seat, and flipped on his headlights. I opened my door, triggering the overhead light.

"That was some music at the bar mitzvah, huh?" he said, his mean mouth smiling at me.

"Some music." I got out of the car and then bent to look in a last time. "Have a happy Thanksgiving." I shivered.

"Happy Thanksgiving." Reaching for something on the floor in back of his seat, he said, "Take this." When he lifted his arm, I saw it was a royal blue hoodie. The blue was bright and distinctive, definitely not the color of every Tom, Dick, or Harry's hoodie.

"You're not thinking," I said, shut the door, and walked toward Brianne's house. From behind me, I heard his motor idling for a little while more, and then his car pull away.

As I passed by Nick at the mailbox, he pulled out his earbuds and asked me, "Were you serious about bringing me a leg before? I'm getting kind of hungry."

"Nick, I will definitely see what I can do."

"What were you doing all that time?" asked Aunt Kathy when I reentered the dining room. From the edge in her voice, I could tell the impact was still fresh from when I laughed at Uncle Kurt for calling out her name. Moreover, my mom had told me that Aunt Kathy had been unthrilled when she saw I'd charged an extra restaurant meal to their hotel bill. I think the direct quote was, "The beautiful dinner we paid fifty dollars a head for wasn't good enough for her?"

Taking my seat at the Kid Table, I tried to end that conversational thread by answering, "I was throwing up."

However, Aunt Kathy wasn't finished. "You don't look like you've been throwing up."

I'd been in the process of shaking out my napkin and lowering it to my lap, but this observation really intrigued me, and so I only got it as far as my waist. "No?"

"You don't look clammy at all. Your skin's a beautiful, healthy color."

"Why, thank you, Aunt Kathy," I said and brought the napkin the rest of the way down. "That's really nice of you to say."

After both my mom and dad had checked to make sure I was okay from their end, the Adult Table and Kid Table (even though they touched borders) went back to being separate countries. The adults talked mortgages and restaurants and us, their voices bouncing off the concrete. As for us, we rarely discussed them.

Instead, Brianne had gone back to the subject of Cricket, saying that if she really was at a tennis camp, then she was only using it as an excuse to avoid deeper issues.

"Right," agreed Dom, his favorite pointer finger coming out for emphasis. "She likes tennis, but it's not like it's her life's passion."

I sat there, cutting my piece of turkey breast into neat, equal pieces, feeling unusually alienated from my cousins. I felt like the dad who comes home from work late after his family's already having dessert, and while they talk about their interlocking lives, he retreats into the parts of his that they don't touch. Now that I knew where both the missing Thanksgiving guests really were, I couldn't think what to do with the information except keep it to myself.

Cricket was the one I probably could have talked to about seeing Trevor. She would have said something about it being no wonder he was using a holiday to vacation from Brianne, but then she would have also said that I'd done the right thing. When I ran back through everything I'd said to him in my mind, I hadn't uttered a single sentence I couldn't also say to Grandma Taylor. Granted, some of them wouldn't have made sense in that context. But there was nothing that would have been scandalous.

I couldn't talk to Brianne about where Cricket was because

that information would send her into a junior-shrink frenzy. She'd want to quiz Brit and Toby on the Hummingbird programs and facilities. I could tell her to play it cool, but ultimately she'd think she could help by offering her early-sophomore-year expertise, and she'd bring the subject up with Brit. Brit had done the right thing by checking Cricket into Hummingbird, but Brit also obviously didn't want anyone to know what she'd done. She didn't deserve my undoing her secret. What would be the point of that? Maybe for once Brit was keeping quiet not because she was embarrassed, but because Cricket was, and if that was the case, of course she didn't want the Kid Table to know. Me included.

I chewed my turkey and studied my cousins one by one.

Brianne I tried to see through Trevor's eyes. She was theorizing about how the jokes Cricket liked to make at Brianne's expense were probably just cries for help. Her cheeks were peachy with cracking the case, like a lovely female Sherlock Holmes, minus the cocaine problem. There was no menace about her.

The unyielding, sprayed-up wall of Dom's white blond bangs made him look more standoffish than he was. At first, I think it gave strangers the impression of him being very "talk to the hand" because he was communicating the same feeling with his hair. Combined with the funnel-neck windbreaker he always kept zipped up to his chin during the colder months, they also made him look like he'd just faced down high gales.

He pointed again at Brianne and said, "Maybe you're on to something there."

He probably loved Cricket as much as me.

Autumn held up a hand, as if to say, "Now, let's not jump to conclusions." Her eyelashes were the longest in the family. She lowered her gaze to her plate, and she looked so sweet it was like she was softly tucking in her eyes for the night.

I looked to Micah. He opened his mouth and stuck out his tongue. On it was a stem from a maraschino cherry, taken from the minibar, and he'd orally tied it into a knot.

Katie was clapping not because she was impressed with Micah's trick, but because a bunch of the women had gone into the kitchen and come back holding the desserts.

Maybe I was the wiliest one at the table.

"Hey, Ingrid, you're being quiet," Dom said, bringing me back to him. "Not feeling any better?"

I didn't know what I was feeling, but I was very in touch with what I was wondering. My questions included: Where was Trevor driving to? What did he and Brianne talk about when it was only the two of them? Would Cricket and I ever talk about where she'd been? And was it really possible for anyone to ever know you better than you knew yourself, or (as I looked around at my Kid Table comrades) should we all just be thankful for the rare true glimpses we actually get of each other?

"I'm just sitting here, sulking for no reason like a teenager," I told him.

"Awesome," Dom said.

Soon around came the pies and everyone's favorite, the brownies, and the cookies shaped like Pilgrim hats, and then the crystal bowl of the Austrian Chocolate Balls made its appearance at the Kid Table. Dom asked my mom what they were called, even though he knew, but he was so wiped from the evening he couldn't even muster the energy to announce how gay Austrian Balls are. I reached for one, staring at my hand. I still had all my fingers. The icing had held up surprisingly well. All was intact. The flash went off on my mom's camera. Had anything changed? I thought I couldn't even tell.

PART III

NEW YEAR'S BRUNCH

CHAPTER 10

A new year, and most of the family was standing in front of Dom's house because they were pretending to admire my dad's new car. He hadn't gotten the Lamborghini. (As he said, we were doing okay, just not *that* okay.) He'd traded in his gray coupe for a red coupe, same model. Granted, the model was a later year, but it looked identical.

Even at ten in the morning, the day was so uncomfortably bright that every single one of us was in sunglasses, lending the group the appearance of a futuristic sect worshipping our new idol god. Katie had on kiddie sunglasses with "Hannah Montana" emblazed down the sides. Great-Great-Aunt Cecily, Grandma Taylor, and Cookie—who I'd always just called Cookie, maybe because she couldn't hear me calling her anyway, so it seemed pointless to tag more onto her name—were in their matching pairs of those glasses that darken into sunglasses when you go outside.

Trevor was standing directly behind me in aviators and the royal blue hoodie. I looked back only once. He hadn't called again.

Brianne, in gigantic Nicole Richie's, was nestled under his arm. Christmas had been postponed because of too many family members finishing vacations and the flu (not worldwide Christmas, I mean—just our collective one), so I hadn't seen her since Thanksgiving, but sometime since then she'd gotten a mom haircut. She'd cut off like ten inches and now it was the kind of hair you actually had to "do" or it would look like shit. Not that it didn't look like shit that morning, but she'd made the effort to get volume at the roots and feather what I guess were supposed to be bangs.

"It's really sexy," Half Uncle Tobias decided about the car, not Brianne's hair.

"The color. I know," my dad said.

"Leather seats?" wondered Uncle Kurt.

"Also sexy," my dad confirmed.

Dom's mom weighed in, probably just because she wanted to wrap up the car beauty pageant and encourage the family to move back in the direction of the house. The Bells had been the last to arrive and the coupe had dragged everyone else out. "The shape is very cute. So, good, good, that's really something, and let's all start . . ." She began inwardly circling with her arm for people to follow her in.

Guys like to say vehicles and houses are sexy and girls like to say they're cute, and really, I thought, there was the crux of so many problems in our society.

"I don't want to argue, but it's not cute," my dad said.

My mom took a photo. "This way the argument will last longer," she said in a pointed way that I thought was for my dad. I'd heard the two of them arguing in their bedroom before we left because my dad's side of the family had thought that she didn't send them holiday cards this year, when really, she was late getting them out to everyone because she'd been so busy with the scrapbooking. So then my mom had scanned the photo card and sent it out as an e-mail, except my dad's family thought she was just being cheap and it snowballed from there after my mom saw an e-mail to my dad in which *his* mom wrote that the sparkling tank top my mom was wearing in the picture was cheap too.

"Let's begin . . . ," Melissa attempted again, and this time everyone started to plod up the orange tile steps of Dom's Mediterranean-style house, tired from celebrations the night before. I'd gone to a party of a friend from school, but the most exciting thing about it had been the glow-in-the-dark arch of balloons over her front gate. I kissed her twin brother at midnight; he was home for the holidays from his military academy and had a tongue like a missile. I felt nothing for him. I felt more for Trevor with him just standing behind me, not even in reach.

When Melissa opened the door, I heard Cricket yell, "Don't let the dog out! He's still learning about streets!"

The two thoughts this warning inspired in me went through my brain backward, seeing as how the thought that mattered way less came in first. First I thought, "I can't believe Melissa and Alec got a dog." They're more into cats. Then I thought, "Cricket is *here.*"

Dom was the cousin nearest me, so I took hold of the hem of his shirt to slow him and asked, "Cricket's here?"

"Yeah." He nodded. "I guess it's not like that tennis camp she went to runs forever, even if it was fake. Wherever she was, she looks good. Everyone's been saying so."

None of the others ever knew Cricket had been away-away. I didn't really have much of an idea about how long the Hummingbird House program took, but I definitely hadn't been expecting to see her until at least after a season had passed. Before Christmas got moved into a hybrid with New Year's, Brit had been hemming about Cricket's coming, saying she might be going for a visit to Yale.

But when I walked into the house, Cricket was standing by Melissa's prized, gigantic Grecian urn, holding a miniature greyhound. She wore a red sweater dress that didn't hang off her. And Dom was right. She did look good. I went straight over and gave her a hug, dog and all, and inadvertently must have squashed him a bit because the little guy gave out a little yelp.

Of course, Brianne was walking through the foyer behind me just as this happened. I hadn't seen her, but then I did hear her say, "Ingrid! What are you doing to that poor daw—"

That's as far as she got because Cricket said from over my shoulder, "Brianne, for New Year's you should resolve not to say 50 percent of what seems smart in your head."

"Hey!" said Brianne, losing her invisible doctor's glasses expression. She'd have to work on maintaining that for when she had real patients; I was sure they were going to say worse.

"Love you," Cricket told her flatly.

Brianne shooed away Cricket's sentiment like she was intercepting a blown kiss in midair. "That's not healthy," she said and walked off toward the terrace. Trevor wasn't next to her anymore.

Cricket and I looked at each other and made peace just like that. That terrible grin in me would have made me wait longer to be her friend again because it always maintained that forgiveness was just around the corner at every step. Maybe it would have even persisted until so much time had passed that we could barely remember how things had gotten strange between us, but I was glad I didn't have to. As my parents passed on the way in, they told Cricket they'd missed her at Thanksgiving.

I said, "I also missed you."

"I heard," she said.

I petted the dog, who had either forgiven me or forgotten the pain because he began to lick my hand. "From your mom?"

"From Nia." Cricket sighed like the jig was up. "I knew you were the only one who would scheme her way to finding out where I was, then have the balls to call."

"Nia," I said, finally able to put a name to the voice. "How has that Nia been treating herself?"

"You didn't tell any of them." She tilted back her head and

peered down at me like a coach taking stock of a player who'd come out for her team. To see how much heart the kid had. "Thanks."

"Why would I have," I said. "And when did Dom's family get a dog?"

Cricket looked at the greyhound and shifted him in her arms so he was sitting upright. "Him? No, he's mine. This is Saucy Evening."

I stared into mournful eyes set far back in the long, serious face. I thought the dog would lounge like that, in Cricket's arms, for all of his remaining years if she'd let him. All remaining, what? Twelve?

"Don't get worried, but he doesn't seem very saucy."

"He's a retired show dog and used to do some racing, so he came with a tragic name."

Ever since we were in our fuzzy jumpers, Cricket had been begging her parents for a dog, especially after I got Long John. But her dad had been bitten by a cocker spaniel when he was, like, three, and since then had considered all dogs, even Yorkie puppies, wild, violent beasts.

I asked, "Did you get him for Christmas? I can't believe your dad finally got over his dog thing."

"No, just a couple of days ago," she said, kissing the top of Saucy Evening's head. "They got him for me when I came home—to help. To be my PSA."

"Oh, he's going to talk to me about staying off drugs?"

Cricket used Saucy's paws to hit an imaginary ba-dum-bum-CHING on an invisible drum kit. "Psychiatric Service Animal. They're like guide dogs except instead of helping me cross the street, which he shouldn't be doing anyway because sight hounds are notorious for having no road sense, and so he's almost guaranteed to get hit by a car, he helps me with my . . ." She seemed reluctant to name what was wrong with her. "My anxiety by just, well, sitting in my arms."

I said, "I didn't know you'd been that anxious." Brianne might have had a better idea of what you were supposed to say, but I kept it simple because I just didn't have any instinct about what was helpful. Or maybe I was just a failure as a friend. I couldn't tell which was worse.

"I'm working on it." She scruffed in back of one of Saucy's ears, and all of a sudden he looked alert. He must have experienced pleasure with quickly diminishing returns because in two seconds he went back to looking depressed. Apparently, Saucy Evening needed his own miniature-miniature-greyhound to sit in his arms. "It's still not good, but it's better. He can even go in restaur—"

Just then, a muscular grown man in a diaper ran tiptoeing barefoot across the archway behind us. He wasn't a family member.

"A grown man in a diaper," Cricket observed, which made him whip around his head to look over.

"You didn't see me," he said.

"Of course not," I said.

"Did I miss *him* at Thanksgiving?" Cricket asked, petting Saucy like she was a Bond villain.

"No. He's brand-new."

Cricket and I joined the rest of the family out on the terrace, which extended from the living room out over a canopy of low palm trees and made it easy to imagine you were someplace like Hawaii—unless you were Dom's dad, who said they took him straight back to Desert Storm. He'd been a war photographer stationed at a palm-heavy hotel in Kuwait, where he'd looked out upon the tree's heads from his room's balcony every morning. He'd seen some terrible things. Because my mom shared his interest in photography, he'd showed her the photos he'd taken of them. Then she borrowed the prints and showed them to me because she found them so powerful.

"Why'd you plant them, then, Dad?" Dom finally asked at last New Year's brunch.

"Your mom likes them," he'd answered.

I remembered wondering, when you loved someone, romantically or otherwise, what was the balance you aimed for? How had Alec measured the amount the trees bothered him against the amount Melissa wanted them? And how did my mom weigh wearing cheap tops in Christmas photos against the obvious response my dad was going to get from his family? My big question was, at what point did holding on to your amount mean you didn't love a person enough? And at what point did the other person letting their amount crush yours mean the opposite for you?

In the time since Thanksgiving, I'd worked out this balance in my relationship to Brianne. But because her love for me obviously didn't translate into her owing me shared use of her boyfriend, I worked it out between me and me instead.

I loved Brianne—I did—so I took the amount that I didn't want to make her miserable in any real way and put it on one side. However, I also loved myself. So on the other side of the scale I put the amount that I wanted to let myself be close to Trevor.

There were clear-cut things that would have tipped the balance, like me resolving never to be alone with him again, or, at the other extreme, me making out with him. Brianne had said that psychopaths have no moral systems. I thought mine was pretty involved.

While shifting amounts from both sides around, I began to realize that in this case, it was best to fall back again on the patience of the terrible grin. That instinct told me there was no rush to be close. I had all the time in the world. After all, I wasn't a miniature greyhound with only a decade or so left before I had to pack it in. I was a human being with a decent life expectancy, judging by my old-person relatives. At some point in the future Brianne and Trevor would probably go their separate ways. And at some point in the future it was likely that I'd go mine too. The terrible grin said there was no good in getting worked up about any of that now. Wait and see what happens. Relationships shift.

In science class we'd learned this theory about a cat in a box named Schrödinger's cat. The idea was that even if this cat died in his box while it was shut, he didn't die until you opened it and actually saw him dead. Whether he was still living or not was all a matter of your perception.

Not that I'm saying Trevor and Brianne ceased to exist as

a couple when my eyes weren't on them. That would be beyond narcissistic. But I believed I had the kind of brain that could allow being close to Trevor when he was in front of me, and then force down the box flap when he wasn't.

That was a decent balance. Brianne could have her boyfriend all to herself, not even have to go halvesies on thinking about him the majority of the year. My amount would be the occasional family get-together. The bar mitzvahs (although, I didn't anticipate there being any more of them), the New Year's brunches, and maybe even the birthday parties the adults threw for members of the Life Alert Table when they hit a new decade.

I wasn't even aiming for the entirety of the family get-together. All I'd take for my amount would be a slice of time where I felt connected to Trevor and he to me. The restaurant at the hotel. His car at Thanksgiving. One moment out of the brunch, that's it.

I began looking for that moment. Out on the terrace, he was listening to Brianne's mom talk over at the railing. She pointed down at the tops of the palm trees. He nodded. Brianne walked up and wrapped her arms around his from the back. He glanced over his shoulder to look at her and saw me. He should have, at most, acknowledged me with his eyes. Why he lifted his right arm, breaking Brianne's hold on him, to wave to me with the warmest, fakest smile on his face, I was at a complete loss. Why he wanted Brianne and Sailor to turn and look at me—which they did, squinting as if I were a DMV eye chart hanging a mile away—I had no clue. But then I realized that you show the world you have nothing to do with someone not by ignoring her, but by waving and smiling at her like you're the mayor of her town, and you'd really love her vote. If only I were as young as he wanted to pretend, he could have come over and kissed the top of my head.

I returned my brightest smile, one that said, yes, of course I'll pretend back that I'm going to vote for you, and then on election day I'm absolutely going to get behind your opponent. That was the best I knew how to do.

Then I went over to the Kid Table, the real and original one with the bite marks. The good old table. It had been festooned with a sparkly tablecloth and an arrangement of prematurely springy flowers in a huge champagne-flute vase. The others were already there, flung loosely in their seats (which were pad-ded lounge chairs instead of our usual folding ones) like teen emperors. I took mine. Katie was off watching the fiftieth rebroadcast of the Rose Parade somewhere.

"How does it get here?" I asked, meaning the table. All these years we'd never discussed how it showed up from place to place. I'd never seen it moved from one house to another in between our family things—it always just *was*.

"Yeah, yeah, I started wondering the same thing," Dom said, reclined and pointing at me as if accusing me of reading his mind. "I pulled in the car after running out for shaving cream this morning, and it was leaning against the wall of the garage. I was half-asleep earlier, but I feel like it wasn't there when I left."

"Brianne's parents had it last," Micah said, "so get her over here and let's kill some mystery."

Brianne and Trevor were taking their seats at the long, rectangular stone table set up along the railing.

"Don't bother her," I said.

Saucy Evening was fast asleep in Cricket's lap, and his extreme relaxation appeared to be seeping into her too. Even her agitation had a lazy, drawn-out quality: "It's like they want us to think it's the Tooth Fairy, isn't it? Is that what they want? Us to believe that it magically travels from house to house like the table version of Santa Claus?"

Autumn, practicing for the day when she'd inevitably have to play diplomat as president of the PTA, said, "I'm sure it's not a secret. It's just we probably never noticed our parents handing it off."

"It's taken on a life of its own," I said. "Maybe it just walks over."

Dom mulled, "In the 'Living Doll' episode of *The Twilight Zone*, Telly Savalas keeps trying to get rid of evil Talky Tina, but she keeps coming back. You can't get rid of her, not even with a blowtorch."

Micah took his lighter out of the waistband of his underwear, where I guess he was storing it because even though his shirt had a pocket, the fabric was see-through, kind of like male lingerie. He flicked on his Bic, pulled back the gold sparkly cover from the table, and held the flame to the edge. From there on out, if there had been any possible way we wouldn't already recognize our table at any meal, anywhere, we'd now definitely know it by that dark burn.

I didn't get the sense Micah wanted to ruin it, though. I

watched his face while he was holding the lighter to the edge, and it was more like he'd been grabbed by the need to leave an updated mark next to the indentations of all our baby teeth.

"Everyone! Everyone!" Dom's mom, standing at the head of the Adult Table, was tapping a normal-sized champagne flute with a knife. "Humor me for a second!"

It might have been that the Kid Table members, in being anchored to the table that had followed us throughout our lives, finally caved to its separatism, but those of us who were facing away from her didn't turn around. Dom and even Autumn, who were facing the adults, didn't look beyond us three who were facing away. All five stared into the center of our table, meeting eyes and closing the ring. We acted as if the other table was at someone else's party.

Behind us, Melissa continued, "Let me just quickly say . . . not to get too sentimental about the new year, but okay, let's get the tiniest possible amount sentimental. Let's always make plans and make sure we sit down together every so often, so we stay friends and not just family." I heard champagne glasses clinking to this. Then I heard some of my relatives starting to make fun of Melissa.

"Here come the tears," said either my half uncle Tobias or Uncle Kurt (who had no business making fun of emotional speeches yet; that right was at least a year away), I couldn't tell over the rustling of the palms in the breeze. The acoustics out on the terrace were horrible.

"No, no tears," Melissa protested, but it sounded like she

was on the verge. Dom tiredly nodded his head, used to his mom's easy waterworks.

"Teeeeeeeeeeeaaaars." That was definitely my half uncle Tobias. Next I heard a sound like a shoulder being hit with an open palm and could guess that was probably his shoulder and probably Brooke's hand.

Melissa must have pulled it together because she was much clearer when she said, "No tears. I'm almost finished."

The members of the Kid Table continued to stare at each other as if we were having a telepathic meeting on the state of our union.

She went on, "Life is short, and full of surprises, like . . ."

"This is mine," Dom said quietly so only we heard him.

"What's yours?" asked Micah.

Dom didn't answer because why use words when the appearance of a muscular, grown man in a diaper can do the talking for you? The guy Cricket and I had "not seen" earlier had put on a few more items of clothing, specifically a top hat and white sash, but he was still erring on the side of naked.

"Baby New Year!" Melissa announced, clapping to his entrance.

Yeah, that's some baby, I thought. Our family's ideas about what constituted a kid were so fucked-up.

"He's here to do a champagne-tasting party for us!"

Micah, not turning around, loudly joined her in the clapping, holding his hands over his head.

"For those of us who are of legal drinking age!" she corrected with undiminished excitement.

Keeping his voice low, Dom said, "He was my idea. I showed her his Web site and talked her into hiring him."

"Subtle," Cricket said.

"I'm not trying to be. I've made my resolution. This is the year I'm getting the family to out me. This is the year." Dom got out of his chair. For that I twisted around. He walked over to where Man New Year was setting up his tasting station on a table not all that much smaller than ours. Taking hold of the guy's arm, Dom asked loudly, "Do you work out?"

My dad didn't help Dom's effort by getting out of his seat too, wanting to know the same. "Yeah, how do you get that kind of definition?" He squeezed his own arm, looking unhappy with it. Dom looked equally unhappy with him.

But there was someone who looked very happy, and that was Tish, also making a beeline for Man New Year. Her eyes were locked on the bottles he was removing from their cases, not his biceps. "Life is short," she echoed. "So don't be so slow with the bubbly."

CHAPTER 11

Dom could barely get a second of Man New Year's time. Tish set up camp at the tasting table, pretending repeatedly that the last champagne he'd served her had been no good, so he needed to scrounge up something better. It turned out Man New Year followed a regular swim regimen, so my dad had his other ear about that.

The adults kept returning for his pouring services based on recommendations made by each other. Autumn, missing the point of his existence at the brunch, even wandered over to his station to find out if he was cold like that, if he'd like her to find him a sweater. Dom could have had a hand down that diaper, and I don't know that the family would have noticed.

I ate vanilla French toast from a plate in my lap, lolled back in the chair, and regarded the Kid Table from a couple feet away. In that moment I hated it without reason. Would I want to be at a table with anyone else but Dom, Cricket, Micah, and Autumn? No, in terms of the company, the table was always the best seat in the house (or in the ballroom, or on the terrace . . .). But still I hated it and felt closer to it because of that hate. Sitting at it was like having your mom still dressing you. The way you were being presented wasn't even your choice.

"How's it going over here?"

In a daze, I looked down to my right.

Trevor was crouching next to my chair, his hoodie gone, revealing what looked like a brand-new thermal. It was the whitest that white comes. His bangs fell toward his right ear as if he'd spent the morning training them.

That question was what a kindergarten teacher asked when you were stringing macaroni on a shoelace. As if there were any way you needed to be asked about a task that was totally impossible to screw up.

"It's going great," I said.

Or, what if this was just what it was like to be oversensitive? Maybe this was what people meant when they said someone had thin skin: getting worked up about the meaning behind a smaller table. About a near-stranger correctly treating you as if you were a near-stranger too.

"Wow," he said.

His eyes didn't look right at all. It wasn't only that they looked bleary, like he hadn't slept since Thanksgiving. They reminded me of when you enter into a staring contest with someone and you cheat by focusing on a point just beyond her, so you won't crack first. He put his hand in the space between my shoulder and neck and squeezed. I'd actually used that move a number of times myself, but only on people who were of equal height. (I think it reads patronizingly otherwise.)

Trevor smiled, distorting the true meanness of his mouth. "How's school?"

In that question he'd turned himself even more into a stranger than when I hadn't known him at all.

I smiled to keep up with him.

"It's fine, but they're making us each sell fifty chocolate bars over break to raise money for graduation. I haven't started, but I'm thinking of hiring Katie to stand outside Trader Joe's for me."

His elbow went onto the arm of my chair, sharing it with mine, no self-consciousness in the act. "When do you have to go back?"

"Next week. How's school for you?"

"There were a few classes I could have done without last term. I'll wait and see about this one."

"Best of luck with that," I said.

If he'd asked how my Thanksgiving was, then I'd have known him. Not that I'd feel right about it, but we'd have been back to playing at secrets and games.

"Thanks," he said. "Same to you. Is the French toast any good? I took the omelet."

"Really good. I can recommend it wholeheartedly."

"I'll have to grab a slice from the kitchen."

"That sounds like a plan."

Trevor's eyes shifted past me to Cricket, who had been

observing this exchange with disinterest because there was really nothing to see. Saucy Evening watched us with an identical expression. "We met at the bar mitzvah, but we never got the chance to talk," he said to her.

"No, we didn't," she said, reminding him, "Cricket."

He rose from the side of my chair to go crouch next to hers, keeping his body angled forward so he wasn't turning his back on either of us. Every move he made was considerate. I felt a twinge.

"I remember," he told Cricket. "Brianne said you play tennis."

"How do you like her new haircut?" she asked.

"I like her hair," he said.

"You do. Interesting." She paused to let him take it back.

"Sure."

He was gone, off in a new conversation, and all of a sudden I was left unsure that the amount he liked me was more than he was showing.

I'd always believed you could make anyone like you on a shallow level if you just remained aware that that's what you were doing. Of course, sometimes you just liked someone, and that person just liked you back. But sometimes you needed to get something out of someone or you needed someone off your back. Or sometimes you just wanted to lock down someone's friendliness if you needed it down the road.

In the end I'm sure it's a selfish thing to line up all those ducks, all those people you put on your side because it's easier to have them there than not, but to get them there takes unselfishness. You think about what they need and what you can do for them. You put aside your boredom and your judgment, and you replace those with your attention and understanding. And time.

I believed that you could make anyone like you, but being liked like that didn't always bring immediate rewards. I mean, sometimes you'd get extra packets of ketchup at McDonald's if you handled your server the right way. But people didn't really trip over themselves for you until you'd convinced them it was their idea. If you wanted, for example, the favorite dress off the back of Lisa, your friend at school, getting to that point where she'd hand it to you freely after PE without hard feelings took some serenity.

But the thing was, I wanted immediate rewards with Trevor, even though the closeness we had was way harder for me to manage than a relationship with a McDonald's server. Even if that was a really naive expectation. Watching him talk and smile, I had to acknowledge that I wanted his falling for me to be real, more than I'd ever wanted anything from anybody before.

Cricket was asking, "Are you two living together?"

"Almost," he said, never looking toward me. "Either she's over at my place, or I'm at hers."

They must do their laundry together, I thought.

Cricket held a piece of her French toast, which I'd seen her actually eating, to Saucy Evening's mouth, but he didn't wake up to take it. I thought that would be great if he was going to not-eat for her too. "I give her a hard time, but she's nothing but good intentions. Those intentions of hers can be a bitch, but I'm glad she's happy with you. She seems to be."

"You're right. She does only have good intentions."

Dom, having reached his tipping point with Man New Year, came trudging over from the champagne station, but he approached from the right and must not have seen Trevor crouching by Cricket because when he got to the table he said, "What do I have to do? Shake a bottle, pop it open, spray it all over his bare chest, then lick—"

Before he said "his nipples" or "his belly button" or whatever had originally been coming, he spotted Trevor and instantly stopped talking. The pause was so abrupt, it was like the *k* in his last word lost a leg.

"Hi," Dom said. No one had ever heard anything like this from him at family events besides the Kid Table members, aside from the occasional visiting toddler, who we could always trust to have the comprehension of a guppy. He wasn't even out at his school because he didn't want to run the risk of the information leaking home; the family had to come to that realization themselves.

Cricket covered Dom right away, forcing Trevor back toward their conversation. "So it's getting serious, then."

Trevor looked at her again. "You could say that."

Behind at the Adult Table, it sounded as if an argument had started, but the bad acoustics prevented me from hearing any intelligible accusations. Also, the rustling of the palms in the breeze created an audio illusion of the fronds weaving through the conversation like they were making baskets with it.

"You'd say that, though?" pressed on Cricket, knowing full well that it's tough to sort through someone else's discomfort when you're busy grappling with your own.

"We're together."

It was definitely an argument—that was becoming clearer—but still nothing concrete was making its way over to our table. I picked up on a stray. "Come on, now" and a "Let's just calm . . ." but figured the disagreement was something along the lines of Micah's dad wanting to go around and hear everyone's resolutions, and Dom's dad, who only hated sentimentality more than he hated voluntarily talking, resisting.

Cricket glanced past me to the adults to see what the commotion was about, and at the clanking of a flute tipping over and hitting the stone table, Saucy Evening opened his eyes to see too.

"The flute's broken," was the first complete sentence that made it underneath the breeze and the noise of the trees. Dom and Autumn looked over then, and so did I.

We were only catching the tail end of it because my dad had already gotten up from the table, finished with his part of the fight. He practically threw aside his chair, which would have gone over if the railing hadn't caught it. Since the arguing had stopped, I followed his sight line to find out who his problem had been with. Solving that mystery wasn't very hard because he was staring down my mom.

She wasn't saying anything to him, just staring back up from her seat.

My relatives *were* saying things, which had become easier

to put together once I could see their lips moving. Things like, "Ace, sit down," and from Uncle Kurt, "You two are making a mountain out of a mogul," which I'm sure, in his head, was a clever ski analogy but to my ear sounded astonishingly douchebaggy.

My dad stormed across the terrace and into the house. Next we heard the front door open and slam.

My mom watched the direction he'd gone in even after he'd left. She didn't cry and her face didn't bunch, but from the way she stared, I could tell how badly he'd hurt her.

Autumn's mom, who was sitting next to her, reached over and started rubbing her arm. I saw more than heard her say, "He'll come back."

My other relatives, who were really my mom's relatives, all began to rally around her, saying that she was right (right about what? I wondered) and that my dad was making a big deal about nothing and that she should just have a good time and let him throw his fit elsewhere. They were so excited by the drama, they didn't notice the Kid Table was listening. I could tell my mom was unconvinced by these lines. After a few seconds, she got up from her table.

"Do you want me to come with you?" Brit asked, thinking, I'm guessing, that my mom was going to the bathroom. Not going-going to the bathroom, but just in there to hide out for a while.

"I'm going to go find Ace," my mom said.

There were multiple protests, but my mom was already walking toward the house.

"What an ass," Grandma Taylor murmured. Cookie was rapidly signing words, none of which looked like the pantomiming of an asshole or a dickhead, but she probably wasn't saying anything nice either.

The door opened and slammed again.

"Why's she chasing after him like *he's* the girl?" asked Half Uncle Tobias. "He should be running after *her*."

"What were they fighting about?" I called out to the Adult Table, and immediately they all went silent and looked over, as if they were only then remembering there was another contingent at the brunch.

"It was stupid," Michelle said.

"How stupid?" I asked.

"They got into a fight over something that's far in the past," Sailor told me. "They'll calm down."

"But. What. Was. It. About?" Cricket overenunciated, talking to the rest of our family as if they were slow.

I scanned the table for someone to spotlight, to guilt with big, vulnerable eyes into the answer, and when I landed on Tish, barely able to keep her head on straight, I knew I didn't even have to exploit any guilt. "Tish?" I said.

She started like I was unexpectedly calling on her in a class. "What?"

"Why were my mom and dad fighting?"

"Your mom . . ." My other relatives tried to shush her, muttering through gritted teeth that they didn't need to drag the kids into it, but Tish was on that drunken cruise control that only allowed her to focus on one goal at a time, and luckily, I had gotten to her first. "Said that your dad kissed *her* on their first date, but then your dad said no, Faith, you kissed *me*, and then that turned into her saying, 'Your family brainwashed you into their opinion of me,' and then your dad said, 'You wore that top in the Christmas photo, so you want to keep that opinion going,' and then your mom told your dad that his family was made up of horrible, judgmental people, and then your dad got up from the tay—"

"That's it?" I asked. They'd had that kind of disagreement before.

"That's it!" agreed Sailor readily, which made me suspicious.

"They have the tape from the episode. My dad says he kisses her on it. And I think that even my dad is in agreement that his family is horrible and judgmental when it comes to my mom."

"Oh, Faith brought up that tape too," Tish went on, then winced because I think someone was kicking her under the table. "Your dad said he lied for the show so your mom wouldn't look like the aggressor. His family's old-fashioned, and he knew what they'd think of her."

"Okay, this is enough," Brianne said, and for some reason, Tish nodded as if the silent treatment finally made sense. "It was a stupid fight, Ingrid. They just need their space."

Evidently Brianne thought this idea of personal space was a scientific one from the manner in which she delivered it. She'd been sitting right there and knew what had happened, but her loyalty was to her diagnosing hobby and not to our history together.

I turned around, giving her my back. I saw Trevor was gone. I figured he was on his way back to her.

"My parents fought over stupid things before their divorce, but now, after all this time, they're finally realizing what a waste of time that was," Autumn said quietly. "They'll talk to your parents so they don't make the same mistake."

The conversation at the Adult Table picked up again, my relatives, from what I heard through the palms, under the impression that Brianne's perspective had put me at ease.

I said, "My parents aren't divorcing." They'd been dealing with my dad's family's disapproval for over twenty years. Sure, this had been the first time I'd ever seen the tension over it reach this level, but one public fight didn't undo a marriage unless you were famous.

"You know, it's probably a rough patch," Dom said.

"What is? This one thing?"

"This is the . . ." Micah thought for a moment. "Third blowout? Third."

Third. Hearing that made me feel crazy for a second. I'd always thought I was a good observer, but what if I just never understood what it was that I was watching? From my end, aside from my mom's sudden nostalgia for everything and my dad's desire to travel back in time to when he was more athletic and drove something sexier, I believed things were mostly fine. But what if I had a gigantic blind spot that didn't just hover over my own emotions, but had me misreading what I saw in others too?

"Third?" I wondered.

Gently, Autumn said, "They had that small but loud fight at the bar mitzvah during cocktail hour." Then she plucked a hydrangea stalk from the table arrangement and pressed it into my open palm. From my suspicion in myself arose a suspicion in her as well. Maybe she wanted to have me in her same boat. She didn't just want to do her usual nurturing thing, but she also wanted to be the expert here; she wanted to school me.

I was about to say that I'd been there for the minichurros and both my parents had been fine, but then I remembered Cricket hiding out in the bathroom stall because of those churros. I'd been gone long enough to miss something.

"What was the second time?" I asked.

"Thanksgiving," Dom said as if he were jogging my memory. But then he added, "Oh, when you were outside."

"I didn't see either of those," Cricket said, also speaking for me.

"That wasn't about their first kiss, though," I said, because, really, how long could you fight over that? And the Christmas card had only recently been shot. And my dad's family hadn't liked my mom since forever.

Dom shook his head. "We couldn't hear what it was about over at our end. Our parents were talking them down before we realized we should start paying attention."

"Why does it suddenly matter who kissed who?" I asked. "That was so long ago."

"Things stay with you," Micah sang like it was a lyric.

I could have sat at the Kid Table and tossed around fruitless theories with the others, but I didn't even trust my ability to evaluate them, so that seemed like a dead end. Instead I fell back on the leftover wisdom of the one observation I still had faith in. My dad may have dragged a dead bird on my mom's carpet, or maybe it was the other way around, but there was always the possibility that they were already to the point of relaxing—not napping, but just relaxing—together again. Then, getting up from my seat, I went just as my parents had gone before me to see if I could be right.

CHAPTER 12

When I got down to the sidewalk outside Dom's house, my mom and dad were nowhere in sight. They weren't even specks. If Saucy Evening had to track them, he wouldn't have had a mark to go on. Still, my dad's new coupe remained parked curbside, and that meant they had to be on foot. No matter how out of their minds with emotion, it didn't seem like them to swipe the brand-new Christmas and Hanukkah bikes of neighborhood kids.

Since the day was nearly blinding, I took my sunglasses out of the pocket of my button-down shirt and put them back on. I was a brunch orphan. Two animatronic reindeer made of wire and lights pretended to feed from the front lawn across from Dom's. Flags with mistletoe and New Year's bells above people's garages rippled in the breeze. That was it as far as activity went on the street.

I called, "Hello!" for no reason, and when no one responded, I got that pleasant feeling you can access if you're out and about at dawn, before everyone else, when you become convinced that you own the world. I decided to hold on to it.

My parents had disappeared. I walked back up the front steps.

Katie was on the floor in the den, planted in front of a wall-mounted plasma. I stopped to watch a float roll down Colorado Boulevard: two huge children made of flowers who, it has to be said, looked as if they were the product of incest. Motion animated, they repeatedly dropped the same dandelion-seed-covered coin into a hot pink piggy bank after pulling it back out again. The female announcer said, "Now there's a great message for kids, presented to us by Bank of America. Especially in this economic climate, don't you think, Bob? And did you know there are over five thousand rose petals on that pig . . ."

Katie must have heard me in the doorway because she twisted to face it. "I got one for Christmas," she said.

"A piggy bank?"

Solemnly, she nodded once.

I patted the pocket in my shirt, but I hadn't brought my wallet because there was nothing that needed paying for when I was with my family. After my dad came back, I'd steal Katie some change out of his jeans.

"What color?" I asked.

"Shiny," she answered.

I took that to mean that Half Uncle Tobias had gotten her a top-of-the-line sterling bank. He'd gone from having no money at the turn of the millennium to being kind of rich when he partnered with an old friend on a new line of styling products for black women. I don't know. Despite his involvement, it did well.

I took a seat on the carpet next to Katie, wanting to be around the only family member who didn't present any complications.

"What else?" I asked.

She looked at me, a little unsure. When you're a kid, or when I was a kid at least, you begin to sense from a very young age how quickly your shit bores adults; you can see it in their eyes. When you first learn to talk (I mean really talk, not like a caveman), there are a ton of details and your accounts are long-winded to the point of being painful for anyone who has a need for sense in the world. With every year that passes, you edit yourself down a little more. Then one day you realize your stories are supposed to be coherent, and right there's the end of childhood-childhood.

Not that I thought of myself as an adult-adult, more like something in between, but already Katie didn't seem to believe me that I actually wanted to hear her laundry list of presents.

"A bear . . . ," she ventured.

"Tell me about him," I said.

"He's soft . . ."

"Bow tie?"

She laughed. "Noooooo."

"A naked bear!" I said and clasped my hand over my mouth as if I were scandalized by teddy nudity. "What else?"

We sat side by side with the parade in the background and Katie took me through all of her thirty-odd Christmas gifts. At first she started tentatively, only giving me colors of things and, in the case of Surf 'N Turf Barbie (she came with both a boogie board and an ATV), all the different ways she could tie her bandanna top.

After a while, when she recognized she had my patience, we delved more into the tangential, batshit crazy particulars that would have gotten her stopped by a policeman had she been wandering down the street, chattering them to herself in twenty years. For example, her plans to affix her new glow-in-the-dark solar system to the ceiling, complete with elaborate, never-before-discovered constellations, including the "Wash & Wear Hair Relaxer" group. Daddy's girl.

"What's that look like?"

She touched the tips of her fingers and thumb on one hand to the other, as if she were holding a ball. "A circle of stars."

I said, "I think I've seen it in the sky before."

In the middle of telling me about her new canopy bed, Katie stopped at the roll call of preschool friends she was going to invite over to sleep up there, and stared at me.

"You're pretty."

I have the kind of looks that are going to get me called handsome a lot when my hair eventually goes silver. Meaning that I'm not traditionally pretty, but Katie thought I was because you become pretty to a kid when you treat her as if you're a Disney princess and she's an adorable dwarf. It's not that when kids tell unattractive people they're pretty, they're seeing inner beauty, I don't think. It's not like they have that magical power, and it evaporates with age like the ability to see wood sprites. It's more like kids find you good-looking when you make them feel good, which isn't all that different from when you come home from a party when you're older, thinking it was a good one because you were especially charming that night.

"Thank you," I said.

"You're my favorite," she told me.

"Favorite what?"

She searched her brain, probably trying to find the concept behind "cousin" or "relative," but it just wasn't there yet. "Person," she finally said.

"I'll take that."

"I got new markers for Christmas too." We were picking back up with the list, resuming somewhere around gift number twenty. "I'm going to draw you a picture. I draw beautiful flowers." She looked at the TV. "I'll put your face in the flower and then you talk to another flower and then you guys sing together—I can teach you the words to the song—"

There were footsteps in the hallway behind us, but they sounded sticky against the tile, not like shoes but feet. Katie and I twisted around to see together. Man New Year first passed by the doorway and then backed up.

"The Rose Parade!" he said.

Katie had never been receptive to strangers, which I guess you're not supposed to be when you're a kid anyway; that's what they deliberately teach you. Ignoring the guy, she straightened, went silent, and returned to watching TV.

"Your diaper," I said. It was slipping at his left hip, revealing a pubic bone so cut he appeared to have the removable leg of a Ken doll. Man New Year looked and tugged up the diaper.

Mesmerized by the parade again, he said, "I used to love to watch this when I was young."

I rotated around on the floor so all of me was facing him. "You're still young." I had a strong feeling only an aspiring actor would agree to dressing up like an infant to serve Veuve Clicquot, rationalizing it as a character piece. That gave me a lot to work with in making us fast friends.

"Nooo," he said, and not to sound like a date rapist, but it was a "yes" if I'd ever heard one. "It's been a rough couple of years, and believe me, they show."

"How old are you?" I put him in his midtwenties. "You bartend, so you *must* be twenty-one."

He smiled, the extreme whiteness of his teeth reminding me of the mime's at the bar mitzvah. (Performers have to be mindful of their Whitestrips.) "Yeah, sure, I just had that birthday. I'm sticking to your version of the story." Then his expression turned abruptly serious. "By the way, thanks for going along with the surprise earlier. I wasn't supposed to let anyone see me."

"When I saw you earlier, or when I didn't see you, I thought you looked familiar."

"You did?"

"I got this feeling like I knew you from somewhere." I would have put the hundred dollars I got from Grandma Taylor for Christmas down on the likelihood that he'd done a commercial, one that had at least run on local cable.

Excited, Man New Year finally entered the room and dropped to the floor in front of me, crouching like a schoolteacher just as Trevor had done. I felt a heaviness in my chest at that move. "Have you seen the commercial where—," he started.

"Sit down," I commanded.

He gestured to Melissa's area rug. "The diaper doesn't give full coverage, and I don't think Mrs. Everard would want my ass on her carpet." He smiled: the teeth again. "Even if my friends joke that I spent fifty percent of my life in the shower." Once I found out he wasn't trying to condescend to me, the invisible but heavy hand on my chest now lifted a few of its fingers. I was also pleased to learn of his commitment to clean living.

"Anyway," he continued, "have you seen the commercial where the guy uses the mouthwash in the club bathroom and then comes out on the dance floor and kisses the girl who's coming up from dropping it like it's hot, and as soon as he does, she falls into his arms and they start to waltz?"

No. Had never seen it. "That's you!" I exclaimed. "That's it! What a strange thing, to think I knew you from my life, but I only knew you from my TV." I slapped my thigh in astonishment. "You made me believe that kiss was real."

"Thank you! Thank you so much. You know what's stranger?" he asked.

"No?"

"To kiss someone for the first time as soon as someone else says, 'Action.' Right before the director called it, I had a flashback to a spelling bee in sixth grade where I misspelled burglar—"

"That tricky *a*," I figured.

"That tricky *a*!" He touched my knee, feeling increasingly connected. "I knew how to spell it, but when they made me spell it right at that second, it was like I never knew how."

I smiled. "When he called for you to kiss that actress, you felt like you were kissing for the first time again."

"Exactly! But it was worse than my first kiss. There was the pressure of all that money and all those people. My career was at stake."

I was still suspicious of my observational skills, so I wasn't going to assume whether Dom was realistically going to get anywhere with this guy. I had to come right out and ask. "Was your first kiss with a boy or a girl?"

"A girl," he said quickly, surprised, his eyes darting over to a completely indifferent Katie as though if he answered otherwise, she was going to try to deprogram him. Then I knew either he was bisexual or lying or that his first kiss had only been an experiment.

"She's four," I said.

Sheepishly, he looked back toward me. "It's Orange County. You never know."

Man New Year thought he'd get in trouble taking his break out in the open, so we found ourselves in the master bedroom, which I'd never been in before. When we went through the doorway at the farthest end of the hall, we were so entertained by the profusion of faux finishes on the surfaces that we were like Hansel and Gretel stumbling in from the woods. Except instead of coming upon walls of candy, we'd discovered a wonderland of fake mosaics.

I didn't know how Alec relaxed enough to fall asleep in that room. It was like a scaled-down version of Saddam's palace.

While I was studying the mantel of the nonfunctioning fireplace, a marble (or, more likely, fake marble) sea nymph statue level with our heads, Man New Year asked, "So how old are you?"

I told the truth. "I'm seventeen."

He yanked on the bottom of his chest sash. "You're still young."

Before he began to give me a lecture about what to expect from life or he disregarded the value of mine completely, I had to bring him back to his vanity. "But you're in your early twenties, aren't you?" I asked. He couldn't bring himself to argue with me. "What's four or five years?"

My head spun a little, realizing I was giving a pep talk on the irrelevancy of our age difference to a man costumed as a baby. Life is funny and inventive like that. Sometimes the daughter goes after the parents like they're the kids, to see if they're all right, and sometimes she finds herself philosophizing with a diapered companion way before she hits the retirement home circuit.

"They're nothing, I guess."

"Then let's just move forward," I said, not even sure what I meant by this, but wanting to see what he'd do. He took off his top hat, almost as if he were about to take a bow, and then he leaned in toward me, and I put my hand on the swath of Mystic Tan that was his stomach. More and more, it was looking like he also went for girls.

"Ingrid!"

I glanced over at Aunt Kathy, who had walked into the master bedroom and was standing by the divan and potted plant. Her attention immediately left me for Man New Year.

"Get away from her!" she ordered. "Away! What was your name? Michael?"

"Oh. Michael," I repeated, surprised that's what he was called.

He still had his top hat in one hand and with his other, he tugged at his diaper as if making sure it were still there. "I was just . . ."

"Do you know how old she is?" Aunt Kathy demanded.

I wanted to cover for Michael so a member of my family wouldn't call his supervisor and tell on him, jeopardizing his champagne-pouring gig. As we'd walked to the bedroom, he'd told me the job paid the bills year-round: in a couple of weeks he'd switch over to champagne-tasting-station Cupid; after that he would get into fuzzy white briefs and ears and do a sexy Easter Bunny, expertly chatting about the science of bubbles through buck-teeth dentures. In between his auditions, there was always work at bachelorette parties and from the foodie gays. There was no need to throw that all away because we hadn't even gotten to kiss.

I shook my head. "No. He didn't know."

Unfortunately, Michael was one of those people who doesn't understand that there are certain cases in which the truth will set no one in the room free, and at the exact same time that I said no, he said, "Yes, I do know."

Aunt Kathy looked at me in astonishment. "Were you just lying?"

I tried to save Michael's ass again. What she meant was, had I just lied to her, but I saw an opportunity to bend the question. "I told him I was older than I am. I thought he knew I was joking, but that's not his fault."

Switching her gaze over to him, she said, "Out of here."

Michael started to move but then stopped, unsure. "The house?"

"Go pour," she commanded.

He exited the bedroom, the plastic lining of his diaper squeaking a little as he went. I had just started to follow him out when Aunt Kathy extended her leg, kicked the door shut, and said, "You stay."

CHAPTER 13

Aunt Kathy may have thrown the man-baby out, but we were still sitting in the bathwater.

The project of soothing her was a daunting one, especially because I was tired and disappointed on a number of fronts and had zero desire to work out where to begin. Did I thank her for walking in on a situation that I'd "lost control" of? After that, did I get her to sit on the edge of the bed and talk to me about her own "teen years"? During that talk did I stare off into the distance, pretending to be really embarrassed, until finally, after fifteen to twenty minutes (long enough to convince her the job was a solid, quality effort, but not to the point of discouraging her) I looked straight at her, letting her know whatever she'd just said had finally done it?

Were any of these the right way to go?

Normally I would have been able to sort through her body

language, personality traits, and current state of mind, coming up with a plan that would have our relationship swiftly moving in a more positive direction. I realize I sound cynical when I talk about dealing with people I love like this. Like they're just a combination of tumblers on a lock I'm going to crack. But the truth of the matter is that usually I know how to sort myself out, and I knew that I had no bad feelings whatsoever about what had just happened with Man New Year. He was a distraction more than anything. I was ready to move on with my life. Now I just needed to get Aunt Kathy to a place where she could look forward too.

The flipped ends of Aunt Kathy's modified bob were practically twitching with disapproval or anger or shock. Like I said, normally I would have sorted out that hair mystery via her body language, but I was feeling out of sorts and impatient, and impatience will do you in every time.

All I offered was a general nod to the fact that she cared about and watched out for me. It seemed a neutral enough move. When in doubt, you add and build slowly.

"Did you come looking after me because I've been gone so long?" I asked. "That's really thoughtful, to notice."

"No." Her mouth was set tight. She was going to answer me but was determined not to lose sight of the bigger conversation. "I needed to use the bathroom."

"This one specifically?" I asked. I wasn't trying to derail her further, I was genuinely curious.

Defensively, she said, "It's my favorite."

Everybody's got their weird, intuitive preferences for

spaces in a house; however, Melissa's bathroom was definitely off-limits, maybe even to Alec.

"Okay. You should go ahead."

"No. I'll hold it."

Holy shit.

"Are you sure?"

She put a hand on the back of the divan as if bracing herself against the will of her bladder. Looking at her outfit, really looking at it, I recognized that what I'd thought was a matching peach button-down blouse and pair of blousy pants rolled to the shin, meeting at a thin silver belt, was really a one-piece jumpsuit. When Aunt Kathy finally made a run for the bathroom, she was going to have to undo that whole thing from the breast down. If I hadn't wanted to keep this short before for my sake, now I was equally concerned for hers.

"Go," I encouraged.

"We need to have a talk," she said.

This was probably about safe sex or promiscuity, I guessed, and it was probably going to be her first time because she didn't have a kid. I was still standing by the fireplace mantel, but to dim the memory of the offending scene in her mind as fast as possible, I realized I should put myself in a new visual context. So I walked over to an easy chair next to the bed and took a seat. "I guess that flirting went a little too far," I said. "I'm glad you walked in."

"Why were you flirting?" she asked, stepping on my last word. It was obvious her patience was even more worn down than mine, so why didn't we just call it a day?

"You didn't think he was good-looking? I know he was older than me, but that only matters when something's actually going to happen, and believe me, nothing ever was."

She stared disbelievingly at me, eyes widening, and for a moment, I thought she was going to accuse me of lying. That's not what it was, though. This wasn't about owning up to how many bases I'd been willing to let Man New Year round. She was disturbed that I'd been able to entertain his company at all.

"How can you even think about flirting with someone after watching your parents come apart like that?"

There went my last bit of patience and good sense. My eyebrows lowered from their open position; the thankful smile left my eyes. "They're not coming apart."

She'd never heard that tone from me before, and it took her aback for a second. "They're having *difficulty*," she started again. "They're off to God knows where. And you're back here in the bedroom, playfully flirting with an inappropriate stranger as if you didn't have a care in the world!"

"What is it with you guys?" I wondered, aghast.

"What is what? With who guys?"

"The family. Always leaping to conclusions." I shook my head. "If my parents are having a few small fights, then they're coming apart. If I'm not back here crying my eyes out, then something's apparently wrong with me too. You know what it is?"

She didn't answer me, just waited, her eyebrows now in that open position, wanting to know.

"You guys need drama. You need the big parties with the big themes, and you need some kind of intrigue at every event. It can't just be that my parents are getting in arguments, the way that people who are married do from time to time in their marriages, right? I'm not married, but even *I* know that happens and that it doesn't have to mean divorce." If someday I did get married and brought my husband to those things and we never fought, they would make something of that too. I crossed my legs, my agitation making me feel like I wanted to compress into a tighter version with greater impact, like a bullet. "Why should I believe there's going to be any major change that comes from this?"

Aunt Kathy, still standing, crossed her legs as well, either mimicking me or doing it for another more physically pressing reason. "I didn't say anything about divorce. Don't put words in my mouth. Don't lump me in."

"What is it that you want me to be back here reacting badly to then?" I asked.

She made an exasperated sound. "It's normal for the child of two people who are fighting to be affected, Ingrid. Even if you had been turning to that"—for a second, she mentally debated how to describe Man New Year—". . . *beefcake* . . ." (an interesting choice) "who, uh-huh, is too old for you, for comfort, then I could almost understand what goes through your head. But when I walked in here, it wasn't that at all."

"Why, what did it look like to you?"

Without having to think about it, she automatically answered, "It looked like you were having fun."

I scanned back through recent memories, searching for the rare times that Aunt Kathy had looked this way too. I stopped on one. And then I said, "After you found out Uncle Kurt was cheating on you, and after we all found out too, you came to the Halloween party at Micah's last year, and you looked like you were having fun."

Her lids dropped some.

I continued, "You acted like things were okay."

Uncle Sam had the family over toward the end of that October, mostly because he needed the extra hands to help him decorate his "haunted condo." No one had expected Aunt Kathy to show up with Uncle Kurt. I think he'd told her only days before. She got to work hanging ghosts with my mom, and everyone knew she had to be miserable, but everything about her behavior was really convincing, from the way that she didn't smile too hard, which would have shown cracks, to the way that she didn't talk more or less than she normally would have. I'd been impressed.

"You hung the ghosts, and you took out your lipstick and made a mouth on one, which is kind of a fun thing to do."

A faint smile crossed Aunt Kathy's lips. I didn't read it as one of happiness at the memory but of her understanding what I was getting at and recognizing the irony of our situation. "I remember that," she said.

"Everyone was whispering behind your back that they couldn't believe how well you were doing. Someone, and I'm not going to say who, said that you could only be having so much fun because you were keeping focus on the fifty percent of the Blimpie's money coming your way."

At this her lids lifted, her lashes practically bending back to touch the crease. "Who said that?"

"I told you," I said. "I'm not going to say who."

She looked around at the room, which was kind of like what Elvis would have dreamed up had he'd been more into Greece than the jungle.

"Melissa," she said.

She was right—it was Melissa who'd called her a Blimpie Digger—but I wouldn't confirm or deny with so much as a blink.

"That doesn't matter," I said. "Whoever thought you were having fun was wrong. You weren't."

She sighed. "No, I wasn't."

"Uncle Kurt cheated on you, and I've never seen you upset with him about it." She seemed possibly on the verge of tearing up, so I stopped there for a second until her eyes had cleared. "I don't think that means you weren't really hurt."

For months I'd been receiving sideways glances and suspicious eyes from Aunt Kathy in particular, the idea of a psychopath in the family having fully captured her imagination. At the beginning of the talk, when she'd shut us in the bedroom, I'd thought that maybe I should get her to talk to me about a similar time when she'd also gotten in over her head. Except that's what *I* ended up doing with *her* instead, and she was looking at me differently afterward, not like I was going to pull the rug out from under her someday, but like we'd both had that happen to us and were standing on the same ground.

"I follow," she said.

I think that back in the coal mining days they taught kids that not losing your shit can be a type of strength, but by the time I got to school, my teachers had reversed that lesson. In sixth grade we had a whole unit on how it was braver to release tears whenever, whyever, which explained why we had so many manipulative criers in my class. So maybe I'm just old-fashioned, but still, I admired that Aunt Kathy had eased herself through her pain, giving herself the space to sort through what she really wanted. I believed she'd always known better than to fool herself.

"I think you're strong," I told her.

"You're not just saying that?"

"No, I really think that."

"Thank you." Aunt Kathy crossed her legs the other way. "I think I'm going to go to the bathroom."

I nodded. "You should."

She briskly walked a diagonal, as if she were on a tightrope, and made for the entrance to the master bath. After she'd shut the door behind her, I got up from the armchair and left the room.

When I returned to the terrace, the party had moved down a level to the base of the palms. Everyone was gone, except for Michael, who was packing his champagne supplies into a black case. Since he was finished with the show, he'd thrown on a flannel, and seeing me, gave a urgent look that said, "We mustn't start this up again; it's too dangerous." I gave him a look that said, "Whoooo boy, what a day."

Down in the yard, my family was playing what appeared to be a hybrid game of Frisbee and soccer, kind of a sports version of patting your head and rubbing your stomach at the same time. My mom and dad were back. I looked at them (they seemed to be purposely not looking at each other) standing on opposite sides of the lawn, but that wasn't their doing, just a function of their teams because my relatives had split into boys versus girls. And looking at them, I remembered the missing detail in the equation of me and my dog. My mom had helped me clean the dead bird off the carpet. When I got home, I was going to make sure the offending Christmas photos went somewhere unknown, never to be found again. Then all we could do was see what the new year was going to bring.

Micah was running around topless as if pretending the division was shirts versus skins. Katie, who they must have wanted to keep sexless, was sitting in a beach chair in the middle of the two groups, and someone had found her a whistle, which she was cautiously testing like it was her new voice.

In order to play with both hands, Cricket had put Saucy Evening down on the sidelines, and he lay there, head on his paws, making no effort to follow the action. Brianne was near him trying to figure out something to do with her hair because evidently, it wasn't staying back in the rubber band she was messing with.

Trevor glanced up at the sky and his gaze jumped to me. I thought that if he smiled and waved, I would pick up one of the empty champagne bottles from the Adult Table behind me and send it down toward his head. He didn't. I didn't back. We only evaluated each other, which was the tiniest relief compared to the friendliness that had gone on earlier. The tiniest because looking at him, I felt almost nothing but sadness. I was telling myself to give up that amount I'd allotted to be close to him, but something in me wouldn't let it go. I wanted to know him. I wanted him to know me.

Michael snapped shut his case behind me. "Well, I'm out of here."

I turned around. "Did you get paid?"

"Oh yeah, up front."

"I'll look for you," I said, meaning on TV.

"You too," he said gravely, and I had no clue what that meant, but I didn't question it. He finally put on a pair of pants and took off through the house.

After Melissa had Alec plant the trees in the backyard, she also had him whitewash and age the stairs leading down to that level. You can't see who's on the stairs from the lawn because there's a white stepped wall that runs alongside them, and you can't see who's about to join you when you're inside the wall either. When I was halfway down, Trevor came to the bottom and took a small glance over his shoulder before he started coming up. I kept going until we were on consecutive steps. When we met, we stood face-to-face, our eyes just about even because of the six or so inches my stair gave me.

He wrapped his hand around the back of my head until his fingers reached and grasped on to my ear. Then he kissed me, the first true thing we'd done together all day. I held on to his bottom lip with my mouth. He fought that lock to get his mouth around mine. A long piece of his bangs was pressed between our foreheads. From light-headedness, I fell off my step onto his.

Standing closer to him, I said, "Schizophrenic."

He said, "Psychopath," probably the rare instance of these two diagnoses being used as declarations of affection, and certainly a pair of pet names that the American Psychiatric Association would find insensitive.

"What were you doing before?" I asked.

"I'm sorry," he said.

"No, really, what were you doing?" I asked again, a panic I hadn't let myself feel while we were making small talk rushing in.

He was still holding on to my ear tightly. "I was treating you like the cousin of my girlfriend, who I was talking to because of our connection through her."

"You were being so ugly."

"How am I not being even less stand-up by doing this?" He kissed me again, my mouth fitting so well into his that I wondered if mine was a mean shape too, and I'd never been able to look at it objectively enough to classify it as that. I had the urge to tell him that if it made him feel any better about cheating, kissing me was almost more like he was being with himself than getting with somebody else.

"I don't know. That's on your head."

He almost smiled. "You think you have nothing to do with this?"

When I let myself ignore the context of the kiss, how happy and alive it made me feel. "I think this might be the worst thing I've ever done intentionally."

He said, "It's a New Year's kiss," trying to come off like that was a reasonable joke. "People kiss for celebration and luck."

I said, "It's a little late."

He put a hand on each side of my face and pressed his fingers on my cheekbones. "Why, who'd you kiss last night?"

"Some guy."

"Was he crazy about you?"

If I wasn't a narcissist, I was asking this question because I wasn't sure of the answer. If I was, then I was asking just because I wanted to hear it out loud: "Are you?"

"No, I'm not crazy about you. I know barely anything about who you are." He looked my face up and down. "I'm crazy for you."

The answer stung. Not that it hurt my heart, but it caught in me and prickled. "Madonna," I said, identifying the first thing I could.

"You know it's true-ah," he sang, putting the valley girl accent on the last syllable.

"I know who you kissed at midnight. Are you crazy about her?"

He pulled me into him again and kissed me. When I heard the squeak of a sneaker on the staircase, I was already past the point of being able to gracefully pretend that I wasn't kissing Brianne's first love. I opened my eyes and pulled back from Trevor. It wasn't Brianne coming up the steps, but Dom. One look at him and I knew what he thought of me.

Trevor looked behind, saw Dom, and went down the stairs toward the lawn, brushing past him. I waited where I was. Dom took the steps slowly, avoiding eye contact until he was almost to me. He stopped a couple away and held his right hand at hip level, pointing crookedly at me, bouncing the finger slightly as if that gesture was the frustration of not being able to find the words.

Still, he threw some together. "You are a fucked-up person," he said. "So fucked-up."

"I know that was a fucked-up thing to do," I said.

"No, *you*. You're fucked-up."

He continued up the stairs, passing me, and I was still for a moment, overwhelmed by how adamant he was that the bad judgment didn't belong to that one decision but ran through me. From the lawn I heard the family wrapping up the game, his mom asking various relatives to pick up things to take inside, and any minute my whole family would be in the staircase with us, coming upstairs for coffee and hot chocolate.

Turning toward Dom, I said, "Okay, maybe that's fair, but it was because it's *him*. I feel like . . . I've felt like—"

He stopped and turned, cutting me off. "No, Ingrid, it's not just him. I also saw you going toward my mom's bedroom with Michael, who, in case you don't remember, I got my mom to hire because *I* was going to drape myself all over him. I needed him to be out here, and I needed him to be smiling and maybe even flirting with me. But that's pretty hard for him to do when you're leading him into the master, which you know my mom has off-limits anyway, and keeping him back there draped all over you. So yeah, I think it's everyone; I think it's everyone and anyone you feel like."

Dom's speech left me numb. At a loss, I picked at the least significant part of it. "I didn't see you in the house."

"Does that matter?"

"Are you going to tell her?"

I heard loud footsteps at the bottom of the stairs. Looking over my shoulder, I saw Brit jogging up first, an ice bucket held above her head. "The trophy is ours!" Spotting me, her eyes softened and that seemed to be her addressing how much better Cricket was doing, which was the most discussion we would ever have on the subject. In the next instant Tish, taking the stairs like they were part of a fun house, knocked into her. Brit muttered something about her being an alcoholic. Next Brianne appeared at the bottom, dancing in victory and shaking out her hair, the rest of my family filing into the stairwell behind her.

I looked back to Dom. "Are you?"

He looked from them to me. "I won't say anything, but only because you have stuff on me too, and I can't risk it." He was already walking up the last step and disappearing onto the terrace before it sank in that he was telling me he believed I was possibly so fucked-up that if he spilled my secret, I would do something terrible with his in return.

"Come on, Dom!" I yelled.

He had to know better of me.

"Come on!"

Brianne came up and threw her arm around the outside of mine.

When I got back to school and turned in the money I'd made last minute selling all fifty chocolate bars to the Roggin twins who lived down the street from us and whose parents didn't let them eat processed sugars, my advisor told me that I was already set. Fifty bars had been picked up over the break in my name. The box had been mailed back from the Pepperdine English department, the return address stamped on the front, and it contained the money. But my advisor was concerned about the message written large on the inside flap of the display, which read, "Professors, buy a chocolate bar and your money goes to world literacy."

"Someone didn't sell this box for you through dishonest means, did they?" he asked me.

I'd been staring at the writing on the inside of the box. "What kind of person would do that?"

"I don't know. What do I do with the money?"

It wasn't only extra money. It was an extra amount of involvement that Trevor was trying to have in my life. It was a token of his thinking about me. And it was a reminder that we both went about things in arguably devious ways. But there was nothing I could do with any of that.

I looked my advisor in the eye and told him, "Why don't we give it to someone who can actually use it."

PART IV

INDEPENDENCE DAY POOL PARTY

CHAPTER 14

I'd asked, "Are you crazy about her?"

He'd answered by kissing me, and I mulled that and the box he mailed to my school through the spring.

Once I took my dad's new red coupe, without permission, and I drove up to Pepperdine after my parents had gone to bed, with my mom's address book in the passenger seat, opened to Brianne's. I didn't have much of an idea why I was going, except that I had to see how his life was progressing because mine felt like it was at a gnawing standstill.

I parked in a lot where I was supposed to have a permit, right in front of Brianne's building. I didn't really believe that I was going to see him, but just being there gave me the sense that I was seeing some new part of who he was.

Trevor and Brianne drove up in his car as I was getting ready to go home. I'd been about to turn on my lights, but I became still and watched them park and pop the trunk.

Trevor got out of the driver's side, his blue hoodie pulled up over his head, and Brianne got out of the passenger's wearing pajamas tucked into galoshes (it had been raining earlier that night). They walked around to the back of the car and she waited while he pulled, of all things, a laundry basket out of the trunk. She looked like a kid, woken out of bed for a late-night errand. *We were all still playing at setting up our lives*, I thought; *remember that this night is one of thousands, and it's come early on in yours.*

I drove back to my house, and my parents were none the wiser, still fast asleep. They hadn't had another fight since New Year's, or at least not one I'd seen, and neither had bothered to pull out the *Love Connection* tape for forgotten clues, but there was still tension. Instead of addressing it, they dove back into their fascinations with the more general past. My mom bought a machine that sucked all the air and dimension out of foods, so she could save, for example, a piece of French toast from the brunch. When her machine was finished with the toast, it was flat as a Jesus wafer and bound almost kinkily in Saran Wrap. Then she stapled it to the designated acid-free page along with its recipe.

My dad dove back literally, increasing the hours he spent exercising in the pool, and signing up for a high-dive class at the college pool on the weekends because ours only went down six feet. He gave me and my mom invitations to his graduation toward the end of May—they were flyers printed out by his diving school, and my mom promptly took hers and glued it down on a new page of her scrapbook—and we went to cheer him on.

When he was up on the high board, my mom put her fingers to her mouth as if she were going to blow him a kiss, but she didn't, and then she looked more like she was suddenly realizing something. Whatever it was, she lifted her camera and took a photo of it.

I was working toward my graduation too. Just barely, though. Since the seventh grade, teachers had been warning us that you couldn't get anywhere without a good education, but they were like the guy at the swap meet who says that his vegetable chopper is the only one that will do the job. From watching my parents, their friends, our relatives, I'd learned that there are many different kinds of educations and that you can succeed with another variety; you just have to choose.

I picked the kind where you exercise the natural abilities your parents and the universe have given you, meaning that I didn't study for any tests or do research for any projects, but instead saw how far I could get with the teachers themselves. I did really well when there was wiggle room, but sometimes I just had to flat-out bomb a pop quiz because the facts were the facts, I didn't know them, and a teacher had to give the cold, hard grade that stared up at him from his calculator, even if he told me it made him sad to do this. When I found out that I was missing two elective credits needed to graduate, I talked the ASB advisor into letting me do the weather on the morning intercom announcements. On the paperwork, we called it "public speaking independent study."

I already knew that I was putting off college for at least a year, and that if and when I did go, I'd do more of the same there. It wasn't even that crazy to think about skipping out on college altogether because I had a feeling that employers didn't actually check on your degree unless you were going to be a policeman or a doctor or the president of something. I was pretty sure that if you sent out a résumé claiming a bachelor's from a decent, big school and gave an excellent interview, you were going to be all right.

Brianne came down alone for my graduation and sat in the bleachers with her parents. Trevor sent his congratulations, she said, but he'd gotten an extension on a final paper and was holed up typing away. Disappointment struck, but I don't know what I would have expected if he'd come. That he would have seen me walking the field and realized that I was out of school and no longer had that life? And what would I say to him? That I thought about him so much that there were thoughts I couldn't grab hold of? That he shouldn't kiss me anymore because he was with Brianne?

My relatives claimed their own section and immediately erected a banner from Kinko's with my name in a font made out of acrobatic caterpillars. Cricket refused to sit behind it, not because she didn't support me, I knew, but because it was just too dumb-looking. We shared a nod acknowledging this from a distance—both the support and the dumbness, I mean. I put on my gown, went onto the field to get into line, and there my friend Katerina offered me use of her waterproof mascara.

"I'm good," I said.

"I can't believe it's over," she said, shaking her head, making it difficult to hit her lashes with the wand. My school friends were popular and couldn't usually be themselves, which was a relief because I never felt like I had a responsibility to be genuine around them, although that probably meant we weren't all that close. We were going to live together with our friend Sarah after the summer, so it wasn't like *our* specific situation was over, but I got the sense Katerina wanted me to empathize with her over missing something.

And I did. The extent to which I missed Trevor astonished me because really, I had never spent all that much time around him to begin with.

Lazily, I told her, "Miss you," before I recognized the insanity of that choice.

I'd made out with the valedictorian a few years back, and as I listened to him deliver his speech, I thought that I didn't remember him being so attractive. Maybe it was just that he'd cleaned himself up for graduation, and he looked so fresh and ready to strike out in the world. He hit all his marks, talking about following dreams (as if they remained constant) and going forth to become good citizens. He mentioned recycling, and I gave him a thumbs-up: on top of that one, man.

"Ingrid Bell."

At the sound of my name over the microphone, I walked onto the stage and got my diploma, and then I no longer had to legally attend school.

Afterward we all went out for Baskin-Robbins, and apparently the family gossip that I was delaying college hadn't reached Brianne because when she asked my mom, "Why can't

I remember which school Ingrid picked? Did she ever tell me?" and my mom told her about my flexible plans, Brianne was so horrified, she yelled at her, which was extremely uncharacteristic behavior.

"And you're letting her do this?" she shouted, echoing a little off the cold glass cases. "Faith, do you understand what a big mistake she's about to make?"

I was at the counter, and I pointed the teenage worker to the upside-down, smiley ice cream clowns with cones for hats. He handed a clown with orange hair to me, which I then presented to Brianne.

"For you," I said.

She took it, distracted while waiting for my mom to answer, but when she glanced down and saw what I'd given her, she held the clown away as if he'd slapped her hand with a giant shoe. "This isn't what I wanted!"

"Oh," Cricket said, her face antagonistically serene, "but have you stopped to consider that maybe it's what you need?" Saucy Evening was tied up outside the window, and she kept looking over there to make sure he was okay.

"What can I get the rest of you?" I asked the huddle of relatives behind me. "Great-Aunt Cookie?"

Micah's dad elbowed her, and she pantomimed blowing a bubble and made a bowl with her palms.

"She can have that? With the dentures?"

Brianne dropped the cone on the nearest table, and the clown's head rolled off from his hat. "You know I hate clowns."

"I thought you were over that." It occurred to me that I

should be treating Brianne more gently than I would have before I kissed her boyfriend, but that would mean our relationship had already started to deteriorate in addition to the betrayal, whether or not she ever learned about it. To the girl behind the counter, I said, "A scoop of bubble gum in a cup, please."

"I'm working on it in cognitive-therapy sessions with a grad student."

I passed back Cookie's bowl to her. "But I saw you talking to the mime at the bar mitzvah."

Brianne's eyes flicked up from the clown's face to mine. She appeared edgy, as if I'd caught her in a lie about her phobia. "You did?"

"In the ballroom."

Fiercely, she said, "Mimes are different than clowns."

"Anything else?" asked the worker.

"Anyone need anything else?" I called.

"Ingrid," said Brianne from behind me, "what we should be talking about is what are you going to do with your life?"

I scanned over the heads of family and realized that Sailor was the only one without some form of ice cream in hand.

"Sailor, what can I get you?" I asked.

"No, no, I can't," she waved me off.

Cricket was watching her carefully as she did this, and I became determined to make Sailor set an example.

Calibrating my voice so it gently straddled the line between jealousy and criticism, I said, "You're too thin, Sailor. I could barely make you out from the bleachers."

That did the job because she broke into a smile and said, "What the hell! Old-fashioned butter pecan."

Cricket went back to watching her dog.

As we were all sitting outside on the curb of the shopping center so Saucy Evening could resume his eternal slumber on Cricket's lap, it was like the afternoon of the Labor Day barbecue all over again, with Brianne hammering away at me while the rest of my relatives ate dessert and listened to her evaluation as if she were the newest mental-health professional endorsed by Oprah.

"Tell me if you can," she said, swirling her spoon around in the cup of strawberry she'd gotten herself after destroying the clown, "where you see yourself in ten years?"

"Is this a job interview?" I asked.

"This is an important indicator."

Since we were sitting in a horizontal line (with the exception of the Life Alert gang, who had been given the metal chairs outside the store), a few family members down by the vacuum repair leaned forward, literally on the edge of their concrete seat, to catch my response.

"Any interest in going into your dad's business?" asked Toby.

"Or sandwiches?" asked Uncle Kurt.

"I was thinking that maybe I'd be a weather girl."

Brianne tried to peer into me. "Is that a joke?"

After a mandatory visit to the career counselor, I'd been considering jobs where amiability contributed to your success (aside from stripping). In the short term I'd lined up a waitress gig at a fancy steakhouse, feeling that I'd make huge tips, and in the long term I thought I wouldn't mind telling people if they needed to bring a jacket or not. I'd liked doing the weather enough over the school intercom. Maybe I'd have to do a few years in a meteorology program, but I'd always had an appreciation for the seasons and could get excited over a new incoming weather system. I also thought I could talk to the viewers at home like we were friends busy figuring out our plans for the week.

"No, I'm being serious."

Brianne nodded as if she'd been expecting to hear me say exactly this position. "The second group of factors in Hare's Psychopathy Checklist includes a lack of realistic, long-term goals. This is not good that you're not going to college and choosing a solid major, Ingrid. This could be a dangerous path."

"There's nothing dangerous about it," Aunt Kathy said, surprisingly coming to my defense. "Why isn't that a realistic goal?"

"It's not easy to just become a weather girl," Brianne argued, a tiny bit stunned to find herself having to give support for her opinion.

"Really hot out today, huh?" I asked, leaning back on my hands to feel the sun on my face. "Am I right or am I right?"

Fortunately, from the very start of the Fourth of July pool party, Micah's banana hammock sidetracked Brianne from picking up where she'd left off with me at graduation. Its sheen— I'm talking even before he got into the water—suggested that it was made from some kind of silk, and its style suggested that he ordered it online from somewhere in Europe. The front was a triangle, the back was a parallelogram, and half-inch bands of scrunched elastic connected the two. The color I couldn't really describe as anything but eggplant.

"It's so gay," Dom said, and not for the benefit of any of the nearby adults. He was more deflated than ever. We weren't at the Kid Table, which for this occasion wasn't the traditional round folding version, but a small concrete table set into the concrete patio area and surrounded on each side by four concrete benches, also secured. There were other tables under the pergola canopy, but they were bigger, taller, and had separate concrete seats instead of the benches. In other words, the gated party area at Micah and Uncle Sam's condo complex, rented out by the family for the holiday, featured its own permanent Kid Table.

Up until this point we had refused to sit at our benches, so the remaining members of the Kid Table, Katie wearing Floaties and sitting atop Dom's shoulders, stood in a huddle by the kiddie pool. We were going to help Katie kick around in a foot of water for a while, but no one was allowed to go in yet because the hired lifeguard hadn't given her safety talk.

Micah was over by the adult pool with Brianne, who had him lying on a plastic lounger as if he were her patient on a couch. In a white one-piece that plunged so far front and back that I'd be willing to put down money it required less fabric than a bikini, she sat upright in a patio chair, with her legs crossed, and her hand was balled on her thigh like she was taking phantom notes on his case. This reminded me of when we used to play at running a doctor's office; I would come in with an injured stuffed bear, and she would treat it with her dad's tool kit.

From time to time her voice skimmed over the water, delivering us nuggets of wisdom like, "I'd say most commonly this is a female psychological maneuver, to reveal yourself bodily as a means of revealing an unfulfilled need . . ."

To that Cricket said, "Glass houses. Pot, kettle." She bent down to pet Saucy Evening, who was hidden in a tote bag because technically the condo complex didn't allow pets near the pool. The sarong over her bathing suit was a new (and Chico's mature) look for her, but she seemed to be increasingly healthy, so I figured, "Baby steps." I bent to scruff Saucy Evening's head with her.

Trevor had volunteered to go pick up bags of ice with Phil at the grocery store because ice was always what my family forgot at every outdoor summer event. Before they left, when Sailor first suggested, "Maybe we should just cool off in the pool and forget it," I argued, "No, we should really have ice. Today's supposed to hit record-breaking temperatures." I wanted him to be sent away so I'd have less opportunity to get anywhere near him.

Aunt Kathy, who had become incredibly supportive of me since our talk over pain, said, "Take her word for it. Right there's our future weather girl."

"It's not that easy to become one on a network," Brianne insisted.

Trevor watched me during this conversation, but we hadn't said so much as hi to each other since he and Brianne walked in through the gate. It wasn't that we hadn't had a chance to talk; without agreeing on a new way of handling things, we were both trying out the silent treatment.

Dom was also giving me a little bit of a silent treatment, not ignoring me outright, but when he spoke to the group, his eyes darted pass mine. Scrutinizing Micah, he said, "I think he's lying there like that because it gets him even more attention."

Autumn, her poolside sensibility the total opposite of Micah's, wore a ruffled cover-up that hung down to her knees. "It looks like he's listening to her. Maybe she's getting through to him."

"Maybe she is," I said, and Dom shot me a sideways glance.

The lifeguard clapped for everyone to assemble in front of her, and my relatives were acting like antsy kids in detention, rebelling against her authority. They kept talking even after she shushed them. Like an asshole, my dad went and dipped a toe in the pool before she'd given the okay, saying, "Help! I'm drowning!" My mom watched him like he wasn't actually there, like he was someone in a movie.

To avoid lawsuits, the condo complex had a rule that if you rented out the pool area, you either had to hire a private life-guard or document that there would be someone eighteen or older who was both trained in CPR and willing to stay out of the water to sit in the high chair and watch the other swimmers. My dad and half uncle Tobias met those requirements, but both wanted to swim.

Half Uncle Tobias and Brooke were off-again, so as the lifeguard attempted to go through all the "no running around the pool" stuff, he was embarrassing himself by flirtatiously teasing her, just coming short of pulling her hair. She had on red running shorts over her red lifeguard suit; one of the legs had "Zander" embroidered in white.

"What kind of name is Zander?" he ribbed while she was in the middle of telling us how to properly enter and exit the pool.

"A last name," she said in a flat way. "So when you climb out of the water, you want to secure your hand around the pole—"

To his credit, Half Uncle Tobias didn't do anything with that material. Instead he pressed on, "What's your first name, then?"

"Laura," she said with a sigh. "If you need to get my attention while you're drowning, either works. So you're going to want to stay holding on to—"

"Do you like going to the movies?"

Autumn reached up above Dom's shoulders and covered Katie's ears from the shame of it.

When finally the lifeguard was finished with her spiel, Cricket took Saucy over to the patch of grass to go to the bathroom behind the shield of a towel, and Dom, Autumn, and I took Katie to the kiddie pool.

However, once we had her in, we realized her Floaties were superfluous because the water wasn't high enough to float her. She was just standing in a circle of water the size of a miniature-golf putting green, soaking her knees.

"Fun?" I asked.

She shook her head, seeming on the verge of tears.

"Crouch," I told her. "Try that, and then pull up your feet."

"You're asking her to tread water. That's too sophisticated for a kid her age," Dom said, refusing to look at me. We were going into our seventh month of icy relations, and I thought we would have had our fight already. He'd never been mad at me like this before, and I'd started to wonder if maybe he expected a grand emotional gesture like he was waiting for from the family. I studied Katie, who was past the verge of tears and silently beginning to cry. Did he need tears?

Autumn applied more of a sunscreen stick to Katie's forehead and cheeks and wiped her tears away with her finger. "Don't sell her short," she scolded Dom. "You have no idea what she's capable of." When Autumn became a mom, she was going to be the kind who told her daughter, "Of course you can be a weather girl." Granted, she was also going to be the kind of mom who told her daughter that running a bank for the leprechauns or being a mermaid gynecologist wasn't out of the question either, but hopefully she was going to marry a guy with a better understanding of the fact that people actually need their limits in order to conduct a meaningful life.

"Here," Dom said, placing his hand in the middle of Katie's back. "Trust me, kiddo. Lean back, I got you. Put your arms out like an airplane."

The gate to the pool area banged shut, and Phil and Trevor walked in carrying huge bags of ice on each shoulder. I only looked over because of the noise, but when I saw who it was, I didn't spend a second longer on them.

Katie held out her arms toward me. "Ingrid."

Dom stared straight at me for the first time since early New Year's Day. "You want her to do it instead?"

"Yeah."

He took his hand off Katie's back as if he'd just become disgusted with her. "You want her? You trust her more? That's who you think's going to look out for your best interests? She's all yours. Excellent judge of character, Katie."

I moved over to Dom's side to take his place. He turned his head away. "Are you ready to talk?" I asked him.

"I'm ready to get out of this piss hole," he said and stepped out of the kiddie pool, grabbing a towel off a nearby lounger to wipe down his ankles. Katie was more interested now than upset, so Autumn also popped out to attend to Dom, in puzzlement about why he'd snapped. She had no clue what was going on between us, but I didn't think she cared about the specifics that much. I thought she seized these kinds of moments in order to be a part of us again, the ones who were her own age. As a kid she'd been like her own parent and then when Katie came along, she just switched over to being like hers.

"Lean back," I told Katie, and I helped lower her onto the

surface of the pool, where she floated on her back in her nautical bikini and sea monster Floaties. I sat on the edge of the pool to watch her in my black bikini and bare arms.

Trevor was watching me while helping Phil empty the ice into the row of coolers. When I made the mistake of becoming aware of this, he touched Phil on the shoulder. He was excusing himself. Phil waved him away; he could handle the rest of the job himself.

With the opposite of purpose in his stride—more like he was walking like he hoped he'd never get where he was going—Trevor came for me at the kiddie pool, his mouth slightly open along the way.

Behind me, Autumn was saying that she hated to see Dom in such an angry state, and Dom, who must have been facing the same way as me, said, "Would you look at this."

"Look at what?" she asked.

I checked on the adult pool. Brianne was in a corner of it, hunched in consultation with Micah.

Trevor was almost to me. I stood up, asking over my shoulder, "Autumn, would you watch Katie float?"

"Okay," she said, maybe with some resignation, and I could also practically hear her squinting at Dom because he hadn't given her an answer. Presumably watching the closing gap between me and Trevor, Dom gave the audio equivalent of eyes rolling with his breath.

When he was near to me, I saw Trevor's hair was dirtier than ever, and I could have made a joke about the pool being the first contact with water his head would have had all year.

"I need to talk to you," he said.

I said, "Not right now."

"No, right now."

In response to that demand I did the most mature thing I could have done, which means that I ran from him and jumped into the adult pool.

CHAPTER 15

As I came up out of the water for breath, my dad was preparing to do a backflip off the low board, old hat for him now after diving school. But if I could have seen his face, I guarantee he would have still looked like there was a thought he couldn't grab hold of.

The lifeguard shouted, "No tricks on the diving board!"

Micah's dad chimed in, "Ace, the sign says so! I signed the agreement and gave them a deposit!"

I'd jumped into the pool because I still hadn't figured out what to say to Trevor after all these months, not even after the imaginary conversations I'd had in my mind. Not after conceiving ways into and out of each conversation, not after testing what it felt like to say, "You shouldn't be with her" out loud.

There wasn't even a split second when I considered giving

him an ultimatum. Forcing a decision out of someone, any kind of decision, fundamentally dooms its success because you're trying to shift time. I'm not talking about fate, like certain decisions have to be made in certain moments or else you create a wormhole that subverts the destined birth of whatever genius invented the Swiffer Duster. I'm talking about how people are ready to act on something only in the moment they're finally ready, and you can influence the decision with gentle or even subliminal guidance, but you can't put it on the clock yourself.

It was just like the serenity prayer said. I'd overheard Tish reciting it in a stall in the women's bathroom before her birthday dinner at the Cheesecake Factory. In a desperate but soft voice, she chanted, "God, grant me the serenity to accept the things I cannot change, courage to change the things I can, and the wisdom to know the difference."

I knew I couldn't change anyone or anything outside of myself, and I followed the wisdom that I couldn't bend time in my favor, psychopath or not.

My dad backflipped off the board, and that brought the lifeguard down from her chair and to the edge of the pool to wait for his head to appear.

"Ingrid," I heard.

Looking back, I saw that Trevor had taken off the jeans he'd just been in and was walking into the pool in a pair of black trunks. He was saying the syllables of my name like someone would say, "Stop it."

With the bulk of my maternal-side relatives in it, the pool

was at maximum capacity, so in order to swim in deeper without interference, I dropped down again. At the very bottom, right below me, was the set of rainbow diving rings that had been around at our pool parties for forever. As kids we used to play treasure hunt; we'd pretend they were real rings, and almost break our ring fingers hanging the weights on them.

I was horrified by my behavior. My temples went hot, even with the coolness of the water pressing in on them. I breaststroked through the tangle of legs with my eyes open. They burned from the chlorine.

Spatial relations compromised, I almost came face-to-face with Micah's swim panties, pulling up just in time to surface to the right of him and Brianne. Brianne was who I needed to stay close to in the pool because if I was swimming near to her, Trevor couldn't come after me. From the reception I got, you'd think I was a patient who'd opened the office door and cut into her three o'clock's appointment.

"Ingrid, what I've said before about boundaries—," she started.

"Micah, why did you start dressing so differently last fall?" I asked. It was the fastest and easiest way to enter their drama. I had to take advantage of his identity crisis.

I thought Brianne would resent me joining in on her line of questioning and instruct him not to answer, as if she'd suddenly become his lawyer too. But after considering my presence for an instant, she adopted her prescription-glasses expression. "Then this has become an intervention," she decided. "We'll do it together." Treading water, she rotated toward Micah again. "Do you know?"

While she was focused on him, I stole a glance over at Trevor, who hadn't moved from where I'd last seen him at the farthest length of the pool. Over by the observation chair, the lifeguard was having an argument with my dad about how he needed to get out of the water—I think she was trying to enforce a time-out—but there was no way she was getting him to go along with the plan.

Micah stared up at the sky instead of down through the water, where he might have looked to remind himself why he'd originally responded to the cut or style of those panties. "You girls are making a big deal out of nothing. Chicken Little. The sky is falling. They're just briefs."

His using that word to describe his swimwear was like a color-blind guy telling you how gloriously orange your blue eyes look in the sun.

I said, "Those aren't briefs." I didn't really know all that much about the proper way to conduct an intervention, but I did know that you had to bring out your toughest love.

"Do you know?" Brianne repeated.

He was becoming exasperated with her, but that bled over into his also losing patience for lying. "I needed a change," he said with a sigh.

"From what?"

Micah slipped deeper into the water, his shoulders going under so only his head was above, the back of it hooked on the lip of the pool. When he spoke, his eyes were halfway shut and his chin tipped upward. He looked like he was singing into a mic. "Not *from* what. Into someone."

"Into who?" I wondered.

He wasn't spilling, and so Brianne announced that this was the part of the intervention where she and I stopped asking questions and just launched into a confrontation about how seeing him like that made us feel.

I shook my head. "It doesn't make me feel much beyond being worried about him, and concerned that he's trying to get naked in front of the family," I told her. To Micah, I said, "You really should be the one who talks."

Brianne shook her head at me. "But you might just be unresponsive to personal relations like this, so he shouldn't go by what you're feeling."

All the time Brianne had been trying to warn me and the family that I might be about as emotionally deficient as a person can get, I hadn't really been bothered by hearing the theory. Sure, it had become inconvenient for a while when my relatives eyed me like I might someday push them off a boat and steal their identities, but I didn't take her seriously. I figured she'd be assigning another cousin another mental problem when mine grew stale.

There she was, though, working on shrinking Micah's head, and still mine was suspect. But since last Labor Day I'd done the research, and I'd read all the qualities and abilities I wasn't supposed to have. I wasn't going to argue with her about how I did have deep feelings for certain other human beings or how I did experience empathy, but there were a number of those kinds of things that didn't fit. Like insight.

If I had nothing else, if my heart was cold and black and dead, I had insight.

"I'm not a psychopath!" I lashed out at Brianne, and hearing myself say that, I thought I hadn't ever actually argued the charge before.

"I'm not saying that you're going to seriously hurt or swindle or murder someone, but—," she began in a tone of voice that implied she thought she was starting to make the peace.

I gave her a piece of advice. "Stay in school."

"At least you have something about you that makes you interesting."

We both looked to Micah, who had just said this.

"Brianne's the one who's good at school and going to be a doctor," he went on.

Maybe, I was tempted to tell him, but I didn't want to stop him from talking.

"Autumn's the mom. You need someone to kiss your forehead, you mosey over to her. Cricket's got her tennis and she's so sharp, you know? Everyone thinks so. No one would ever say that about me. Dom's going to have his pride parades when he finally comes out." He realized a greater injustice. "And he has his vintage sci-fi stuff too. He's got the uptight dorkiness to fall back on, even beyond being gay." I waited, but his list stopped there.

"What about me?" I asked and then added, in case he hadn't abandoned Brianne's reading of my personality, "I'm not a psychopath."

He looked down at me from beneath his eyelids. "You're

the one with the mystery. You're the one who no one knows what she's up to." I'd worked so hard at the appearance of transparency that the surprise of him saying this left me quiet. He might have just been latching on to an idea that Brianne had put into his head last year, but I felt like he was accusing me from a more personal standpoint.

"You think that swimsuit makes you interesting?" Brianne was astounded. It seemed like she asked this because she wanted to know and not because she was following a therapeutic technique.

"What, you think it doesn't?" Micah asked, sounding as if a carefully laid plan was unraveling from the tug of that one possibility—that the clothes, or lack thereof, didn't actually make the man.

"Ingrid!" yelled Trevor suddenly from over near the barbecue. He yelled. His voice rang across the pool, from ear to ear of each of my family members, into the ears of his girlfriend, who looked over at him when he called my name.

"What?" I yelled back, having no choice but to stare helplessly at him and trust him to be smart about this. Brianne looked back toward me. I hoped the rest of the relatives behind us were wrapped up in themselves, so she wouldn't have reason to take greater notice in the back and forth. I couldn't bring myself to check to see if anyone was interested, especially Dom.

"Whoever used the grill before us left it a mess." Trevor ran a towel across the dirty grate and held it up, showing the dark lines. It was a nice touch. "I know you're particular. You want to clean it? Or I will."

I couldn't decide if that was some kind of veiled threat, like he was telling me that if I didn't come talk to him, he was going to . . . what? It gave the impression that there was something I could be about to lose, but I just didn't know what yet.

"How does he know that about me?" I asked.

"He's read my notes," Brianne casually explained. "For the study I'm writing on you."

I looked at her. "There's no paper there."

For a second she appeared taken aback, as if now *I* were threatening *her*, and then she turned thoughtful and seemed to be examining my face, her gaze jumping from part to part. "Or that I might not," she said. "Don't be defensive. I suggested that he should get to know you guys better, and he's just trying to be nice."

"Okay," I said.

I pressed my hand to Micah's chest, still shaved, right above his heart. "You're the ballsy one."

"Don't pun with me," he said. He was right. It wasn't a good time.

Micah and I had always related to each other as the ones who could be counted on for a good time at the family events. Me, because I could always fake it. Micah, because historically he had a truly easygoing nature that let him believe if life wasn't a party, then it wasn't less than an amusement. So together we were the first to set off the illegal fireworks or face paint with cocktail sauce or pull out the Twister (this is partying when you're nine). That had seemed like enough for him for a long time, but now he needed more. He was waiting for a better answer about who he was to me.

I said, "You're the one who doesn't have to have a *thing* because you're just so much who you are—and it comes easy to you, so you can't even see yourself from the outside."

Micah lowered his chin under the water and became pensive, chomping at the pool's surface like a fish, but I couldn't tell if I'd let him down further. He only said, "I'm counting on you to save my burger from the dregs of the riffraff who were here barbecuing before us."

I swam over to the nearest ladder and climbed out of the pool. Trevor bent down to one of the coolers and made a motion to ask if I wanted him to grab me anything. With my hands I slicked my wet hair off my face. I was acutely aware that from the neck up, I looked about the same as when I first met him.

"Do you?" he asked when I reached him, because I hadn't indicated if I did or didn't want a drink. Feeling around in the ice, he pulled himself out a root beer in a bottle—the family had gone completely nonalcoholic for the party in support of Tish's recent induction into Alcoholics Anonymous: soda, juice, water.

"No thanks."

Straightening, he pried the cap off the bottle with the opener on Phil's sterling *P* keychain. He took a sip. He kept his eyes on mine. I thought he might be trying not to look at my bikini or me in it. While walking up to him, I had already spent time on him. His body gave me the mental image of a childhood that involved a lot of climbing and hanging from trees instead of playing sports. He was long—every proportion.

"We need to look around for the brush and cleaning supplies," I said.

I knew they were in the clubhouse next to the bathrooms, but that would take us out of everyone's sight. "Maybe in the clubhouse," he said, which again sounded like a veiled threat coming from him, or at least that's the reason I gave myself for leading him in there.

The clubhouse party room was empty of things. The folding tables were collapsed and pushed back against a far wall, and the plastic chairs had been stacked. We didn't turn the fluorescents on, but the skylights let in enough filtered sun to give us long shadows on the sisal carpet. I mean, mine was long; Trevor's was lonnnnnng.

I went to the storage area, which you could see from the party room through the cutout above the serving bar. I opened a cabinet, jam-packed with the property's Fun Noodles, which I began to toss aside. "I remember the supplies being in here."

"Hold on," Trevor said from the other side of the cutout. He rested his arms on the ledge and held them out, as if I were supposed to seriously come hold on to him. "Before we get anything, I want to talk to you."

"Sure, let's talk. So I graduated from high school," I said, starting to tell him the first of the three, and only three, things that I was going to say on the subject of him and me. High school graduation came first because I wanted to remind him that we were now in the same bracket of life steps.

"I know. Congratulations."

"Thank you."

The second thing was harder to say. It was that he shouldn't be with Brianne. Not that he should be with me either—that would be some serious backstabbing—but just that he didn't fit with her. I was silent, and Trevor continued, "I have a graduation present for you."

"You have it here?"

"Right here in my pocket," he said, unable to stop every muscle in his face except for his mouth from smiling at the obvious joke. I saw the entertainment in his cheeks, in between his eyebrows. "I swear," he said, "I do have a present."

"Then throw it through the hole," I told him, and the same entertainment crept into my features when I realized I was making what was already a sad, easy joke even sadder and easier.

He reached into the pocket of his trunks and pulled out a small square box, tied with a black ribbon. He took a pretend underhand swing, raising an eyebrow to check if I was ready, and I said, "Throw it."

I caught it and undid the ribbon. When I pulled off the lid, I was looking at a stone with two painted eyes on it.

"It's a pet rock. There's no way you can hurt it."

I removed the rock from the box, turning it around in my hand, and I began to laugh. Not for as long as when I laughed at Uncle Kurt (an eternity), but it kept Trevor waiting. After

I'd finally calmed down, I tightened the bikini string around my neck, which had somehow loosened in the process. "Thank you."

"I have one more present, but it's not here."

"Oh really," I said, "this is plenty."

"No," Trevor insisted, leaving his place at the opening and walking around to the doorway. Then he came close to me, stepping over the Fun Noodles. "The present's already yours. You just have to check with your parents first."

The condition on the gift was like a slap in that it filled my face with that same kind of hotness. Whether I was still as naive as he once accused me of being, I wasn't the eternal kid his condition suggested I was.

"I'm moving out at the end of next month," I said crisply, telling him the third thing.

A barely perceptible wrinkle appeared in his forehead from the surprise. "I thought Brianne said you weren't going to college."

"I'm not. There are other things you can do with yourself when you're eighteen."

This small piece of information seemed to throw off his picture of the world, or maybe just *his* world, and I watched him as he made whatever sense of it he wanted to.

"Then this present is all yours, from me to you," he said and drew an envelope out of his back pocket.

Every envelope I'd received at my actual graduation had contained cash or a check, and I hoped he wasn't trying to give me money. I was curious, though. I accepted his envelope and ran a nail across the top because he'd gone through the bother of licking it shut. It was thin. I really hoped it wasn't a letter, regardless of what it might say.

But it wasn't a letter. It was a photo. I slid it out of the envelope. A beagle puppy lay on a fleece bed, face sunk between big paws and ears looking too big for her head. I knew she was a girl because someone had tied a pink bow around her neck, and people don't tend to care about teaching gender neutrality to their dogs.

"What does this mean?" I asked.

I loved her right away.

"It means she's yours if you want her. My brother's dog had puppies a few months ago." He smiled minimally. "She's the most charming of the bunch, so I had him set her aside for you."

"I'm not very charming lately," I said. "This is for real?"

"The first time I met you and you were so mad that Brianne didn't think you loved your dog, I thought you missed having one."

I studied her in the photo again. My dog. After Long John died, my parents had said they weren't ready to get a new dog. I'd been ready for a while, and it wasn't because I didn't mourn Long John, but because I couldn't stop.

"I'm driving up to San Francisco next week to visit my family, so I'll pick her up then."

I glanced at him. "The rough patch is over?"

He didn't sound all that happy when he said, "Things are better for now."

"What happened?"

"Not important." He shook his head twice.

I could have kissed him, even just on the forehead, where the wrinkle had been, or on the shoulder, but I couldn't start with that stuff, so I made him a promise. "I'll take really good care of her," I said.

"I'm not worried at all."

"I'll take her straight to the best vet in town the day she comes home."

"Where are you going to be?"

Before I could tell him that I was going to live near the beach (the one down in Orange County, not the Malibu coast), Brianne's dad had entered the clubhouse already talking. "You guys find the grill brushes?" He'd been following our earlier line of question and answer. "It's like animals cooked on that thing!"

There was nowhere big enough on my bikini to hide the photo of my new dog, so I palmed it like I'd learned from the magic book. The dimensions were a little unwieldy, but I got it to buckle so I could keep an almost straight hand.

"That's a dark image," Trevor called back to Phil over his shoulder, turning his head sideways.

I turned and resumed my search through the cabinet. Phil came into the storage area, and when he saw all the Fun Noodles on the floor, he said, "All right! Fun Noodles!" He picked a lime-colored Noodle up from the ground and hung it around his neck, throwing his arms protectively over like it was a limp swimmer he was going to rescue. "We should get these into the pool for everyone."

"We should," I said and fake jabbed him in the side, using my free fist. He laughed and clutched his ribs, pretending I'd hurt him. "You grab them, I'll grab the brushes."

The first thing my eye went to after returning outside was a shining clump of purple lying at the edge of the pool. A sea cucumber that had gotten itself mixed up with the wrong body of water, then was stepped on and killed. I considered that maybe it was a mirage created by the sun, so I went toward the clump to break the illusion, but from a few feet away, there was no confusing Micah's swim panties.

I didn't know whether Brianne's method of intervention relied on Micah getting worse before he could get better, but at any rate, wherever he was, he was nude.

I'd left my sunglasses in one of the bags, so I cupped a hand over my eyes to find him. As if deliberately guiding me, the lifeguard shouted, "Hands off the board! Hands off the board!"

I looked that way and found Micah hanging on to the lip of the diving board, pulling himself just enough out of the water that you could see the very dawn of his crack. His head was thrown back, same as it had been when he'd been onstage at Uncle Kurt's bar mitzvah and same as earlier, when he'd been using it to hook himself onto the rim of the pool. But this version struck me as joyous somehow, like when dolphins get so happy they jump and curve their heads toward their tails, or when cheerleaders erupt in herkies.

The cumulative pain-in-the-assness of assorted relatives must have dampened the lifeguard's enthusiasm for keeping us all from harm, because instead of coming down to remove Micah's hands from the board, she just gave a dismissive wave to the sky.

I walked over, stepped onto the board, and sat down near the tips of Micah's fingers. This was definitely not allowed, but the lifeguard sighed, or just looked so much like she was sighing that that's what I thought I heard. Leaning over the end of the board, I asked Micah's Adam's apple, "How are you holding up?"

"I'm enough!" was his joyous response. I hadn't been imagining the joyousness in his body language.

"Of course you are," I said.

"I'm enough just as I am. There's no greater degree of nakedness I can reach."

Katie had wandered over to his discarded bikini and was poking it with an ambivalent toe.

He began to use the diving board as a pull-up bar, lifting himself from the pool, and from behind him his dad, who didn't believe in cursing, hollered, "Micah, keep your heinie down in the water! No one needs to see it!"

Micah's chin was now on the board, and he looked up into my eyes. "They do need to see it. Because this is what I was most scared of anyone seeing. This is me without any of the gimmicks . . . it's me *uninteresting.*"

He pushed off the board, arching backward into the water, exclaiming happily, "All there is!"

Before Micah came back up, Phil called from over at the barbecue, "Everybody to the tables! It's time for the announcement!"

"What announcement?" I asked.

CHAPTER 16

"Everybody get a drink!" Phil ordered the group. That meant a toast.

Autumn had wrapped Micah in a huge body towel, which he wore over his shoulders like a cape, and he took a seat at one of the Kid Table benches without protest. The rest of us were still practicing some level of resistance. Dom was sitting on the table itself. Katie was lying on her back under it, I don't know why, other than that maybe she wasn't yet finished with the floating. Autumn sat cross-legged on the ground, trying to talk Katie out ("Honey, it's dirty"), and Cricket had put Saucy Evening in her place on the bench. She touched the back of his neck to wake him from what we presumed was a bad dream— he'd fallen asleep almost the second he hit the warm concrete and had begun to convulse with a puppy nightmare.

I stretched in the sunlight a couple of inches from the table.

I had the photo of my dog pressed between my hands, extended above my head.

Brianne's mom came over to the Kid Table and dropped a six-pack of Cokes off in the middle. "Everybody's cool with soda?" she asked. Droplets of the pool glistened at the ends of her buzzed hair. Her head was a field of water globes.

Dom reached forward and opened a can. "Soda's better than when you give us grape juice and call it wine."

"It's not you," Autumn reassured Sailor. "He's been in a bad mood."

Sailor just stuck out her tongue and scruffed the back of Dom's head, joking, "Girl problems?" The way she asked that, I thought she'd put an especially sarcastic emphasis on "girl," as if she knew that was the biggest part of the joke.

Dom must have heard the same thing in her delivery because he gave her a look made of hope almost immediately stepped on by fear. It was like, if this was how the adults were going to go about confronting him about being gay, with jokey pretense like that, then he'd never have the milestone he'd been holding out for. They'd be letting him know they knew without ever really saying they did.

He mumbled, "Yeah, girl problems."

"Look, you have a bunch of girls around you to help you figure them out . . ." Sailor's head swiveled as Tish passed by, Tish being a real, pressing problem that everyone in the family had been briefed about before the party: "Tish, can I get you something to drink?"

Still moving, Tish raised the bottled water she was holding.

The motion was so angry it had the same quality as though she were giving Sailor the finger or that sign people sometimes make while slapping their forearms to add to the insult.

Right then I began to worry that maybe my reintroduction of alcohol into her life had altered her personality for good. She'd definitely been more reserved before I gave her "punch."

Sailor watched Tish go, saying, "I think I liked her better before." I couldn't be sure which before she was referring to, but I guessed it was the drunk and not the prude.

"Everybody good? Everybody sit!" instructed Phil. Saucy Evening woke up, recognizing the second command, but you could practically see him deciding that going from lie to sit was too much effort, so he fell back asleep. Sailor gave a little clap and took off for her table. "Everybody park it! We have some news!"

I took a seat at the bench.

Important news usually traveled fast in my family—just like the Kid Table had our conference calls, the adults kept up a phone tree—so it was hard to believe that anyone had anything big to share unless it had secretly happened behind one of the pool area's shrubs within the past hour. The summer had been quiet, with everyone humming along. Even if one of us had gotten a bad sunburn, it would have made the rounds.

What was this business about? Maybe Phil and Sailor were taking off for Mexico like they'd always threatened to do once Brianne left for college. Or, if they wanted to stay in California but had gotten melancholy about their empty concrete nest, maybe they were taking in an exchange student to fill the void. Phil could be telling us he was going into business for himself; he'd been complaining about the lack of inspiration at his architecture firm for ages.

In the same class that I learned about the cat in the box, I also learned about a principle called Occam's razor, which says the simplest route to an answer is the best one. If I thought about the most direct path between an announcement from a family member and its probable content, then I couldn't arrive at any solution other than that we were about to get a new occasion. Of course they were throwing a party.

Maybe Phil and Sailor were going to renew their vows.

There were no spoons to tap with and no glasses to tap on, so Phil got the talking to stop by taking a wet towel and snapping it against the air. The crack first set off a fast debate about whether or not the towel made that noise because it was breaking the sound barrier, but then the general lack of that kind of scientific knowledge in our family trickled into silence.

"When I look at Brianne," Phil started, "I still see that little girl—" This was about Brianne, then, not them, and I began to adjust my theories. She was getting an award. A medical school had accepted her earlier than they'd ever accepted anybody before.

"—who was an old soul from the first day we met her. So cute, but so very smart." I glanced over at Brianne, to see how she was taking this. I was reminded of how much I could like her when I caught her staring out the bars of the gate, looking like she wanted to run. Trevor's back was stiff. I'd never seen him so perfectly straight.

"I'm not a sentimental person, but when Trevor came to me last week, asking for her hand in marriage—"

Say what now?

There were gasps.

Not mine.

I was too surprised to open my mouth. The shock of knowing what was to come went directly to my spine, straightening me too. The day stopped. Time stopped, I mean. Not for long, but for just long enough to crack through me painfully (not unlike a wet towel) as I fell behind and tried to stall in the present to do a little more math.

I took a good few seconds to realize that the gasps were happy. Applause came next. I would say it was downright wild. All the women, except for Tish and my mom, leaped up from their chairs and faced Brianne and Trevor to clap and say things like, "You two!" and "I can't believe it!"

If my mouth had been working, I could have echoed the latter and meant it. Phil whistled, trying to win back everyone's attention. I wanted them all to be quiet because if they would do this simple thing, then maybe he would go on to explain how this could possibly be the situation.

Because what was this, 1919, and Brianne and Trevor needed to marry young so they could have some able-bodied kids to work the farm? Had they found religion out of nowhere, one that still allowed for Brianne to wear bathing suits like the one she was in, but which had suddenly panicked them about living in sin? Had they gotten themselves involved in some fucked-up psychological experiment at school like the egg-baby thing my health teacher had implemented at mine, except this time with marriage? Did one or both of them badly need a tax break?

Brianne was twenty and Trevor was twenty-one, and maybe those were the ages that some of our parents used to marry at, but back then they were newly scared about AIDS and drunk on the romance of a strong economy, or at least that's how Bruce started the story he told Autumn when she got older and wanted to know why he'd stopped loving her mom.

Was Brianne pregnant?

Fortunately, Tish was asking this exactly as I was wondering it.

"I'm not pregnant!" Brianne laughed. The edge of my vision stopped with her. It didn't include Trevor, even if he was right there.

Phil whistled. "Hey, people, I wasn't finished!"

Uncle Kurt, possibly still wounded from the time he gave a rudely interrupted speech, acted in support of Phil. "The man's trying to make a statement about his daughter growing up! What's wrong with you guys? Show some respect!"

"Okay, yes, okay, we're respecting you," said Michelle, bouncing flat hands lower and lower. I had a flashback to seeing her perform this very move on the night of the bar mitzvah to the end part of the song "Shout," where it tells everybody to get softer.

Other relatives encouraged him to continue, but you could feel—and even Phil appeared to feel—that he was already the relic and they were eager to trade him out and hear from Brianne instead. I didn't care who stepped up to explain why it was the case that marriage was on the table. *Someone* needed to continue.

"Dad?" Brianne prompted.

Phil? I sent out that message by thinking it with as much power as I could.

He took a step back toward the coolers. Even before he spoke, I saw the embarrassment that had seeped into his whole body and face. "I feel stupid now," he announced.

"Why?" asked Brit, who was really susceptible to embarrassment, so maybe she, of all people, should have understood that sometimes you just feel like an asshole for reasons that would be hard to explain. Like say there was this guy who had just recently proposed to your cousin, except he'd also just pulled you aside to give you *a dog*, and yet you felt like an asshole for still believing that he wasn't ready to spend the rest of his life with his new fiancée, that would be hard to explain to your family. "What happened?" she asked.

Yes, Phil, what happened.

"Nothing, nothing," he said, dropping his head and absentmindedly spreading around a puddle of water on the ground with his loafer. "I had a joke I came up with to go with the announcement, but now the moment doesn't seem right anymore, and I just realized it won't be funny."

"Sure it will," said Autumn.

"The wording has to be right too. I had it down last night, now I can't . . ." As that sentence drifted off, we could tell he was going to try. "I was going to start with the stuff about Brianne still being a little girl, and then something like—" He shifted to a voice that was more presentable. "When Trevor came to me last week, asking for her hand in marriage, and I said yes, I thought to myself, what is this guy, a pedophile?"

No one laughed. With all the other circumstances factored in, I came close.

"Yeah, that wasn't funny," said Michelle, looking to her ex-husband for backing. Bruce said, "Nope." Who knew what was going on with them, but it was a fact that after giving young marriage a shot, they had ultimately returned to dating. Why could they not just date?

Belatedly, Tish gave a short laugh and decided, "It's not bad."

That set off some whispering between Sailor and my mom, but Phil began to talk to Tish as if she were the only one who related to him and the only one at the pool. Flipping his palms up, he explained, "The wording came out differently from how I solved it before. I don't think I used pedophile in the final version."

Tish, no longer of any help, shrugged and gave a single barking laugh again.

"Never mind," Phil said loudly, coming back to the rest of us. "It's not important." Trevor had told me the same thing.

Phil threw up his hands, and I had "Shout" déjà vu of him doing the louder part of the song. He took a deep breath. "I said yes, and I'm proud to announce that Trevor and Brianne will be getting married at the end of the summer. Raise your cans and your bottles, and Katie, get up that juice box, because we're going to toast!"

Phil's line was that there was no rush. It was just that he had been the lead architect on a new reception venue in Newport Beach, and when he shared the good news in a conversation with the client, he'd been offered use of the space before it officially opened in late September. Brianne had come down from Malibu for the day, and they went to the site for her to take a look. By all accounts, the building was completely romantic. She liked the space, but she loved that Phil had built it and loved it even more that she was going to be the first person to be married inside it.

Everyone else went over to Brianne and Trevor to give congratulations. A swarm formed around them, so that I didn't have to avoid seeing him anymore. I never knew they even liked him that much.

I heard a lot of the women asking to see the ring, and Brianne saying something about how she and Trevor were going to replace it later. That meant small or simple. He was a student. The ring was a band, maybe. I tried to think back to her treading water in the pool next to me and recall if she'd had something sparkling around her finger. Had I missed it? Had I naively thought it was her own?

While I was hanging back, I felt a gentle scratch at my leg and looked down to find Saucy Evening with a paw up on my shin. He was panting, his tongue hanging from his mouth.

"You thirsty, Saucy?" I asked.

Happy to have something legitimate to do to keep from joining the group, I scanned the nearest table for some water to pour in his plastic bowl. Tish's bottle was still half-full and cold, so I poured the rest of it for Saucy and petted his head, saying, "There you go."

He sniffed at the bowl warily—mistrustful, I thought, of anyone who wasn't Cricket. "I'm okay," I told him. "Don't listen to any of what you've heard."

Eyeballing me once, he dropped his head to lick at the water. I gave him a kiss behind his ear.

"Wait, where's Ingrid?" Brianne was asking over the other voices.

I stood from kneeling next to Saucy so she could see me. She was standing on a seat, looking for me over the heads of the aunts and cousins and mother and grandma hanging around her and talking excitedly about plans for the big day.

"I was giving the dog something to drink. It's really hot out." I even pointed to the sun as if I needed to give proof.

Now Trevor was surrounded by the guys, facing the other direction. All I could make of him were pieces of hair.

"Why aren't you congratulating me?" Brianne called, not mad but astounded again, like she'd been earlier with Micah.

"I am," I said.

"How?"

In that moment I missed the day when it would have been second nature to fake it. I would have put my arms around her and told her I'd only been waiting to give a more personal congratulations. This was bigger than a first peek at the ring. I'd wanted to wait until things weren't so crazy around her and we could talk. I'm sorry it seemed like I didn't care, I'd say. Forgive me. You're going to be beautiful.

I walked toward Brianne and said, nodding, "Congratulations."

She stepped down from the seat. Michelle came up from behind her to hug her giddily across her chest, rocking her from side to side. As Michelle did this she was in profile, talking to Sailor about centerpiece flowers, and she didn't have any awareness of what Brianne looked like as she looked at me. How instantaneously I'd sombered her up.

Brianne rocked, wild-eyed. "This may not be important to you, but it's important to me."

"I know it's important," I said.

"Then be over here."

I did as she asked and stood next to her, our hips practically glued together as the group conversation drifted into dresses and honeymoon islands. When Cricket grew weary of the conversation, she abruptly seemed to realize that she'd gone too long without her dog.

"Where's Saucy?" she asked, checking at her feet, and I said, "Last I saw him he was at his bowl by our table."

She went to get him. Aunt Kathy suggested that Brianne, "Do Hawaii, but not *Hawaii*. You want to go to the secret parts," which, from the way she said it, sounded like sex advice in code.

"Ace and I did tourist Hawaii," my mom said.

My parents had only taken one picture the entire time they were there—a waiter with a Polaroid offered to do it for them, and if he hadn't, they wouldn't even have the one. In it, they're so in love that you could never doubt it. Their mad love is like the tiny red lamp on their table in the photo. It's definitely there.

That was before the scrapbooking and the photography, so you can see in the Polaroid that my mom is just being there with my dad. And that was before my dad started looking backward at himself, so you can also see him just being there with my mom.

"We liked it fine," she added.

"Well, we're not going anywhere until at least winter break because the fall semester starts right after the wedding—"

"Help!" screamed Cricket. "Oh God, please come help!"

The terror in her voice had us immediately running over to where she was, huddled under the Kid Table with Saucy Evening convulsing violently in her arms. She locked eyes with me first and asked desperately, the tears beginning to come, "He was hunched over his bowl! What did you give him?!"

Toby ducked under the table to help her with her shaking dog, who now had foam coming from the side of his mouth. The sight filled me with apprehension, and I answered just as desperately, "I only gave him water! Bottled water!"

Relatives were all shouting out different things, like Uncle Sam was telling Toby to grab Saucy's tongue, so he didn't bite it while seizing, and Brit was asking Sam where the nearest emergency animal hospital was. Except he didn't know because they'd never had pets. The lifeguard, who'd been reading up on her chair while we were out of the water, jumped down and came sprinting around the pool.

I grabbed the empty bottle from the table and said, "Just this! I took Tish's water! He was really thirsty!"

Tish had been hovering on the edge of our cluster, but she pushed through the shoulders of my dad and Uncle Kurt at mention of her name. "You poured him water from mine?"

"Yes! It wasn't even tap!"

The lifeguard dropped under the table and started to examine Saucy's eyes and feel his chest.

"*That was mostly vodka,*" said Tish, her hand flying to her mouth in horror.

I turned toward her, feeling myself begin to tremble a little. "You're saying that I gave the dog vodka?"

From behind her fingers, she moaned, "I was hiding my drink in the water bottle."

"He drank vodka!" exploded Toby, freshly panicked, and my other family members yelled, "It's vodka!" and "Oh my God, vodka," and "Jesus Christ, he's probably dying," and hurried to get car keys and find the closest hospital on their iPhones and BlackBerries.

I looked to the bowl, which had the smallest amount of alcohol left shining at the bottom. Cricket, belatedly grasping that her dog had been poisoned and that this was worse than she'd even imagined, scrambled out from under the table with Saucy still in her arms and cried, "Get us to a fucking vet *now!*"

I yelled, "Get them to the vet!" and pushed her dad, fumbling with his keys, toward the gate. "Just go!"

Clutching Saucy to her, Cricket tore after him. Brit took Michelle's better handheld smartphone and ran to catch up.

After their car peeled out of the lot, the pool went even quieter than it had when Phil made his announcement. Everyone scattered from the crowd around our table, shaking their heads and exhaling and that kind of thing. Tish was especially rattled and her gaze swung from family member to family member, like she was asking if she was accountable. Generally, people avoided eye contact. I felt as if someone was watching me, but I didn't look to see who. Sailor said, mostly to herself, "When I heard her scream, I thought she'd hurt herself. Thank God it was the dog." But I knew if her dog died, then Cricket would be lost because in many ways, she'd handed herself off into his care.

I burst into tears.

CHAPTER 17

As I was crying, I felt like a baby. Not inside myself, I'm saying, not that I had reverted to a primal state I knew from way
back, but in how my relatives were outwardly looking at me.

When the doctor delivers a baby, turns her upside down,
and spanks her, the people who watched the birth make their
relief-and-miracle face—or, they do on all the hospital shows
I've seen. My relatives wore variations of that face, and it
made me feel like they saw me as someone new to the world.
That, in turn, made me angrier than I already was to begin
with.

I didn't believe in God, but I was angry with something
big like a god. With whatever force of nature made it so that
Brianne's bullshit about my animal cruelty appeared to come
true in the form of a coincidence that could also seem, if you
couldn't look into my heart, like proof about me.

I wasn't waking up to the universe of human emotion. I hadn't cried in probably a couple of years or so, maybe more, but it wasn't like puberty and suddenly I had all these questions about what was happening to me. Put simply, tears were still a familiar thing.

Breaking the silence, Brianne assured me, "Don't begin to think that I think you did anything."

She was a wavy figure through my tears, which were streaming down both my cheeks, but I did my best to locate the boundaries of her head.

I said, "You shut your unlicensed trap."

"Whoa, whoa, whoa," said Uncle Kurt, not without some amusement, I thought. I know that after he'd admitted the affair to the family, Brianne had offered him some counsel about why he was a man who needed to cheat. At the time, I think he'd appreciated her giving him the source of his fuck-up—it was his brain that had gone wrong—but since his bar mitzvah, he hadn't wanted to hear more from her, I'm guessing because he stopped believing he had to be permanently defective.

Reflexively, Autumn launched into, "Now, we don't need to—," but stopped because you could easily make the argument that Brianne and I did.

"I wasn't being passive-aggressive," Brianne told me. "That was straightforward."

Next to Brianne, Trevor was wavy too, which was also how my understanding of him had gone after finding out that he had decided to get married. Before Saucy Evening had done the equivalent of ten shots, I'd been too depressed and perplexed by Trevor's behavior to even look straight at him. Now that I was so angry, though, I was ready to gawk at him. I wiped away tears from the rims of my eyes, so I had a clearer view.

He was looking back at me with something like concern, holding his hair back off his forehead with his hand like he couldn't comprehend, I don't know, his own life.

My mom tossed the offending water bottle in the trash. I'm not saying this as a joke or a dig at her, but that move surprised me because I thought she'd hide it away in her bag for the party's scrapbook page. She said, "It's not your fault. It's not even Tish's."

"I know it is, I know it is, I know it is," Tish chanted, her head down on her table.

"They'll pump his stomach," my mom continued. "This isn't like Sweetie, he's a heartier animal."

Remembering my hamster, who died young and left a good-looking corpse with residue of the glitter she'd been vomiting on her muzzle, I was electrified with the unfairness of life. It didn't matter that I knew I wasn't owed anything or that in my life I'd had so much good come to me that the bad couldn't make a dent in my balance. I felt the loss of pets, the future loss of Trevor, who I'd never even really had, and the fear that we'd all lose Cricket again if the vet couldn't pump dog stomachs. But most of all, I felt how all of these were things I couldn't really do anything about.

"Ingrid, you're not alone. We're all worried about Cricket together," Brianne said with a shiver.

I didn't have any pull over death, of course, so the lone item on that list that I could even begin to touch was Trevor.

"Trevor—," I said.

I'd gotten as far as that when Dom put his hand in mine and declared, "I want to go with you on a walk."

Dom was the only person in my family who knew what I could have said. I closed my hand around his. Relationships shift.

Before pulling me to the gate, Dom pretended to lower his voice to confide in Brianne (while still keeping it loud enough so everyone could hear), "Before she tells him he's not really part of the family and should leave."

Dom had his cell phone with him, and we took turns holding it so we wouldn't miss any news from the vet. We walked the outer pathways of the condo complex, casually looking in the windows of the people who lived on the ground floor.

"I don't know if you shouldn't say what you were about to say to him. Maybe you should. But I thought that if you were going to anyway, you should take at least a minute to decide." He pointed to a window where an obese cat was lying on the back of a leather couch and making the whole middle sink in.

I whistled at its size. People slowly kill their animals with excessive kibble in condos all through the nation, and no one's pointing a finger except if they're doing it like Dom, at the cat.

"Why would they get married?" I asked.

He shoved his hands in the pockets of his trunks in contemplation. "I don't know. Maybe he did it out of guilt about you."

I'd been so blown away by the announcement that I hadn't tried out any of the more complicated yet stupider reasons that Trevor might have proposed. "I promise, Dom, the only time we kissed was the time you saw us."

He pointed at me, but it was gentle pointing, the kind you get as a kid when you've worried someone older but they love you too much to hold whatever you've done against you. "You know, I do believe that it's about him and that he's not just anyone to you." The pointing became firmer. "Not that I'm saying you should be kissing him or that that wasn't fucked-up."

"I'm really sorry I hogged the bartender. It's no excuse, but I thought you were done with him."

Dom lowered his finger from its aim at my collarbone and let that hand fall to his thigh, slapping it in regret. "He wasn't getting my point across anyway."

"We'll figure something better out."

"I hope so."

"Your day will come."

We reached Uncle Sam's first-floor condo and stepped over the half wall surrounding their front patio. We took seats in two of the three mesh chairs out there and threw our feet up on the wall, letting our flip-flops drop off on the other side. The phone wasn't doing anything. I pressed a button to make sure the volume was up and the battery was charged. Dom had Rod Serling on his wallpaper.

I'd almost forgotten I still had the photo of my beagle

palmed, but when I reached around Dom to rest my arm along the back of his chair, it flapped against the metal bar like the telltale card of someone trying to cheat at poker.

"What's that sound?" asked Dom, looking toward his shoulder.

I placed the picture in his lap, and he picked it up to study it closer. "A beagle?"

"Trevor's brother's dog had a litter, and that's the one Trevor wants me to have."

He'd been leaning forward to look at the photo, but when I told him from whence my dog came, his neck and chin jerked back. It was as if he'd just been pushed in the throat while an invisible force steadied the rest of him. "He's giving you a puppy? Isn't giving a puppy a sign of love?"

"Is it?"

Dom's eyes were saucers as he rolled his ankles around on the wall.

"He did it before I knew about the proposal, so I feel strange about the gift now." I took the picture from under Dom's hold and looked at my puppy again. "I do really want her, though."

"What a weird thing to do."

Weird or strange or not, it was the best gift I'd ever gotten from someone without any defined ties to me. "In some universe, it's a nice thought."

"For a psycho to have," laughed Dom, and I smiled at him. "What are you going to do when Brianne comes over, sees the puppy that eerily resembles her brother-in-law's dog, and asks where you got her?"

Not being serious, I said, "I'm going to tell her she was a stray that came running up to me on the street, and instantly I knew we were meant to be."

"You think she's going to believe you just *found* a homeless purebred?"

"Why not."

Some kids came racing down the pathway on the other side of the wall on their bikes, red, white, and blue streamers flying from their handlebars and laced into their wheels. The curly-headed one wasn't looking where he was going and almost crashed his bike riding over our flip-flops. He skidded away from the wall a second before there wouldn't be any other option but to go into it.

The bikers took off, communally excited about the near-death experience.

"Is he a bad guy?" Dom asked, meaning Trevor.

I returned my arm to the back of his chair. "Not totally."

About an hour later, Dom's phone chimed. I picked it up from the ground between us. Brit had sent out a group text to the family: Saucy Evening had gone into a coma.

"Hey, he's not dead." I was a tiny bit more hopeful.

"I think a coma's promising," Dom said. "Maybe his body went unconscious to protect itself, and he'll wake up when he's burned through all the vodka."

By the minute, the air was smelling less and less of charcoal, the hot dogs and hamburgers cooked and the grills all over the complex cooling. The sun had dropped notice-ably lower in the sky. "That's a hard way to go about sober-ing up."

"You'll see, it'll be like an alien abduction, and when he opens his eyes, he won't remember a thing."

Dom's phone chimed again not long afterward. The incom-ing text let us know that the doctor had just come in for the consult and to give Saucy's prognosis. While we were waiting for the next message, Cricket was waiting for the vet to get to the only part that mattered: if her dog was going to make it back to be her dog. My heart twitched like I was in the room with her, scared of every next word.

It turned out that watching the phone made time grueling, so I stared off into the sliding glass door of the opposite condo, trying to figure out which scenes were depicted in their hung artwork. I couldn't decide if the print by the built-in aquarium was a woman under a sheet or melting ice cream in a bowl. The strokes were abstract, and that red blotch to the left was either her upswept hair or a maraschino cherry. Ultimately, I went with the painting being a woman, since women make more likely decorations.

The phone chimed again. "Read it to me," I asked, and Dom went ahead.

Saucy was expected to wake from the coma and recover within the next eight to twelve hours.

Raising my arms in hallelujah, I said, "Okay, let's go back."

∞

The lone Fun Noodle lying by the barbecue and the set of clean, untouched scrubbing brushes were evidence of a party that had never gotten anywhere near its potential. When Dom and I returned to the pool, everyone was in the midst of packing up the unopened bags of buns, the incredible amount of sunscreen that could have covered the family six times over, and the wet towels. Melissa was shouting that someone needed to dive into the pool and get the rings.

I said I'd do it, took off the sundress that Dom had managed to get on me when we left the party, and walked to the edge of the pool. Under the high chair, the lifeguard, Laura, was zipping up her bag as my half uncle Tobias resumed his attempts to date her. He touched her foot and asked her where she got the scar on top, saying it was cute. She said it had come from the time a neighbor, aerating his lawn, reversed the tractor and sent the spike straight down through the bones.

"You grew up around tractors?" he marveled. "That's so different and cute."

I dove into the water to get the rings. They hadn't moved from where I'd last seen them, and I easily stacked them on my wrist like a pile of awkward bangles. This had always been my end-of-party job as a kid.

Somewhere in the complex someone was blaring his Fourth of July playlist, and one of Sousa's marches had advanced upon the pool. In light of recent events involving marriage and dogs, the music sounded less pompous than in years before. More like it was trying to overcompensate for a gaping hole at its core.

David Bowie's "Young Americans" kicked in next.

I pulled myself out of the pool and found Trevor helping Brianne dump out the bags of melted ice into the planters. After dropping the rings, I pointed at him like I was Uncle Sam (not *my* Uncle Sam, but the one that looks like a goat in a top hat) and said loudly enough for the group to hear, "Trevor, I want to apologize to you."

He shot me a glance that asked who I thought I was kidding. The answer was right there next to him because Brianne took hold of the bag they were sharing and said to him, "I don't get what the problem is, but go talk to each other."

"There's no problem," he said, coming over to join me and keeping the ironic expression in his eyes.

To me she said, "You should probably start considering him family."

"I should." As soon as he was by me, I threw an arm around his waist. "Come on, new family member, let's go have a heart-to-heart." Inside I was conflicted between how good it felt to pull him close and how angry I was. The hand clasped around his side was itching to do harm.

At the very least I'd hoped my arm would make him uncomfortable, but as soon as I'd placed it, he threw his arm around *my* shoulder.

"What a great idea," he said, using the same fake cheer that I'd just showed him.

The sudden chumminess appeared to mystify Brianne. She stared at us, half smiling, her head slightly tipped. She was right to sense that the picture before her didn't make any sense. Having spoken to each other less than a handful of times, why would Trevor and I be fighting to the extent that we'd have to make up?

But then, as if she were hearing a newborn baby cry for the first time, the trouble was washed over by relief. She told us, "Good. This looks promising."

"I'll be right back to help you," he said.

When we were a few yards off, having strolled (arms still wrapped around each other) toward the playground outside the gate, I said, "I don't want to apologize to you."

"I figured."

We slipped our arms off each other.

I made crazy circles next to my temple with my finger. "What's wrong with you? Proposing? You couldn't go with a promise ring or a smaller step?"

"I couldn't have just given her a dog?" he built onto my suggestion, his grin starting. It was an outward manifestation of the terrible grin that had taken up residence in my brain. We both had a reflex that caused us to keep humoring all the shit that had flown out of our hands.

"You're going to make a terrible husband if you become one now," I said.

The grin held and became nearly desperate. "She's my girlfriend, remember? I love her. Your family's thrilled, and my family's thrilled . . ."

I thought back to our conversation in the clubhouse and how he'd told me that things were better between him and his family and how he hadn't seemed happier about the shift.

"Did your relationship with your family get fixed because you're getting married?"

The grin broke. "What does it matter, why this? Why that? Do you think you're going to understand it no matter what I say?"

That question could have meant he was still painting me to be so young and naive that I couldn't understand the real reasons that people decide to get married. But I didn't think that was it. It seemed more like he was pleading with me that we not spend tons of energy going through all the angles of a situation that was already taking its own course anyway. I felt like he was saying there was no beautiful, elegant reason he could offer for his decision, so why torture ourselves looking for it?

For once in my life, though, I wanted to spend the energy, even if it wasn't going to get us anywhere, so I begged, "Just start talking."

"I'll be a better husband than boyfriend," he tried.

Phil came through the gate, his arms piled with towels and coolers. "Hey, guys," he mumbled, his teeth closed around his metal *P* keychain, keys jangling. The cars were parked in the lot in front. "We're moving it to Uncle Sam's." The party was over. It was about to turn into a visit.

He went to go load the stuff into his trunk, and I looked and saw that everyone else was seconds away from filing out too. If Trevor and I were going to come up with some kind of closure, it had better be quick.

"You're really doing this?" I asked.

"It's time to grow up," he answered flatly. I got the impression he'd taken that sentence straight out of one of his parents' or brothers' mouths, because his went slack and lost its natural meanness.

"Do we have everything?" called Sailor, walking through the gate. There was a whole bunch of thinking so in response.

My relatives were spinning around one last time, making sure no pair of sunglasses or child (Katie) got left behind. My dad spotted the diving rings, where I'd dropped them on the cement, and put them into their nylon bag.

"I think that's it," called back Brianne, and, as if Grandma Taylor were deaf too, at top volume Autumn said to her, "Let me carry that for you," because Taylor had shouldered a full bag of charcoal, and Micah let out something like a primal yell. They were coming.

What was left to do? I looked up at Trevor and said, "See you at the wedding." And hearing myself say those words, I was suddenly hit with the full, panicky power of adult institutions and their relative permanency.

PART V

THE WEDDING

CHAPTER 18

In the bridal suite, my main responsibility as a bridesmaid was to keep Brianne distracted while a hairdresser put in long blond extensions. I was doing this by giving her a lengthy quiz on social psychology I'd found online. After all, it was her day, and from what I understood, that meant she should find everything about it enjoyable. The room got sideways light from the French doors looking out on the garden. I tilted the paper to read.

"The dominant theory which explains 'bystander apathy' blames it on . . ." I paused as the hairdresser attached another section of fake hair to the loosely gathered cascade in the back. Brianne had been letting her hair grow out ever since the cut, but it had underachieved.

"Okay."

"Your first choice is 'alienation in modern life.'"

She turned her head to say, "But that could include a number of things." Forcing Brianne's head forward again, the hairdresser told her, "Sweetheart, if you don't keep still, you're going to end up with a beard."

"Okay, let me hear the rest," Brianne said, making eye contact with me through the mirror. "I'll do this by process of elimination."

Her maid of honor, Cara, an old and best friend since junior high, kneeled down in front to start rolling lacey thighhighs up her legs. Brianne was like a paraplegic, showing no signs of awareness that this was happening to her.

"Your second choice is 'modern city life,'" I continued.

Because the wedding had been planned so quickly, our bridesmaid dresses were black strapless columns from J. Crew. Thus, we weren't subject to the tradition of making a wedding party look simultaneously twenty years older yet two decades behind; then again, Brianne had never had bad taste. Her theme colors were black and white and the light-but-not-mint green of the roses the hairdresser was pinning into her hair.

"Okay, next one," Brianne said with a nod. The hairdresser steadied her head again.

In a gunmetal cocktail dress and looking more like weaponry than ever, Sailor came hustling in with the wedding planner. I recognized her as the same woman from Uncle Kurt's bar mitzvah. While Sailor was advising Brianne to put shimmer on her clavicle (Sweetie the Hamster still voted no), I waved over the planner and confided, "I fall asleep to your snow globe every night."

"I remember you," she said, and we shook hands. She smiled quizzically. "The ski lodge can't still be glowing, can it?"

"I change its battery."

"I never thought of it as anything but ephemeral. Do you really?"

"Of course I do."

She glanced to the side as if getting ready to slip me confidential information. "I made the centerpieces myself again for today."

"Can I have another choice?" asked Brianne, gently tugging at my dress.

"Excuse me," I said to the planner, who was already being pulled off by Sailor to go see to the flowers at the altar. They worried that the black dyed roses intertwined with the white and the green were both too morbid and too blue.

I returned to the quiz in my hands. "Your next choice is 'less feeling of responsibility when there are many witnesses.'"

"Okay, now *that's* a good one," said Brianne. It occurred to me that the opposite was true for a wedding: that you felt more obligated to go through with it because you'd invited so many people to watch.

"Fourth choice: 'hostility toward strangers.'"

"No, that's not it."

Cara put down satin heels in front of Brianne's feet and instructed her to slip into them. Another longtime friend, Erin, reclined on the green velvet couch next to Brianne's dress, which was reclining like a headless person next to her.

Cricket and Autumn, also bridesmaids, were outside

standing at the fountain to greet the weird people who can't stop themselves from showing up too early. This was Saucy Evening's job, too. He wasn't attending the wedding itself because Phil's clients weren't honoring his Psychiatric Service Animal certificate, but Brianne had tied a green bow around his neck and told Cricket to keep him with her before the ceremony as long as she could.

"This is your last choice," I warned Brianne. "Bystander apathy. 'People being afraid a criminal will find out they reported him and strike back.'"

"You can never be too careful," said the hairdresser as she took a can of aerosol to Brianne's hair and sprayed the shit out of it. You couldn't really tell if she was talking about getting the style to hold or about neglecting to call the police after you'd witnessed a neighbor get stabbed.

Brianne scrunched up her nose at the mist settling down upon her. "I feel so sticky." She wiped at her clavicle. "And my mom put that shimmer gel on me . . ."

I grabbed one of the hairdresser's hand towels and poured some water on it from one of the bottles that had been stocked for the bride's party. "Here."

"Oh. Thank you." She began to towel off her shoulders and neck like it was the height and not the end of summer. In a distracted way she murmured, "I think I'm going to take my chances and just hope that when I walk down the aisle, I naturally glow." Then suddenly she stopped what she was doing and fixed on me, intensely alert.

"That wasn't vodka you just gave me, was it?"

I looked at the bottle, doubting what was in it for a second. We started laughing.

Saucy had come out of his coma overnight, and while we had few ways of testing his personality because he was such a lethargic guy, mostly he seemed the same. Cricket had called me immediately when he woke up, and I went to stay with her at the animal hospital while he went through a day of tests. From the instant I got in the door, I began swearing to her that I didn't know the bottle of water wasn't water. "Give me some credit," she said. I did.

After he was released, I drove the two of them over to Petco. Unable to think of anything he'd like better, I let him pick out a new luxury bed. He did this by walking to the one nearest to where we'd put him down. Even if Cricket and I were fine, I still felt like I should make some amends with him.

Time plus tragedy equals comedy and, considering that the vodka incident was only an almost-tragedy, the passage of less than two months didn't seem unreasonably soon to be laughing about it.

Almost in tears, Brianne asked, "Can you imagine? I get too close to the votives, and—" She acted out her own explosion, which really amused her. "*Poof!*" With her joking around with me, it was like it used to be between us—lighthearted—before she'd gotten serious about pinning down what was wrong with me.

"She shouldn't be laughing," Erin said to me from the couch. "Her makeup."

I checked on Brianne's eyes and face. "Don't worry, nothing's budging."

"All set," said the hairdresser, patting one of the white roses in Brianne's hair to make sure it wasn't going anywhere either. "You look gorgeous."

Erin leaped to, checking a delicate silver watch on her delicate wrist. All other pieces had finally fallen into place for her to be able to carry out her assigned task. "Bree, let's get you into your dress."

"Wait, I want to finish that question," she protested, wearing her eyeglasses expression. It was slightly disconcerting against the romance and whimsy of her hair and makeup, like if you happened to catch a Disney princess working on her taxes. "Run through my choices quickly again. We have time—the wedding can't start without me."

"Brianne," cautioned Erin in a tone that said she was about to start using middle and last names.

I consulted the paper. "You have your pick of alienation in modern life, modern city life, relying on other witnesses, hostility toward strangers, or fear you're going to get cut if you narc."

"Then it has to be the one about people feeling less responsible when there are others around."

I nodded. "Right. The answer key says, 'This is the so-called "diffusion of responsibility" theory.'"

Brianne made a gun with her thumb and forefinger and said, "That's it. Diffusion of responsibility. All these fumes in the air slowed me down, but I got it."

I began to wonder if the concept also applied to weddings. Not that they're crimes, but if there was a person in attendance who could hardly bear to see the couple marry, did she have this feeling like someone else was going to take care of it when the justice of the peace asked for objections? Would she believe someone else was going to protest for her even after the room had remained completely silent and the justice had moved on? Did she believe someone in the crowd was going to say something, up until the couple was running down the steps by the fountain as guests threw petals at them? Would the person hang back at the open doors, still convinced there was time?

Erin's patience snapped. "That's it, I'm putting you in this. I'm not going to have a late start on my head."

We bridesmaids were also operating according to a kind of diffusion of responsibility, but Erin appeared to be feeling the weight of her part more heavily.

"Okay, calm down," Brianne said. "I was just having a moment of victory."

Erin carried the dress over and, as if she were an officer taking Brianne in for that handgun she'd made a minute earlier, told her, "Stand and put up your arms."

Brianne stood from the chair she'd been sitting in at the vanity. In a white satin bustier, silk shorts underwear, lace thigh-highs, and heels, she looked like one of the paper dolls I used to have as a little girl. They were always in lingerie you could never imagine wearing under a number of the outfit options you'd been given, like the patent raincoat and galoshes. But they usually came with a wedding dress too (or at least a formal gown that could double as one), and only in that lone showstopping outfit did their corsets seem like the right foundational choice.

The dress was thin and simple. The bottom had a gauzy effect, not to make Brianne sound like a post-op surgical patient; it was more angelic than that. She held up her arms and Erin pulled the dress down over her, never getting anywhere close to messing with her hair or her makeup—that's how flowy we're talking. When it was on, I took the two silk halter ribbons at the scoop of the bustline and tied them gently around her neck, careful not to entangle any of the hair.

"Now go look at yourself," said Erin, still bossy. Brianne walked over to the full-length mirror by the French doors.

For a minute she touched something, like a rose in her hair or the ribbon around her neck, then dropped her hand back to her side like she wasn't supposed to be doing that. Finally, she said, "I love it all."

"You look beautiful," I said.

"So beautiful," echoed Cara.

"What do you think Trevor's doing?" Brianne asked me dreamily, staring at the mirror like it could potentially become a closed-circuit television.

"Oh, he's touching the flowers in his hair too," I said, and she smiled.

Erin smoothed out the back of the dress and flattened a stubborn, folded edge of one of the ribbons. "Why don't you take some time for yourself before the wedding starts? Just to think about things before your mom and dad come to get you. Soak in the feelings you're having."

"Yeah, okay," Brianne said. "I could do that."

∞

It was about a half hour until the start of the ceremony when Erin, Cara, and I coaxed the hairdresser out with us and left Brianne in the suite by herself. Normally I would have already become chummy with the others. We would have exchanged cell numbers, to be used later when I took them up on the impulsive offers they'd made (I was aware that Cara's dad owned a cruise ship line). If a bridal suite isn't the perfect bonding environment, then there's no such thing.

But I hadn't asked them a single question about themselves or treated the similarities between us like they were big enough deals, so we were walking toward the front with none of the giddiness I could have generated if I'd put in some effort. Erin and Cara wanted to find Sailor and tell her that Brianne was ready to go. I pretended to be on that train until we reached the hallway to the groom's suite, and then I broke off and took a right.

The venue was stone and ivy on the outside and wood and glass on the inside, built to look like it was someone's sprawling, one-story villa. Its lived-in feel and year of construction could have simultaneously counted for Brianne's something old and something new. I followed the runner on the floor down to the end of the hall and opened the door on the left by the farthest window.

Dom was sitting in a club chair. "What if there were pants being put on?"

"Ingrid, hey," said Micah, fully dressed in a suit complete with a buttoned shirt, sitting on the window seat, smoking a cigar. They were the only two remaining in the room. Trevor had made them groomsmen because he needed to plug two holes in his party, the other three filled by his brothers and a mysterious friend he'd produced at the last minute. "Trevor's a loner," Brianne had explained when Dom asked, why him? "He doesn't open up to many people besides me."

I would never have said that I knew him better than she did, just that I was familiar with different sides. She knew what he was like as a boyfriend. I knew what he was like when that role failed him.

"Brianne's ready to go," I said.

"How's she doing?"

"She seems calm. Where is he?"

Dom pointed somewhere out the window behind Micah. You couldn't even make out separate trees or grass. From where I stood, it was just a world of green. "He went to go take a walk before the wedding."

I nodded and lingered in the doorway, enjoying the stillness and deep smokiness of the room.

"You aren't going to try to stop the wedding, are you?" asked Dom.

It was a good question.

CHAPTER 19

If I really *was* going to stop the wedding, why would I have waited until the wedding to do it? There were so many times in the weeks leading up to the event where I'd been doing bridesmaid things with Brianne, and I could have wrecked the wedding in a thousand quieter, more private ways. I could have destroyed her life when we went to the bookstore for bridal magazines. When I drove up and met her in downtown LA to browse the flower mart. When we flipped through old family albums, searching for funny baby pictures for the reception slide show. The point being, I had left the decision to the last and most brutal minute.

Though I tried not to let that point factor into my decision.

While Brianne and I had been going through the albums, we found a picture of us—all six of us cousins, I mean—sitting at the collapsible poker table. I was in the sea foam green full-body jumper with the hood cinched so tight that I was looking out a fleecy porthole.

Brianne smiled and brushed the image of the jumper with her finger. "I think one of my first memories is of you in that thing. Do you remember it at all, or were you too young?"

"No, I remember," I said.

She touched the image of her little face. "Look how angry I am."

"Therapy could have helped you with that."

"I'd go back there in a heartbeat now."

Maybe in the next hour I'd be wishing I could travel back in time too. It would probably mean I was one of the crueler people in the world if the terrible grin led me to believe I wasn't going to cause trouble during the wedding, when really, I was. *If* the grin was going to take me right up to the altar, where I could cause Brianne the most humiliation and pain, and then let me loose, then the fact that I was hanging out with Dom and Micah instead of coming clean to her was going to be disturbing in hindsight.

"Are you?" asked Dom, snapping me back to attention.

"Am I?" I said.

I needed somewhere to think where I could be alone. If I was going to stop the wedding, I needed to be available to the realization that *holy shit*, that was what I was going to do.

"What does that mean?" asked Dom.

"I'll catch you guys later."

I let go of the door, and it shut on Micah and Dom. Seeing as how time was already in short-enough supply, I opened the window right by the groom's suite, hiked up my tasteful J. Crew column to my thighs, and climbed out of the annex. The reception hall was across the lawn behind a gleaming row of French doors. That's where I wanted to be. By Brianne's request, the room had been kept a surprise; she'd demanded that no one be allowed to see it. Fortunately, one of the doors was cracked open.

I ran across the lawn and heard feet crunching on the freshly laid grass behind me.

The party planner was in close pursuit, calling, "Are you looking for me? Is something wrong with the bride?"

I waved at her while running backward. "No, I just thought I'd sneak a peek at your centerpieces before everyone messes them up!"

"No one's supposed to—," she started.

"I really love your work!"

"The bride said—"

"The snow globe . . . ," I reminded.

I watched as the artist in her won out over the party planner. Sighing affectionately, she waved me off and whisper-yelled, "Find me later and tell me what you think!"

I saluted. "Will do."

There had to be over a hundred frosted jars hanging from the beams and five times that number of tiny lights blinking inside. At the sight of them, a new memory emerged from the mountain cabin trip belonging to the sea foam jumper: the six of us being put to sleep together in the same room, a firefly night-light glowing in a corner. The younger kids standing up in our vacation cribs, in awe of the firefly because our parents had mutually agreed to raise us not to be fearful of the dark, after passing around a popular child care book that outlawed night-lights at home. Brianne throwing a fit from atop a twin bed and screaming, "Lights are for babies!"

The bugs in the hanging jars were electric too. I was walking in a wood-sy won-der-land.

I strolled around the room. In the middles of the tables, green rose heads began in piles, but then it was like God had run an invisible thread through the bottom of each heap and tugged because the roses—well, they rose toward the ceiling. They stopped in midair. I leaned forward to touch a centerpiece and felt the thinnest filaments holding it together. You couldn't even see the wires unless you were going to be a real jerk of a guest, climb onto your table, and poke your grubby hands around.

The planner had a clever eye, but I wasn't there to earmark a blinking jar to take home later. Regardless of whether the wedding made it to the party stage or not, the day was about to get ugly (if only in watching the wedding), and I didn't need a memento of that.

I'd come to the room for the Kid Table because it was the seating equivalent of a security blanket, the one place I could think of where relationships had always been mutually clear. Through the years the six of us had had our differences, and sometimes we'd pretended like one or the other of us wasn't actually at the table, but even if we weren't talking, we had to sit there together.

When I asked myself if I was in love with Trevor, I barely had a clue. I'd never been in love before. So who knew? I could say that it was more than wanting to lose my virginity to him, more than being curious about what it would feel like to do our laundry together. But still, it seemed crazy to pledge ourselves to forever, even if you argued that I'd loved him at first sight.

You just don't stop a wedding unless you're ready to take the person yourself, I think.

I scanned round table after round table, searching for the one unlike the others. Thinking it was a trick of the sunlight bouncing off the glowing jars or something about the depth of the room, at first glance they all appeared to be the same size. I changed my vantage point in case it was a perception issue, but they still all looked the same, so I began winding through the room. As I did this, I counted. Ten chairs, ten chairs, ten chairs, ten chairs, ten chairs, ten chairs, and on it went . . . ten chairs at every single table, every single table of identical size.

That's how I found out Brianne had done away with a Kid Table for her wedding.

On one hand, I found this to be a touching gesture of solidarity and respect. It was the end of an era. She was in love and getting married. She was bringing us all along with her. Even if Trevor had four young relatives she was throwing at a table with us, this would only make it a table that happened to sit some kids.

On the other hand, there was no Kid Table.

I could have gone to the place card table to find out whether I was supposed to be at "The Rambling Rose" or "The Owl Prowl," but it didn't really matter where my assigned seat was because every option was interchangeable. I eeny, meeny, miny, moed my selection and landed on a table near the dance floor. It was a random table, and I pulled out a random chair and lowered myself into it. A small piece of cellophane, probably wrapping from the flowers, sat on the table, glinting in the light. I picked it up and since there was no trash can around, tucked it into my shoe.

That's how you come of age: a table gone from the room. I leaned back in the chair and waited for my mind to tell me what kinds of things I was capable of doing.

"You must be Ingrid," a voice called from behind me.

I glanced over my shoulder toward the row of French doors. It was the same assistant the wedding planner had brought with her to the bar mitzvah, and she vibrated with the same agitation of being someone who knew the true darkness that lurked in the hearts of organized celebrations. "They need you outside the great hall—it's almost time."

I said, "I'm on my way." This was a bold-faced lie because I hadn't moved from the table, but the assistant must have trusted that I could supervise myself because she took off running across the lawn.

The sun through the trees on the walls, the fireflies in the jars, the displays on the DJ's equipment: everything was blinking but warning signs in my head.

So I pulled myself out of the seat and followed in the same path the assistant had taken—her sensible pumps had heels so thick they'd left divots in the grass. When the guests got wasted at the party later, they could use the pieces of turf like bread crumbs to find their way back to their cars.

I returned to the annex through a door this time, contemplating that there was always the wide-open potential of divorce. A guy in a suit and black tie turning out of the bridal-suite offshoot almost bumped into me.

"Sorry about that," he said.

"No harm done." I lingered on his face as if we were abruptly falling in love. He looked incredibly serious and he looked familiar, except I couldn't place how I knew him. This was unsettling considering I prided myself on remembering faces, names, hobbies, and insecurities.

"Don't I know you?" I asked as we began to travel down the hall toward the front together.

"We met at your uncle's bar mitzvah," he said, his eyes darting sideways. He wouldn't give me another good look at his face. "Dennis."

"Ingrid." I thought back on the bar mitzvah and the handful of people I'd been introduced to, most of them from Blimpie's corporate. I could remember each individual meeting. For example, there was Troy with the dimples, who enjoyed biking but feared being too chatty because he kept cutting himself off midsentence. But a guy from Blimpie's wouldn't have made

Brianne's guest list. I ran through the other introductions in my mind: the waiters, the bass player in the band, the valet; none of them fit.

For my next trick I asked something I never ask because coming after, "Don't I know you?" it's like spitting in your conversational partner's face. "I'm sorry, but why don't I remember us meeting?"

"It was brief," he said, quickening his pace, trying to pull ahead of me. His obvious discomfort made me feel even more that I had to solve how I knew him. Now he had my full attention, and I needed to shake him from it. I attempted to match his stride, but the J. Crew column only let my legs out so far.

I said, "Remind me."

"During cocktail hour. It's all right if you don't remember. I'm not insulted."

I reached out and grabbed his hand because he was moving too fast. When he looked back, confounded, his top lip pulled upward to reveal some impressively straight, white teeth. The visual clicked a memory into place. I knew exactly who he was.

"You're the mime!" I said, relieved to put that mystery to bed. "I couldn't place you because of the makeup."

"Yeah, I'm the mime." He was looking straight at me now, but he still didn't seem comfortable in his own skin. I thought maybe that was because he was out of his mime outfit and greasepaint. Or, I thought, maybe he still held it against me from when I rejected him almost a year ago. When I'd left him for Trevor.

I let go of Dennis's hand. "It's good to see you again." But why *was* he out of his mime outfit and greasepaint, I wondered. "Are you working the party?"

"No, I'm just here." We began walking again.

Considering that I'd only been slow to recognize him because he didn't have his face on, I thought it was fair to keep with the questioning. "But for who?"

He gave me another sideways look, not answering.

"Bride or groom?"

"The wedding," Dennis said, sounding like I'd really pissed him off.

The hallway ended, spilling us out into the lobby outside the ceremony hall, where the other bridesmaids and the grooms-men were huddled with the wedding planner and her assistant. When the planner spotted me, she frantically waved me over. "It's almost time." The door out to the courtyard clicked shut, and Dennis was gone.

"You're always going to think you're going too slowly down the aisle, but I promise you, it's all in your head," the planner was saying. "You're going to be tempted to speed up, but you've got to fight the impulse, or there isn't going to be enough anticipation for the bride, okay?"

I went and stood next to Cricket, who already looked dispirited without Saucy Evening nearby. Her posture had crumbled. With her shoulders curved in and her backbone popping out from the top of the strapless dress, it was like in the course of half a day, she'd gone from being healthy to having lost all that weight again.

"It'll be short," I whispered to her.

"How do you know?" she whispered back.

"Brianne said they didn't write their own vows."

Cricket frowned (the wedding planner, thinking it was intended for her, did a double take). "But then there's the party."

The assistant took over the directions, suggesting that we "try becoming metronomes . . ."

"All the food . . . ," Cricket whispered. If another big, formal party was going to set her off, I'd bring Saucy Evening into the reception hall—health codes, schmealth codes—and put him right down on her lap.

"—and then become a statue once you get up to the altar because even if you scratch your nose, it's a distraction. Do whatever you have to do to stay still. Meditate. Find your Zen."

"All the people staring at us like we're supposed to do something cute . . ."

"You can all do your part to make this the most beautiful wedding it can be."

Cricket gave a sigh sadder than any I'd ever heard and whispered, ". . . like we're their last hope. Like we're their past selves."

"There's no Kid Table," I told her to stop the downward spiral.

She looked into and through me, absorbing this news. "There isn't?"

"Ladies, ladies," the wedding planner was saying, "I need you to listen or this is going to be chaos."

"I'm engrossed. Go on," Cricket said absentmindedly.

"Go ahead," Autumn encouraged the planner with the firm but compassionate support of a speech pathologist who's attempting to get a stutterer to try again.

After getting her focus back by putting a few checks on her clipboard, the planner said, "The groom is going to enter first to meet the justice. He'll already be standing there. Then groomsman and bridesmaid pair one go, pair two go, and so on down the line." The first two to go were Erin and Trevor's friend. Next were Autumn and Micah. Cricket and Dom followed them.

I was walking down the aisle with Trevor's younger brother, Kyle. Brianne hadn't wanted to do a rehearsal because, one, she said that everybody involved was intelligent and could manage walking a direct path between two set points. And two, that she and Trevor were definitely intelligent enough to repeat word for word after the justice. So I'd only met Kyle that morning. His face shared no features with Trevor's. We didn't have much time to talk about hobbies, but he did express concern over whether there was going to be a vegetarian dish at the reception. That could be useful.

"Then together, the father and I will get the bride," said the planner. "Is everyone on board? Everyone know what they're supposed to do and where they're supposed to be?"

We nodded, then were told to mill around for a few more minutes. "Go *nowhere*," added the assistant. My parents popped their heads in through the side door to say hi before going to their seats. When they'd gotten ready for the wedding that morning, I'd heard them laughing hard together. They had their arms around each other, and there seemed to be a bouncing energy between them, like all of this was theirs too. Almost like the wedding was a time machine that had zipped them back to a point where they thought everything could only work out.

My mom eyeballed the wedding party. "Looks like everything's going smoothly."

"It should, unless someone objects," I said.

She leaned her head against my dad's shoulder. "Oh, no one does that anymore."

"Objects?"

"Gets the priest or justice to ask. Most couples have given up that tradition. We should have."

My dad smiled down at her. "Nothing could have stopped me," he said and kissed her hand. It felt like he was trying to reset something between them, and in turn my mom seemed to be more than willing to go along.

My brain tingled with the realization that there was no way I was going to stop the wedding, because I wouldn't be given the opportunity. I smiled, and my parents thought I was smiling at them. They smiled more.

The wedding was a runaway train. I was free.

Brooke came in to drop off Katie, who was acting as flower girl, except that whenever someone handed her the basket of flowers, she began angrily flinging petals onto the ground. She didn't toss them charmingly like she was supposed to, just chucked them in disgust. Still, we thought if we could just get her to the aisle with some left in her basket, she could at least hurl a few of them at the top. That would work.

(Brooke and my half uncle Tobias hadn't gotten back together like they usually did. In fact, he'd brought the lifeguard from the Fourth of July as his date.)

"We're ready to start!" The planner shooed out everyone who wasn't in the wedding, and then she opened the door to the courtyard, letting in the sunshine and the justice of the peace. Trevor walked through last. I turned my head. I wasn't going to play the game where he gave me a loaded stare and I gave him a loaded stare. This was it. He was a memory. I scratched an itch on my cheek with a fully extended middle finger.

"Groom, I need you," said the wedding planner, beckoning him with her clipboard.

The rest of us lined up boys on one side, girls on the other. Autumn held Katie in one arm and kept her free hand firmly pressed over the top of the basket.

CHAPTER 20

Through the door we heard the music start, but it wasn't the traditional wedding march. Phil and Sailor had poached the guitarist from Uncle Kurt's band, and he was playing an acoustic version of Sinéad O'Connor's "Nothing Compares 2 U," which I doubted was Brianne's first choice, but it was probably the most contemporary song he had in his repertoire on such short notice.

Dom leaned toward me from out of his line and asked, "So are you going to?"

I leaned in so our heads almost met. "No."

"But did you see the way he was looking at you when he came in?"

I couldn't even have told Dom if Trevor had grown a mustache or if he was getting married in an undershirt, that's how little I made myself see of him before the planner sent him out. "No."

"I don't know, Ingrid," he whispered, adjusting his tie like he was the one nervous about getting married. "If he looks at you like that when he's up there, maybe you *should* do something."

Erin and Cara were practicing the pacing of their steps like they were Laker Girls going over a halftime routine.

"There's no chance," I said.

He tugged on my hand like we used to do to our parents when we really needed them to listen. "I'm not sure this is right."

"What, do *you* have cold feet?" I tried to joke, but he wasn't having it.

"I'm going to watch him."

"Sure." I nodded. Dom would be lined up behind Trevor, so he'd be watching the back of his head.

The wedding planner cracked the door from the other side. "Bridesmaid one, groomsman one, we're ready for you! Pair two get on deck." Erin and Trevor's friend hurried through the door, arms linked like they were the oldest of friends. Autumn and Micah stepped up, next to go. "Will you take her?" Autumn asked me, meaning Katie, but she sounded as if she were marrying the two of us off.

"I will," I said, and we made the transfer. Once Autumn's hand was off the top of the basket, Katie tried to get hers in. "And watch the flowers," Autumn cautioned. I placed my hand over the petals and told Katie, "When we get to the party, I promise there will be millions of flowers for you to tear apart."

The planner's profile appeared again. "Number twos, off

you go! The first couple walked like they had somewhere else to be. Keep it slow, keep it steady."

I thought the planner was being kind of an asshole about this pacing stuff, when everybody just wanted to see the bride and realistically welcomed the fast-forwarding. But Autumn, being Autumn, said, "We'll do our best" in the sweetest way imaginable. Micah seemed to be taking the walk seriously too because he took a second to check his buttons, pocket square, and fly before escorting her through the door.

Dom and Cricket were next to go. As he looked back at me and said, "I don't know" with a haunted expression on his face, she gave me eyes that asked, "What's his problem?" I half regretted never telling Cricket about what had gone on between Trevor and me, but there had been so much going on her life. I never saw a good time.

I put my hands on Dom's shoulders and squeezed. "Be a metronome."

"That's the gayest thing I've ever heard," he said and smiled in spite of himself.

"Say it a little louder," Cricket told him. "Maybe someone out there will finally start your perfect storm."

"This wedding is gay!" he whisper-yelled.

The planner popped her head through the crack in the door and said, "Bridesmaid and groomsman three, it's your turn."

Dom made one last motion, swiveling his pointer and middle finger from his eyes to an imaginary groom for my benefit. "One look," he said, then he and Cricket joined the ceremony.

Kyle and I stepped up to the door, and I passed Katie off to the surprised assistant, who tried to keep her from the petals by asking if she didn't want Brianne's wedding to be pretty and magical, as if the kid cared. Kyle said, "I hope the flowers were grown organically," and I said, "Yeah, Kyle, me too."

When it was our turn, we entered the corridor leading into the great wedding hall, its double doors flung open. Everyone in the audience had twisted around in their seats to watch the procession from the top, so we were walking past rows and rows of vigilant faces, just like criminals must have done during the public trials of yore. Kyle was loosely trying to find the beat of the music as we traveled down the aisle, so he had a mellow bounce that I used in place of having to become a metronome myself.

As I passed all of my adult relatives, they did things like wave and wink and mouth (or sign) "hi" as if we were meeting by coincidence and needed to greet each other. They'd taken over both sides of the aisle because my mom said Trevor hadn't had a very long invite list. On the right, Tish was in a black, conservative sack, looking like her old self, if that was a good thing. On the left, Autumn's parents were openly holding hands on Bruce's thigh, and I could see the veins in his hand straining as he squeezed Michelle's. Farther down my parents gave me an indistinguishable look, as if they'd built up one powerful feeling together and split it between them. They were proud of me, but they weren't aware of what I'd been sitting on all that afternoon.

Sailor was already crying in the front row, and I blew her a small kiss before taking my place at the altar.

I kept my eyes forward toward the doors.

I watched the maid of honor and best man walk down at a respectable speed, and next came Katie, who looked as if she'd been pushed into the room because she entered it running, as if to keep her balance. Once she'd found it, she immediately stopped. The word "cute" fluttered around in whispers. She jammed a fist into the basket and even though she had tiny hands, it appeared that she got the whole supply of petals in one grasp. She opened her fist and dumped them on the floor like they were trash.

At last the guitarist switched to playing the chorus of the song, maybe to entice Katie down the aisle with its greater emotional momentum. Indifferent, she dumped the basket and made for her mom's row, climbing over guests' legs to get to her.

The planner's assistant ran into the aisle hunched over to get the basket out of the way.

The guitarist faded out of the song, strumming more and more lightly on his strings, until suddenly he'd transitioned into the opening notes of "She's Got a Way."

Brianne and Phil stepped through the doorway framed with a swag of white roses. The chairs creaked as everyone turned even more sharply to get their first look at her. Although I'd already seen her in her dress, I'd been looking at her from close-up. Looking at her from the end of the aisle was something else altogether. She was a bride. It was like when you became one, you not only put on the outfit—the dress, the something old, the something borrowed, the something blue, all of that—but you put on a new self too.

When Brianne was first getting into psychology she told me about a true story she'd read for class about a man who mistook his wife for a hat because he had a disorder that kept him from recognizing faces; he kept mixing up objects and people. Seeing Brianne at the other end of the aisle was like that. I knew she was the bride because she was in the right things, but I don't know that I would have recognized that was her if she didn't have them on.

Phil was also crying, like Sailor, but Brianne seemed peaceful as she walked toward the altar. For half the way, she glanced at both sides, acknowledging the guests. For the final half she looked straight on. Before letting her go, Phil kissed her on the side of her head, loosening one of the roses in her hair in the process and sending it down to the carpet.

As Brianne took the last few steps up to the altar, I turned and focused on the justice of the peace, waiting for him to speak.

"Friends and family, we are gathered here today to share with Brianne and Trevor a pivotal day in their lives. These two have come together and decided to make their love concrete before us . . . and that makes us lucky." I didn't know if I'd put it *that* way, but I wanted to be standing up there believing in what he was saying. "But before I get too poetic here, the bride and groom have requested that I keep this ceremony short and sweet." I sent thanks out to them for that. The wedding was going to be a runaway train between two commuter stops.

I thought that meant we'd be jumping to a quick prayer, although I didn't know what Brianne believed in these days. Last I'd heard her talking on the subject, she said that our brains were programmed to need a god, and I didn't ever find out if that meant she thought he'd programmed us himself or if he only existed in there and nowhere else. The lack of a church and a priest had me leaning toward the latter.

"Which I thought was apt—," the justice of the peace was continuing, his voice picking up volume, and then I knew that he wasn't going to be able to keep himself from doing some poetry. I zoned in and out during the next few minutes. I zoned in on him reciting the part of a Matthew Arnold poem on time that referenced "two young, fair lovers," and then as soon as I heard that reference, I zoned back out. I decided the justice of the peace looked a lot like a young, fairer Abe Lincoln. He didn't have the moles, though.

"And so it makes perfect sense that we should keep the ceremony short and sweet because, as the poem says, the lovers cry, 'Time, stand still here!' " is what I came back in on again, but the justice seemed to be wrapping things up, his voice dipping back down. "That's what a wedding should be: a perfect moment that doesn't overstay its welcome or spill over into any other. It should be perfectly its own."

I guessed that Brianne and Trevor were probably looking at each other in that moment, but I didn't torture myself by looking at them.

The justice clapped his hands together softly. "Okay, then, so here we go. Brianne and Trevor, have you come here freely and without reservations to give yourselves to each other in marriage?"

They both said, "Yes."

First the justice asked Brianne if she would love and honor and cherish and protect and forsake, in sickness and in health, for richer or for poorer (although with Phil and Sailor's money as a cushion, they were never going to have to test that last one out), and Brianne said, "I do."

The same was asked of Trevor. When he said, "I do," the sound of his voice troubled me more than I thought it would.

I started to feel alarmingly uneasy about myself, and I began practically willing the rings to lift up out of their hiding places and thrust themselves onto Brianne's and Trevor's fingers, so the marriage could be sealed. The justice had paused. "The rings," I wanted to say to him, since I was gripped with the fear that he'd forgotten what came next. "With these rings, they thee wed."

But instead of asking them to produce the rings, the justice lifted his gaze over their heads and out toward the guests. There was a playful smile in his eyes.

"Before we get to the rings," he said, "if there is anybody who objects to this marriage between Brianne and Trevor, speak now or forever hold your peace."

I was so stunned to hear this offer made that I almost spoke immediately.

Not to say that I objected, but to say that I'd been told no one made that offer anymore at weddings. The people in attendance weren't supposed to be given the chance to speak. This was the couple's show.

I couldn't understand why the justice would have thrown such an ugly offer into the ceremony if it was something he didn't have to do, but in the next second I had an insight. I looked at Brianne. When I did, I knew I was right and that this was her idea of a fun time.

She was looking over her shoulder at her guests, wanting to see their reactions. Not because she imagined that anyone would actually object, but because she was curious to see how the awkward question fell. I knew her. She was conducting a psychological field study in the midst of her own wedding.

In watching Brianne, I accidentally saw Trevor. He was behind her and out of my focus, so his face was a blur. When Brianne first turned to look at the guests, one dark dot hovered below the greater darkness of his hair. But as the justice took in a breath to proceed with the rings, there were suddenly two.

I'd thought that Dom wouldn't be able to see what Trevor was doing with his face because Dom would be behind Trevor's head, but I didn't count on the fact that the groomsmen (and us bridesmaids) had lined up at an angle. Dom, having been third to enter, was the third farthest away from Trevor on a diagonal. That meant if Trevor were to turn his head to the left, Dom would have a decent view of his profile.

This all happened in a matter of seconds, but here was the order:

The justice breathed in.

One dark spot went to two dark spots above Brianne's head.

I realized that Trevor had turned his head to look at me.

I looked at Dom, who was also realizing the same thing.

The justice said, "Now—"

Dom looked at me.

Then he shouted out, "She can't marry him!"

The room went silent before anyone gasped, and you could see that people really do put their hands up over their mouths when they're in shock. Seeing the guests from the vantage point of the altar, it was like they were choreographed. Like they were doing a Bob Fosse chair number.

Brianne and Trevor had whipped around to look at Dom. The justice, flustered because I guessed he'd practiced his part and done these things so many times that he didn't expect anyone to fall out of line, asked meekly, "What's your objection then?"

Dom's eyes darted to me and then back. "She can't marry him because I'm in love with her!"

There were gasps again. I wasn't expecting him to give that reason, and I almost laughed over the thumping of my heart. Dom's pronouncement wasn't as incestuous as it seemed because Brianne's grandpa Baron, now dead, was the half brother of Dom's great-grandma Cecily, mom of Cookie, so they were cousins far removed, but I'm sure that didn't make it sound any less bizarre to half the guests' ears.

"No, you're not!" someone shouted from the gallery, and

we all turned around to see his dad, Alec, standing up from his seat. "You can't be in love with her."

"Why can't I?" yelled Dom defiantly.

Alec threw up his hands. "You're gay!"

CHAPTER 21

"What?" Dom asked, pointing to his right ear like he had a hearing aid and needed that last statement repeated louder with it in mind.

I'd never seen Alec exasperated. "Besides her being your cousin that you've grown up with since you were in diapers, you're gay." To his side, Cookie had begun signing something that looked like the letter g tapped against her chin, and you had to assume that she too was informing Dom that he was gay, as if his hearing problem were a real thing.

I scanned the faces of our adult relatives and they were all, *all of them*, nodding their heads, their expressions mystified. Who knows how long they had known or how many conversations they'd had about him, never letting on that they knew for sure? The millions of things he had declared gay over the past seven or so years, and not one knowing glance bounced around from person to person? It was almost cruel.

Of course there were many guests who weren't family, and they were easy to distinguish because they looked around at each other, wondering if Dom was playing a joke. They included Trevor's mom and dad, who were sitting in the second row. They'd started uncommitted smiles, like they wanted to be halfway there when that turned out to be the case.

"What are you doing?" Trevor asked Dom.

I looked at Trevor.

He had bags under his eyes, like he'd spent the night up at a bachelor party that I knew he didn't have; his mysterious friend hadn't organized one. His suit was sharp and pressed, his tie black. His hair was clean and uncombed. He also looked like he was daring Dom to ask the same thing of him, but Dom, after considering him for a moment, ignored the challenge and faced his parents again.

"Just like that?" Dom asked them.

His mom misunderstood. "No, the way it works is that you were gay since you were born."

"No." Dom switched his pointing to his dad. "You tell me"—the pointing went back to his chest, incredulous—"that I'm gay? Just like that?"

"Maybe we could finish the ceremony first, since the objection doesn't appear to be real?" suggested the justice, his eyes wide.

"Please," Trevor's mom said. "This is inappropriate."

Alec sat back down. "We've been waiting for you to want to tell us, but you just pushed our hand."

The justice was recalling his lines about the rings when Brianne must have realized she couldn't let the objection go.

"What is this about, Dom? In the middle of my wedding?" She'd asked him in her normal, soft voice, ignoring the curiosity of her guests. You could see her old self pushing through the bride because on one hand, she looked about to strangle him, and on the other, she looked like she wanted to get him to the nearest couch and herself to the nearest notepad. Trevor had the decency not to look perplexed. He put an arm around her protectively, readying her.

He glanced over at me and gave a wistful smile with his chin atop her head.

I thought he was saying we were the like ones. That we were the two who were about to be outed as the breakers of her heart, and we were going to have to be there for her together. It occurred to me then that maybe Trevor had proposed out of love and protection because he would do anything not to hurt her, and for all the times I'd thought he was treating me like a kid, it was her he'd really been coddling. Then I felt even more strongly that they couldn't get married.

He was right. We probably were alike. After all, he'd thought that in time his relationship would shift with Brianne past the infatuation between him and me. Looking ahead had once seemed like the best idea to me too. Where he was wrong was that he thought once Brianne pressed Dom to tell her what was behind his objection, Dom would.

But I knew that Dom never would have dragged me into it. Now he was nervous facing Brianne. The first time he'd lied without thinking, and he couldn't do that twice. So instead he picked a fight with our relatives.

"No one's surprised?" he asked. "Not one person in the whole family thinks I'm straight?"

"Not for a few years," my mom said gently. I looked out at *her*, surprised because she'd done sneaky things in the past like ask me if I knew if there was a girl he wanted to take to junior prom.

"Brianne, please, do something," asked Trevor's mom. "It's your wedding."

"Hold on, Jules," Brianne said nicely.

Stepping out of line as if in a trance, Dom drifted to the edge of the altar, stopped there, and fixed his stare on the swag of roses across the entrance. "It wasn't that I didn't think some of you wouldn't have had suspicions. I was dropping hints all the time, you know?"

No one said, "Yeah, we know," but that was the tone of the silence that followed.

"None of you ever said anything to me . . ."—his voice trembled—". . . so I thought if somewhere in the back of your mind you knew, you didn't want to."

Even Brianne had been unaware that our parents and relatives had come to basic terms with Dom's sexuality without our involvement, and she faced out toward them too. "Did you guys have a meeting about him or something?" She blinked slowly in disbelief. "Not all of you could have been comfortable with his homosexuality." If I had to guess, she was especially thinking of Half Uncle Tobias, who also had a habit of saying things were gay, except his usage was a lot less innocent.

Dom's mom stood. "Everybody's working on acceptance at their own speed."

"What does that mean?" Dom asked.

She shrugged, her massive breasts helplessly going upward with her shoulders. "I had to work past some difficulty at the beginning because I've always secretly wanted a daughter, and I'd built up this fantasy of you getting married to a girl who I became close with, and she and I would meet for coffee regularly, and we'd—" She stopped herself before going into detail about what kind of treatments they'd get at the spa. "Never mind about the girl. I'm past that now."

"You accept him for who he is anyway—," Brianne prompted.

"I think you all probably have had to accept that I'm gay to varying degrees by now," Dom interrupted. I was looking mostly at his back, and when it heaved, I could tell he'd released a sigh that was years in the making. It reminded me of the one Cricket gave earlier that day, when she said that the adults looked at us like we were their last hopes.

"You're all at different places with this. Obviously, some of you must have been better with the news than others. But no one's in a fresh state of shock anymore?" His mom's dream had been of a girl, but there went his dream of spectacularly bursting through the other side of their gay issues.

"No," answered Half Uncle Tobias. "I've been trying to call less things gay in support of you, if you've felt it."

"Just like that," Dom repeated to himself. For a second he looked about to take a seat on the top step of the stage, but then he turned and walked back to his place in the grooms-men's line.

"Way to go," Cricket told our relatives.

The justice may have resembled Abe Lincoln a little bit, but he didn't share his power to pull together a crowd. When he said, "If everyone's ready to move forward, then let's move forward," suddenly Uncle Kurt stood from his seat at the outer edge. "Look, I know how you feel, Dom," he said.

Dom was already a skeptic from all the *Twilight Zone* lessons he'd internalized, but this was a claim that pushed him above and beyond. "You do?"

"I think I do. This news is supposed to be big, but no one's treating it like it is. Take me, for example. When I decided to get my life back in order—" I saw Aunt Kathy's face tighten at his side, but she didn't stop him from talking. "—I wanted that to be acknowledged, but it was like this universal shrug back. *We'll see how it goes over time.*"

"I hope you're not saying that my being gay is the same as you breaking your marriage."

"Not like that," Uncle Kurt said, leaning backward on his heels. "I'm thinking more that I felt like I was going through a rite of passage that I didn't want to seem so invisible. Maybe I was doing it too late for other people to care."

Tish stood up. I wondered if all the AA meetings had made standing and speaking into a reflex that happened whenever there was a group of people standing and speaking around her. "Well, it's also that this family tends to think that things are easier to do from the outside than they are, so they write off your personal achievement as something obvious."

Uncle Kurt faced her and said, "That's so true. That's better than I put it."

"We can talk about this later?" proposed the justice, using some weird version of the royal "we" that didn't actually include him.

"Later," Uncle Kurt agreed. But as he took his seat, he called out, "So you know what you do then?" and punched into the air.

Dom pointed to himself, although there wasn't anyone else Uncle Kurt would have been talking to. "What?"

"You throw yourself a party."

"A party," Dom repeated, mulling it.

"A party," Uncle Kurt repeated back, as if that were the secret password that gets you through the door to adulthood.

The justice saw his opening and hurried to shut it. "Yes, then. You can make arrangements for the party after we finish here." Maybe having picked up on my family's affection for any party, he smartly used the one waiting in the other room as his dangling carrot. "As a matter of fact, let's wrap up this ceremony so we can all get to the party for the couple. There's a beautiful party waiting for all of us if we can just get these two married."

"Please, let's move on," said Jules, whose name I now knew. The room was still.

The justice nodded and resituated himself. Addressing

Brianne and Trevor, he asked, "Are you both ready to continue?"

"Yes," Trevor said.

Brianne turned to Dom. "I'm going to go back to my wedding," she said, "but you're going to have to explain why you tried to stop it later."

"Later," Dom said, giving her an apologetic smile. Then he looked to me. His coming out had derailed the objection he'd really wanted to make, and as soon as Brianne had faced toward the justice, his mouth pulled back at the corners in a grimace, because he didn't know what else he could do.

I smiled at him to let him know that he had enough of his own shit to handle, and I was good on my own.

"We're ready," said Brianne.

"Here we go then. I think we can safely skip past asking for objections . . . ," the justice began.

It was one thing to have your family be suspicious of you because you didn't cry enough. It was another for them to think you were a ruthless person because you stopped your cousin's wedding by admitting to the questionable secrets you'd kept.

I tried to imagine what it would be like in the future if I told the justice, "But there is another objection," and went on to confess the events of the past year that would grind the ceremony to a screeching halt. (I imagined Sailor screeching first at Trevor and then at me.) It wouldn't be my relatives just giving me watchful eyes and treating me with strange politeness at—what was next? Dom's coming-out party? Tish's sixty-days chip bash?

Whatever the occasion, it would be cousins and aunts and uncles (and past and present girlfriends of half uncles) and great-aunts and lone living grandma and parents having a real reason to doubt that I could ever be up to any good.

Of course, they wouldn't turn against me *forever*. I'm certain that things would level out with enough time. Brianne's happiness would return, but in the meantime, I'd be stuck. Compliments would only read as bribery, so I couldn't toss them around. Any attempts at humor would seem insensitive to what I'd done.

If I simply made the rounds at the parties, smiling but quiet, for a long while after the wedding they'd wonder what damage I had up my sleeve. They'd have learned that I was willing to play those cards on even the most sacred occasions. They wouldn't think they could count on whatever kind of conscience I had. I mean, if they still believed I had one.

The theory behind love between family members is that it's unconditional, and I'm not saying that theirs would go away. But it's so hard to get anything accomplished in a roomful of people who don't find your antics at least somewhat charming. I'd be a carnival worker trying to get their money after they'd already decided I was a complete and total rip-off.

That was the rest of them. Then there would be Brianne, who might never forgive me. Not for stopping her wedding— she might be thankful for that someday—but for sitting down in the hotel restaurant with her boyfriend when I knew, even then, that it wasn't going to be the last I saw of him alone.

Our relationship would shift just like any other, except maybe it would never be the same.

I thought I could see Brianne's left hand releasing from around her bouquet of roses in preparation to receive her ring. The justice had just shuttled past asking for objections, and he was an instant away from reciting the next part.

I let the terrible grin have its moment. They were all going to be scandalized anyway.

"I object too!" I shouted before he could get out another word.

CHAPTER 22

I thought I must be delusional when I heard a male voice echoing mine. Like I'd reached the heights of narcissism and was
hearing God speak my words from the mountain.

What tipped me off that I wasn't the only person who
heard the voice was that when I looked out across the guests,
only a few of them looked at me. Most were looking into the far
left corner of the room, where the mime stood with his arm
raised like a schoolkid.

"But I object!" he'd yelled.

Confused, I swept my gaze back to Brianne and Trevor.
He didn't appear very confused, staring at me. In fact, his look
struck me as an accepting one, as if he understood why it had
to come to this.

"Brianne, you can't marry him!" yelled the mime, whom
I knew was named Dennis, but still I said to myself, mystified,

"Hey, that's the mime." Trevor looked out at him, more confused by his intrusion. Brianne, however, whom I expected to be squinting at Dennis, trying to place why he looked so familiar like I'd done in the hall, didn't appear confused at all.

"This isn't right for you!" he kept on while walking up the left wall with his arm still raised, although now it seemed less a request to let him speak and more a demand for her to stop what she was doing.

"You've got to be kidding me," said the justice.

Brianne cupped a hand on the back of her neck, right on the bow that I'd tied there. I'd figured out that she'd recognized him immediately because she wasn't asking who he was. But what especially surprised me was that she seemed to know why he was coming toward her, because she wasn't asking, "Why is the mime from my cousin's bar mitzvah objecting to my getting married?"

It was Trevor who asked, "How do I know you?"

Dennis's pissed-off look, which Trevor had already seen before, must have clicked his identity into place.

"You're the balloon twister, aren't you?"

"That's my balloon twister!" confirmed Uncle Kurt, now recognizing Dennis as well.

"A Chesapeake Bay retriever," Trevor remembered out loud.

When I voiced my objection, my heart had jumped into my throat. As Dennis took the heat for interrupting the wedding, it started to mosey back down. I wasn't sure who'd heard me beyond the wedding party, but no matter who did, I could now divide their outrage by 50 percent.

"That's Dennis," Brianne said to Uncle Kurt and Trevor. Then to him, she said forlornly, "Dennis . . ."

He'd almost made his way to the stairs at the side of the altar, but he stopped when she spoke his name.

"What's going on, Brianne?" asked Sailor, staring at the guy who was hanging around just a few feet in front of her.

The great hall we were in had homey touches like double-hung windows and a river-rock chimney, and with Dennis so close to the altar, it took on the feel of one of those interactive dinner party shows, where a guest at your table turns out to be part of the action. Everyone was riveted watching him. They were on the edges of their seats.

Dennis said, "You shouldn't be doing this."

"What is it I should do here?" the justice asked.

"What do you know that I don't?" whispered Cricket, giving me eyes.

"*You* shouldn't be doing this," Brianne told Dennis. She was clearly upset, and not the photogenic kind of upset you're supposed to be as a bride. Her eyebrows crumbled in like they used to do before she'd cry as a little girl (come to think of it, I hadn't seen her crying for years, not out of sadness), and she looked more and more like a person, less and less like her hairdo made any kind of sense.

She didn't cry, though. She'd always been tough, and that's why, despite everything that was going on, she hadn't forgotten my involvement.

Taking a step back so she could get a good look at me, she asked, "But why did *you* say something?"

As bad as I felt about having been in the way of her

relationship for almost a year, I couldn't pass over her reaction to Dennis. If he'd been a stranger, she wouldn't have given him the time of day. If he'd been her obsessed stalker, she would have had Phil throwing him out of there already.

I thought back to the bar mitzvah and how I'd seen her huddled with Dennis at the bar. At the time I'd noticed that the conversation seemed very intense, but I'd been too wrapped up in my own circumstance with Trevor to really pay attention.

Then, when I'd brought up seeing her talking to the mime at the party, she'd abruptly let up on bugging me about my college plans. I remembered thinking that she'd looked like someone caught in a lie. And she even went so far as to defend mimes. They were different from clowns, she'd argued with more passion than that argument probably needed.

I was positive that something romantic had gone on between Brianne and Dennis. For sure I wasn't in a position to judge her for it—really, I felt closer to her knowing that we'd been keeping secrets alongside each other. But I also wasn't crazy enough to let the secret slide when it could refocus everyone's energies onto her role in all this.

"I don't see the rush. I think it's early in your relationship," I said. "But is that why Dennis objects too?"

"Their relationship has nothing to do with this!" Dennis said, which is basically what I hoped would happen.

On the afternoon of the Labor Day barbecue, when Brianne said I didn't love Long John because I didn't mourn him openly, I could only defend myself by saying, "If you love something, you set it free." I wasn't sure anymore whether I believed that in all cases, but I thought that Dennis probably loved Brianne. He just couldn't do that last part. So he was getting ready to defend the truth, and even if that wasn't going to set him free, the fact was, it couldn't hurt my chances.

Brianne finally looked confused by his presence. It seemed like they had made a deal, and she couldn't believe he was going back on it. She shook her head slowly. "You know we already talked about this, and you know we came to a decision."

"What decision is that?" Trevor asked.

The hand that had been around her neck dropped down and swung against her dress, rippling the cloth. "I wanted you more," she said.

"More."

Maybe Dennis was frustrated from all the time he spent as a mime, not being able to talk, because the words just poured out of him, and even though Trevor's parents and Sailor and Phil were getting upset, telling him that everybody had gotten the picture, he wouldn't stop.

"We've been seeing each other for a year. She came up to me and asked if I could tell what people were like right away, judging from what they asked me to make them. I talked to her voluntarily, and I'm not supposed to. I'm a fucking mime." He glared at Trevor. "Or, as you said, a balloon twister. We had the best conversation. I'll remember it forever. It was about people and the human mind and dreams and loneliness and purpose in life. We hid in the elevator and she kissed me. Do you hear that? I didn't kiss her first. *She kissed me.* Okay, I knew she had a boyfriend because I'd seen her kissing you too, but when she said that she had to go back to the party, I said, let's just see how this goes. Let's be something to each other. We can't just never talk to each other again."

Although Dennis wasn't finished, the wedding party started to take a beating. The bridesmaids' and groomsmen's lines busted apart. The guys had unclasped their hands from their backs, and the girls, who'd been clasping smaller bouquets in front of them, let the flowers hang from one hand.

Brianne had taken a step forward when Dennis began speaking, as if to take the pummeling by herself.

The way the two lines staggered, the five of us from the Kid Table had pulled closer to Brianne. If you imagined a line starting with her and whipping around us, we made up an inner circle on the stage. A squashed one, but still, you'd be able to see it.

"She was the one to say that she loved me first too. Do you know what she said exactly? She said, 'I love you, and I also love him.' She loves two people. She admitted to it. So I asked her, 'How can you marry one guy when you love two?' Get ready for what she said, brother. She said, 'You make the choice between them.'"

Dennis was unexpectedly tan and passionate too. He stood rooted to the ground, and the legs of his suit pants twitched from the flexing of the muscles underneath. Shards of light came in the upper windows through the trees, and they quivered on his slacks. His arms tensed inside the sleeves of his coat. I got the impression that were I to drive him to a bar when he was finished, he would punch a hole right through someone's head.

While listening to Dennis, Trevor began taking off his coat. The justice tried to get him to keep it on because he thought it meant that Trevor was getting ready to go punch a hole through *Dennis's* head. But Trevor turned to him and said, "The wedding's over. I don't want to wear a coat." He handed it to the justice to hold.

"But that's no good, is it?" Dennis asked Brianne, not any of us. "You don't go and marry him because you need to quantify your degrees of love. We're a separate thing, so keep us separate! Please just keep us separate. You might love me less, but you love me."

"Who said I didn't?" Brianne asked as if he were being ridiculous. "Who said that people aren't capable of loving differently but at the same time?"

Whereas Dennis was pretty much shaking with emotion, I could nearly see Trevor's spiraling down into him. As the hits kept coming, he swallowed them fully, making them into a private torture.

At this point Trevor wandered over toward the rear of the altar, and it looked as if he were going to step over the wall of rose arrangements and head out the back door. Instead he stared at the flowers for a second. Then he picked a black one. Breaking off the stem, he put it behind his ear. I was almost convinced I loved him when he turned back around.

"Please don't act like you're normal!" Dennis begged Brianne. "Does everyone here understand who you are?

Secret phone conversations, secret letters, secret meetings, secret sex—"

A couple minutes before, Sailor had told Dennis that everyone had gotten the picture when he was talking in generalities, but when he brought up the secret sex, she finally looked at it. "That's all," she said, walking up the aisle. "I'm pulling the plug."

Dennis looked up at Brianne, his eyes shining. "Brianne, are you getting married?"

"How could I?"

I think he took that to mean that she couldn't go through with the wedding based on the argument he'd made, but it was more likely she was saying that the wedding had been stopped for her.

"Okay then," Dennis said, backing from the altar before Phil could get his hands on his shoulders. "That's all."

"So we're finished here?" asked the justice.

Brianne and Trevor stared at each other with apparent hurt and disappointment. He removed the rose from behind his ear and tucked it behind hers, which didn't look anywhere as sweet as it sounds. It was like damage he was passing forth between them, because instead of doing what he could have done, which was blame her for the bad idea of agreeing to marriage, he said to her, "I haven't been a saint either, but I was trying to turn into one by marrying you."

"You've been seeing someone else too?" she asked, sounding more wounded than she had a right to be.

Trevor couldn't really achieve anything by exposing me,

other than giving Brianne an even bigger shock than the one he got, but still my heart caught, because you never know what a betrayed person will do.

"I've done some flirting. It's not important."

He had his back to me, but I mentally nodded at him and said to him as powerfully as I could think it, "See you later." I didn't assume anymore that things had to work out for us somewhere down the line. I didn't believe, not even a little, that we'd meet again.

But I did have a fleeting thought about how nice that could be.

"I can't believe you, Brianne," Sailor scolded, walking onto the stage. "Agreeing to a wedding when you have another boyfriend."

Phil joined in the dressing-down. "Sweetheart, really, this is not your finest moment."

"I didn't think it would go this way."

The guests were getting together their purses and coats, leaving the wedding programs on the floor. The friends and acquaintances milled around in the rows, talking in clumps and stealing nervous glances at the altar, because they couldn't figure out if they were just supposed to grab back their gifts and take off. Our relatives were standing too, but they faced Brianne and channeled all the earlier exasperation they'd summoned for Dom.

Aunt Kathy said, "Darling Brianne, for someone getting a degree in psychology, you did a bang-up job of misreading your second boyfriend."

"Well, that was romantic," said Tish.

Along with Trevor's dad, Jules edged toward the altar, refusing eye contact with anyone in our family, and called out to Trevor, "Let's go. You don't need her." To her husband she said, "Thank God we weren't paying for any of this."

Trevor didn't move. "You go ahead. She and I have some things to talk about."

"We're going to talk about some things, too, daughter of mine," said Sailor. "You know I love you, but you have to take responsibility for the havoc you wreaked. Not just the wedding, but on him." She tipped her buzz in the direction of Dennis. We watched as he slipped out the side exit.

Looking across the hall, I finally noticed that the wedding planner and her assistant had been playing dead like opossums at the other end. They leaned against the closed double doors, flat and motionless, as if hoping everyone would just leave them there until dark, when they could steal away. All that work and nothing to show for it, just like when you toilet-paper someone's house, and their parents have it all cleaned up by the time you drive by in the morning.

Dom looked so relieved that Brianne wasn't going to marry a guy who'd cheated on her he was practically making the sign of the cross. Micah blew out a slow, sinking whistle. "I haven't been to many weddings, but hands down, this was the most intense of them yet," he said.

"You knew she'd been seeing that guy," Cricket said to me, tugging on the zipper of my J. Crew column. "I know you did."

"I swear on my life, I didn't."

The justice hadn't budged since he last spoke, as if trauma-
tized by what had unfolded before him, but he suddenly came
to, clapping his hands twice. "So we're finished here, yes? Do I
get in my car and drive home?"

Trevor took back his coat, still hanging in the crook of the
justice's arm. He put it on. "I'm going for a walk." Looking at
Brianne, he said, "I'll be back for you."

The justice clapped again, needing finality. "That's a yes,
then."

Trevor walked past me, touching his shoulder to mine on his
way down the steps. It sounds crazy to say that people can have
a conversation through a moment of touched shoulders, but we
did. There was even a somber joke in it about our bad timing.
Then I heard the side door open and click shut; I never turned.

"Yes," said Brianne. Autumn had come over to stand by
her, since no one else was feeling overly sympathetic. Erin and
Cara got a clue and also went over to her, shell-shocked but
still alert enough to do things like fix the tendril of hair that
had fallen onto her forehead and straighten the neckline of her
dress that had tilted when Brianne messed with the bow.

"I hope you take care," the justice said and left. Trevor's
parents followed him out, and their other two sons followed.

The rest of our relatives gathered around at the base of the
stage and cluck-clucked with Sailor and Phil. Michelle came
up onto the altar and surveyed the room. She sighed. "It's such
a waste of beautiful flower arrangements and such a beautiful
hall."

"Tell me about it," said Phil.

"And a waste of a party," Uncle Kurt emphasized.

Bruce joined Michelle at the top of the altar. He took her hand, a gesture that grabbed Autumn's attention away from Brianne. The former spouses stared at each other, appearing to have a short and silent conversation before becoming tickled by whatever it was they'd just wordlessly agreed to. Raising his voice, Bruce said, "It doesn't have to be. Why throw away such a nice place and a reception that's ready to go when we're all together anyway?"

"Because there's not going to be a wedding," answered Sailor.

Bruce looked at Michelle once more. "We weren't going to say anything until after Brianne had her day to herself, but—"

He paused.

"Michelle and I are getting remarried."

"What?" Autumn said, almost hitting Brianne when her hands flew to either side of her head so she could jam her fingertips into her temples.

"The afternoon is still young," he went on. "We might as well make use of all this. Why don't Michelle and I marry today, and then we'll go celebrate that instead?"

Before any of us could react, Michelle burst out with the rest of the news. "Also because I'm pregnant!"

That set off a lot of chatter and excitement, but even through all the commotion you could still hear Autumn scream, "What in the hell is wrong with you two, keeping this from me? You're fucking evil!"

∞

Bruce and Michelle got married in the beautiful hall amid all the white, black, and green roses.

After their announcement, I volunteered to go out into the parking lot and stop the justice's car because I needed a walk myself. When I tapped on his window and told him that his presence had been requested back inside, he placed his forehead on the steering wheel for a second before taking off his seat belt.

Their ceremony was completed without interruption, and the same people who weren't sure if it was rude to leave once Trevor and Brianne's wedding fell apart stayed for Bruce and Michelle's because they weren't sure if it was rude to leave once it started. Autumn had cooled down a little by the time her parents took their vows, but she didn't applaud or whistle when they were pronounced man and wife. It wasn't that she didn't want this—for them to be together again—because she'd been wishing for their family back for so much of her life. It was just that she felt left out and maybe even nervous that she was going to be the first of us not to be an only child.

Then we all continued on to the party, except for Brianne and Trevor, who went somewhere to talk.

As my relatives lost themselves to "Celebration" (come on!) beneath the glowing jars, and Michelle and Bruce locked in an embrace in the middle, I had the thought that none of the adults ever had any business crying psychopath. Just a short while earlier they'd witnessed Brianne's relationship and future plans crumble, but there they were, whooping it up on the dance floor. If that wasn't a poor ability to defer gratification, I didn't know what was.

There was a definite lack of guilt. A predilection for turning situations in their favor with a disregard for others' feelings. With the exception of Tish, they'd all been knocking back shots and flutes of champagne, which indicated poor impulse control. But maybe most tellingly was a failure to learn from experience, as demonstrated by Bruce and Michelle in trying for a second run. They kissed and appeared madly in love, and no one would have found it possible to disbelieve them.

My dad did a flip by the DJ's booth and change went flying out of his pants pocket. Cricket was outside on the dark lawn, spending quality still time with Saucy Evening. My new beagle puppy was waiting for me at my new apartment. I looked up at the ceiling, admiring the blinking jars, and made sure to stop the wedding planner when she passed by.

Looking up with me, she said, "I might just go into making the decorations instead of coordination. This one was almost the death of me."

"I really think that's a fantastic idea." Tilting my head toward hers, I asked, "Is there any way I could get you to pull me down a few of those jars at the end of the night?"

She sighed with contentment. "You like them that much?"

"They're charming," I said.

ACKNOWLEDGMENTS

First and foremost, this book is for my dad. He was diagnosed with brain cancer in the middle of my writing it, and he died a week before I finished with the edits. His biggest complaint about my previous books was that I have too many characters, so it figures that the book dedicated to him would be the one that needs a family tree at the front to help keep everyone straight. He was the best guy—everyone agrees—and I miss and love him. When I was little, I could always count on him to let me come sit with him at the Adult Table.

Thank you to those who donated to the Leukemia & Lymphoma Society even before the brain cancer diagnosis, my dad among them (Bonnie Bauman, Ann Beirne, Kathy Bradey, Sarah Christensen, Sandy Gellhorn, Hannah Eklund, Rhonda Kaufman-Malkin, Cheryl Klein, Geoffrey Litwack, Katerina Martin, Russell Merritt, Michael Newstat, Eileen Roggin, Eileen Seigel, Larry Seigel, Pam Seigel, and Laura Zander). If I forgot to list anyone, I'm sorry, but my computer gave out before I finished writing the book, and I lost my files. Let me know, and you'll go in the next book.

I thank anyone who continues to donate to cancer funding and research, and I'm particularly excited about the Kanzius Project, which you can read about here: http://www.kanziuscancerresearch.com/.

∞

Thank you to my agent, Doug Stewart, who defended this book against naysayers and who pronounces my name like no other.

Thank you to my editor, Caroline Abbey, who was so enthusiastic about this book from the beginning and brought it home to Bloomsbury.

(And also a thank you to Claudia Gabel for originally wanting to make this book happen at Random House.)

On the film side, thank you to Jeremy Bell, Eddie Gamarra, and Luke Sandler at the Gotham Group.

More thanks to Kassie Evashevski, Rio Hernandez, and Rich Klubeck at UTA.

How could I not thank Dave Bernad, even if I won't believe him when he tells me he likes something?

Thank you to Dr. Russell Dewey, who let me pull from his online social psychology quiz and who asked me to encourage others to search for and take it.

Love to my mom, Eileen, who always thinks whatever I do is going to be a big hit. To my brother, Brian, who has supported me and my work in his monosyllabic but endearing way.

My greatest appreciation to Pam, who took such loving, phenomenal care of my dad.

And then there's Brent Bradshaw, who I want to say is the light of my life, except that's too hokey, so—the lantern of my life. The substantial glow of my life. I love you.